Clearwater Romance

Volume One

Marissa Dobson

Published by Sunshine Press

Printed in the United States of America

ISBN-13: 978-1-939978-29-5

Contents

Dedication

To Thomas—my wonderful husband.

My amazing sister Jenifer. Thanks for all your support and work.

My readers, you rock. Thank you for everything. I hope you enjoy the Clearwater series as much as I did writing it.

Winterbloom

What she needs....

Prepping Winterbloom for the incoming snowstorm is the only thing on Chloe Frost's agenda when a stranger comes in from the cold.

What he's looking for...

Tortured by the past, Jordan Sheppard fled everything he knew until his car broke down and sidelined him.

Trapped together...

When this unexpected guest needs a room, these two lonely souls find refuge in each other. Can Chloe help Jordan discover a path through the pain and anger to find love?

Chapter One

Chloe Frost danced around the living room. She enjoyed having the place to herself. She sang in tune with the song playing on the local country radio station while she finished her storm preparations. Everything needed to be in order before the blizzard lashed her sleepy little town. It would be her first time at Winterbloom alone during a storm and she wanted to be prepared.

Slipping out to bring in another arm full of firewood, a strong, unforgiving wind assaulted her. Hurrying she grabbed as much wood as she could carry, the snow drifted deep already. *Thank God I am not out in that.* Inside, she fought the door shut.

Carved right in the side of a mountain, Clearwater, Wyoming always received a lot of snow but this storm promised to put even the most seasoned residents to a test. They expected Ezekiel to stall over the area, and last four to five days, dumping up to ten feet of snow.

Dropping the wood next to the fireplace, someone called out behind her. She whipped around and fumbling for a log to wield in her defense. Not expecting anyone, the radio was louder than normal. She liked listening while she worked.

"Ahem do you always ignore paying customers?" The deeply masculine and unfamiliar voice set her heart racing.

"I see the hospitality continues. Are you really prepared to beat away a customer?" A man loomed in the doorway to the living room, filling the space. Annoyance harshened his voice and his rumpled clothes looked as though he slept in them.

Holding onto the log, she fought to get her shallow breathing under control. "I wasn't expecting anyone. I'm sorry, but we're closed."

"Uh, that could be a problem. My car died about a mile up the road. I was hoping I could call a tow and find a warm place to wait out the snow. It's supposed to be a hell of a storm." He lowered his duffle bag to the floor.

His clothes were soaked through and crusted white with snow. The man wasn't an attacker out to get her, but someone genuinely in need. Guilt poked through her unease and she put the log down.

"I'll call Pete's, but I'm sure he won't be able to look at your car until after the storm passes. Why don't you go upstairs to the first room on the right and change? I'll give him a call and get you some hot coffee. The bathroom is at the end of the hall."

He nodded gave her a brief, but grateful smile and swung around, his boots making a thumping noise as he made his way to the staircase.

Picking up the cordless phone, she wondered why he would be traveling with such a storm heading their way. It has been on the news for days, everyone rushing around to prepare, it was impossible not to know what was headed towards them. His rumpled clothes and unshaven face made her think he had been traveling for a while. He might be stranded by the storm, but everyone had a story— maybe his went deeper than just stuck on the side of the road.

"Morning, Pete. This is Chloe. I have a guest that says his car broke down about a mile up the road. When you get a chance, could you tow it back and see what's wrong with it?"

As expected, Pete raged about the storm, and the number of calls he already received. His life was tougher than anyone else's. The best way to deal with it was with sympathetic noises and acceptance. He moved at his own pace.

"Yeah, it's going to be bad. Whenever you get to the car is fine. I told the guest it most likely wouldn't be until after the storm. I'd hate to see you out in this when it's obvious he's not going anywhere until this passes." She grabbed two coffee cups from the cabinet and filled them with steaming coffee. The front door slammed closed startling her. She spilled a couple of drops on her chest and hissed at the scalding heat. *Is he leaving?*

"Pete, don't rush. I have rooms available. He can wait out the storm here. Just give us a call when you know what's wrong with the car."

Sheriff Ryan Ryder walked into the room and she ended the call. His tall frame stood in the kitchen doorway, a hand on his gun like a character leaping out of the pages of some novel from the old west. It was a natural pose for him. His thick winter jacket open enough to show the dark blue uniform shirt pulled tight against his broad chest.

"Chloe, is someone here? I found a broken down car about a mile from here and there are faint tracks leading this way."

"Yes. A man came in about ten minutes ago. His car broke down." She handed him a cup of coffee. She would have to pour another for the guest.

"You don't know him, Chloe." He frowned, temper stewing in his voice. He had been on her case since Granny passed. The bed and breakfast was too far out. She was alone. Running it on her own was dangerous. Over the last few weeks, the number of fights they had about Winterbloom escalated. It was her life. She grew up here, helping her Granny with chores for as long as she could remember.

"Ryan, I run a bed and breakfast. I rarely know my guests. This is no different than any other time. Why are you so upset?" Impatiently she glared at him. She didn't have time to have this conversation with him *again*. There was still a long list of things she needed to be done before the storm, not to mention she now had a guest. Granny always taught her to be prepared for anything, the refrigerator and pantry were both full.

"Where is he?"

"Upstairs. He was covered in snow, I assumed he wanted to shower and change. Why?" She took a sip of coffee and watched him over the rim of the mug. If she kept it casual, it might relax his overprotective instincts.

"I want to meet him. I can take him into town; you don't need to be here alone with him. You have no idea who he is or what he wants."

"I run a bed and breakfast." She repeated the stance. If she said it enough, he might finally believe her. "He wants a room to wait out the storm. I'm not going to have you interrogating my guest. It's bad for business."

"I don't like you running this place all by yourself. I've seen too much in my line of work not to be concerned about you. I don't want anything to happen." The fear in his eyes aroused a fresh wave of pain through her. His concern for her safety was the same reason he went into law enforcement. Crime marred his life long before he came to Clearwater. When he arrived, fresh out of the police academy they became instant friends. Their friendship grew closer as he rose from deputy to sheriff.

"Clearwater is one of the safest places because we have you as Sheriff." Placating him never used to be this hard. When Granny passed, he took on the role of her protector.

"Flattery will get you nowhere, Miss Frost." But he laughed. "If you insist on running this place by yourself, how about a dog?"

"We talked about this before. I want to find the right one. Winterbloom takes a lot of work, and I don't have time to train a dog."

"So you will take a dog if it's trained already?"

Was that a trick question?

"Of course." She agreed. "I'd love the company, but I can't take the time right now to do dog training justice."

"Good, because I have just the one for you." He placed his empty cup in the sink and strolled out of the kitchen.

Shock rippled through her. *Did he just say he had a dog for me?* "What?" She jogged after him. "I didn't agree to anything."

He turned to face her. "Chloe, you want me off your back and this is the only way. I will be worried sick with you out here by yourself with a strange man. In this weather, the response time won't be good, especially with the mountain roads. I want to know you are safe. Goldie will keep you safe."

"Blackmail is illegal." She'd already lost the battle. Amusement edged her frustration over the very neat trap he set for her. She agreed before he told her, so it wasn't like she could really argue with him. Ryan was like a brother to her, and she didn't want him to worry about her. If a dog alleviated his concerns, then apparently she'd take the dog.

Plus, it would be nice having some company until the paperwork clears to open Winterbloom again.

He winked at her. "I'll be back with Goldie and her things shortly and when I do I want to meet your guest."

Chapter Two

Ryan left and she climbed the curved staircase to bring her guest—
she didn't know his name—coffee and a sandwich. It was unusual,
but she hadn't asked, and he wasn't very forthcoming with
information.

The chill raced over her skin. She had turned down the upstairs
heat while the bed and breakfast was closed. No use heating the
whole place when her quarters were downstairs. She needed to turn it
back up for her guest.

Balancing the tray, she knocked lightly on his door.

It jerked open swiftly and she took a step back. Her guest glared
at her, anger flushing his face, bringing a warm red glow to his checks
and neck.

"What do you want?" Hostility rolled off him in waves.

"I brought you something to eat, and coffee. I thought you
might be hungry." She nodded to the tray.

"Don't bother. I can walk to the diner if I get hungry."
Apparently, Mr. Surly arrived with a hard chip of rude on his
shoulder.

Even with the tension in the air, she couldn't help but smile.
Most of the local shops closed on weekends, and during nasty
weather. He was out of luck, if he didn't eat what she offered.

"The diner will be closed. No one will go out in this weather. If
you want something to eat, it's here or starve." When he didn't take
the tray, she nodded to him. "Have it your way."

She carried the food back down the stairs. If the stranger wanted
to be a jerk, he could starve. Allowing him to stay was as far out of
her way as she planned to go—especially with his attitude.

* * *

*What is wrong with her? Doesn't she realize I'm dangerous? That I can snap her
like a twig?* He paced the small bedroom. He didn't want to hurt
her—he didn't want to hurt anyone. His training drove him—his
body reacted, and his mind shut down. It shouldn't work that way,
but it did and he didn't always know where he was or what he was

doing. Running proved to be the best solution. He needed to get away, far away from people.

The sexy redhead's bed and breakfast didn't qualify as far from people.

Why did the car have to break down here? Where a delicious woman with a hot temper to match drilled holes in his reserve and cracked the shell around his heart.

The sheriff made his objections loud and clear. He heard the stress in the man's voice from the top of the stairs. He hadn't planned to eavesdrop and retreated before the Sheriff left the kitchen. Too bad the man hadn't dragged him out of here in cuffs. Then he wouldn't be anywhere near Chloe—even her name beckoned him. But he was here and the least he could do was stay in the room. Starving didn't bother him.

If things were only different, like before the war. He stared out the window, hands drumming against his knees. The world hadn't changed...

...I have.

* * *

Chloe settled at the dining room table with her mystery guest's unwanted sandwich and coffee. She still didn't know his name and she didn't care. Storm prep took hours and exhaustion nibbled at her. Smothering a yawn, she stretched her legs. *Eat first, nap later.* Ryan would be back soon if the pending storm didn't delay him.

Despite her irritation, her thoughts returned to the man upstairs. Pain flickered in the depths of his furious eyes. Pain—and something more. Something rattled him, deep inside. Like a cornered animal, he lashed out, and snarled at the world.

Seriously? Maybe he's just tired and cold and doesn't like strangers...

But what if there was more? She didn't usually indulge whimsy or imagination, but he reminded her of the kids in school who ran as far and as fast as they could from the problems in their life. Not that it ever worked. Problems chased a person and sooner or later, when a body stopped running—those problems caught up.

The sound of a truck door slamming brought Chloe out of her thoughts.

Ryan's back. She rose from her chair and headed for the front door, anxious to meet Goldie.

"Chloe?" Ryan called.

"In here."

"Go get her." Ryan whispered.

She barely turned into the foyer when a beautiful golden retriever sprinted across the wooden floors. Kneeling, she held out her hand to the beauty. Snow crystals glittered against the downy fur—giving her a blinged out look.

Ryan stepped into the living room as Goldie sniffed her. "Chloe, meet Goldie. She is fully trained and will protect you."

"She's adorable. How old is she?"

"She's four. She was trained to be a Seeing Eye dog and knows how to look after her people. The owner died a month ago. Her daughter and I went through the police academy together and she asked if I knew anyone who needed a good dog. I thought of you. Goldie has been with me for a little over a week. I was waiting for the perfect time to bring it up, and since you were closed and dealing with your grandmother passing, I didn't want to rush you. But with a guest staying here, I want Goldie here."

"Ryan, you worry too much. This isn't my first rodeo, I've been looking after Winterbloom for years." She ran her fingers through Goldie's coat. "Hello beautiful."

He nodded, but looked undeterred. "Yes, but Granny was here with you."

She was so busy, she'd buried her loneliness without Granny. Trying to cover with a fake smile never worked but she wouldn't give up. "It doesn't mean I can't do it on my own."

"I know that, but Goldie will be good for you. Give it a try, for me."

She nodded, and returned her attention to the dog. "I don't have anything for her."

"Don't worry. I brought her food and stuff."

Of course, he did. Ryan headed back out into the snow and Chloe looked at Goldie. "You're more than welcome sweetie...I just have to give him a hard time." The retriever gave her a slurp.

Ryan returned with supplies and cornered her in the kitchen. "I put her dog bed in your room, and here's her food. Where's your guest?"

"In his room. He's tired." The lie escaped before she had time to rein it in. She sat on the floor petting Goldie and ignored his glare. She could tell he wasn't pleased, but she held onto her patience.

"He's a guest Ryan. In a few weeks this place will be full with them again and you'll have to get used to it. Now stop worrying. I can protect myself."

His radio crackled and interrupted them. "Sheriff, 11-81 in front of Express Ohh's."

"ETA five minutes."

Chloe spent enough time with him she knew most of the police codes. An 11-81 was an accident with minor injuries. She jumped to her feet. "Jennifer?"

"Stay, you don't need to be out in this. You run a bed and breakfast, remember? You'll get in an accident and I can't be in two places at once. Stay here. I'm sure she's fine. I'll call you once I know." Ryan gave her a quick hug before hurrying out the door. "Stay inside."

She knew he was right, but Jennifer was her best friend. They'd been friends since they were in diapers and went to school together and were inseparable. *From cradle to grave...* If something happened to Jennifer, she wanted to be there.

Sinking back down, she comforted herself by petting her new dog. She wasn't sure how long she sat there. Time seemed to stop until Goldie nudged her hand. "Oh girl, I'll bet you're hungry. Ryan said you might be. Come on, let's get your food."

Rising, she examined a large box with toys, bowls and anything else you needed for a dog. Sitting beside the counter was a large bag of food. "Looks like he came prepared."

As she set the bowl of food down, the phone rang. Her heart was beating rapidly against her ribcage. She reached for the phone but her hand froze in midair. *What if it's bad news?*

"Hello?"

"Chloe, Jennifer's fine. Someone hit her car."

Sighing, the tension in her shoulders relaxed. Her stomach stopped doing flip-flops.

On the other end of the phone, he spoke to someone. "Jennifer's trying to steal my phone. See, I told you she was fine."

She could hear Jennifer arguing with Ryan but she couldn't make out what she was saying. Ryan shushed her and was trying his best to keep her from getting her hands on the phone. Jen's voice came on the line. "Chloe, I'm fine. I should beat your ass. Ryan said you tried to storm out of the house when the call came over the radio."

"Sorry Jen, I was just worried about you." Her friend didn't sound upset, only concerned. It made her feel guilty for trying to rush out in the blizzard.

"Wait for the call next time. Don't rush out in a blizzard."

"Yes, Mom." She teased. "I'm sorry. But after losing Granny, I couldn't bear to lose you, too."

"I'm not going anywhere. Ryan needs his phone, but call me later. After this storm passes, I'm coming out to meet your new dog. Got to go."

"Bye." She managed before Ryan came back on the line.

"Now, are you satisfied? You won't do anything crazy like getting in your car?" The authority in his voice carried across the line. She had a vision of him putting her in the slammer to teach her a lesson. He would do it, too. Ryan was like the older brother she never wanted.

"I'm just going to stay here with Goldie. Thank you for calling me."

"No problem, Chloe. Call if you need anything. I'm on call until the storm passes, so I'll be available."

"Thanks, Ryan."

Chapter Three

Outside the snow came down heavily, making it impossible to see further than a few feet. The wind beat against the house, as though nature wanted inside. Dinner baked in the oven, and Chloe curled up by the fire with a new murder mystery that Alyssa talked her into during her last trip to Happy Ever After Books. Goldie slept at her feet. A quiet evening at home, with a good book in front of the fire. There was nothing better in her mind, until the creaking of the steps. Still smarting from his earlier attitude, she didn't look up from her book.

"Excuse me." He paused behind her.

She looked up and studied him via the mirror over the fireplace. He wore jeans and a blue tee shirt that pulled tight over his chest. It was a well-built chest, a wall of solid muscle. Goldie lifted her head, watching him intently. *Goldie doesn't see him as a threat. I told Ryan he had nothing to worry about.*

"I wondered if I could take you up on that sandwich now." His rich voice teased her like a piece of delicious chocolate.

His attempt at making nice earned him a pass. "I have a roast in the oven. It should be done in an hour if you want to wait. You could grab something to tide you over if you want."

For the first time since he walked through her door, a smile softened the dour expression on his face. "Roast sounds great. It has been a long time since I had a home-cooked meal."

Laying her book aside, she rose and Goldie followed closely on her heels. "Come on, I have the perfect thing." She really didn't want to leave the coziness of the fireplace, but if he could make an effort, then so could she.

In the kitchen, she placed a small veggie tray on the counter. "A few weeks ago, my Grandmother passed away. Since then, the residents of Clearwater continue to bring food over. Most of the ladies around here said they had extra and thought I would like it, so I didn't have to cook just for myself. Yesterday, Sarah and John Kelly brought over this veggie tray. John owns the hardware store in town.

She said the grocery store messed up on their order and gave them two of the same tray for the school's party. I know she ordered two so she could bring one to me with an excuse, but what could I do. Tell her no?" She knew she rambled.

His initial attitude was as frosty as the storm but there was something to him hidden under the hard shell. She only glimpsed it, but wanted to explore. There was a pain in his eyes she didn't understand, but wanted to erase.

"That was nice of them. I always hated cooking for myself." He moved to the kitchen counter and the plates she sat out for dinner.

"Me too. I can't wait to reopen Winterbloom and have guests to cook for. I had to close while the paperwork was transferred into my name. It was fine, because we had some work going on in three of the rooms upstairs, and that just finished last week. I hope to draw up plans for the other two rooms and cabins. Then I can get a construction team in here." She hated the fact that she was over sharing, especially when she didn't even know his name. But it eased the earlier tension. "What would you like to drink?"

"Do you have beer?"

"I do." Pulling open the fridge, she grabbed one off the top shelf and handed it to him, choosing a bottle of water for herself. "It seems that since we are having dinner together, I should at least know your name."

"Oh sorry, I should have introduced myself. I'm Gunnery Sergeant..." He shook his head. "Sorry, Jordan Sheppard."

"Marines?"

"Yes. I was just discharged. I'm so used to having that be a part of me. It feels different just being Jordan Sheppard."

"It will always be a part of who you are. Just because you retired, doesn't mean that you stopped being who you are. How long were you in the Marines?"

"Fifteen years." His lightness fled leaving only a cold and lonely man.

"Jordan, if it meant so much to you, why did you give it up?"

"I didn't have a choice." He took another swig of his beer, and she waited to see if he would explain, but his eyes shuttered, closing her out. "I don't want to talk about it."

The rest of the evening he seemed to be tense and withdrawn. She tried to start a conversation throughout dinner, but all she received were grunts and short answers. Finally, she gave up trying and they ate in silence.

She cleaned up and he excused himself back to his room. She loaded the dishwasher, and wiped off the counter before moving towards the door to let Goldie out.

The snow had been blown against the house and fell onto the kitchen floor. She grabbed the broom and tried to brush it out before it melted as Goldie slipped out in the whiteness. "Stay close, girl."

Chapter Four

Screaming woke her. She looked at the bedside clock, *one o'clock in the morning*, before dashing up the stairs to check on her guest. Goldie rushed ahead of her.

"Come on James, stay with me. Don't you dare die on me!" Pain laced through his shouts.

Tears welled in her eyes. Climbing the stairs two at a time, she didn't bother knocking and pushed open the door. Jordan lay in a tangle of sheets. He reminded her of a lost little boy, curled in a ball, but ready to spring to action.

She went to him warily, Goldie following close on her heels.

"Jordan." She raised her voice as she neared, but he didn't wake. His screams drowned out her voice. "Jordan, come on, wake up."

Uncertainty warred with the desire to help. She touched his arm. That woke him. His hand shot up and wrapped around her throat. Her throat constricted and she fought to breath. Goldie barked like mad, and growled at him.

"Who are you?" His grip loosened, but his hand stayed firmly in place.

"Jordan, it's Chloe." She wheezed the words. "Winterbloom's owner."

His hand dropped to his side and his head fell in despair. "Chloe…what are you doing here?"

She retreated, putting distance and Goldie between them. Heart hammering, she coughed and tried to catch her breath. "I heard you scream. You were having a nightmare."

"It wasn't a nightmare. It happened." He ran his hand over this face. "Get out."

* * *

It was late, but her body was on edge. Sleep wouldn't be coming. She curled up on the couch in her quarters, a hot cup of tea in hand and Goldie stretched out beside her. Uninterested in reading, she set aside her earlier book. The television was out, leaving her alone with her thoughts.

What happened to cause him so much pain? Who was James and what happened to him? The questions nagged at her. She set the tea aside, and scooted down on the couch. Resting her head on one of the throw pillow, she tried to think of a way to help him.

A gentle knock woke her. Rubbing her eyes the bedside clock came into view. *Three. It's going to be a long night.*

She slipped the afghan around her shoulders to ward off the chill creeping up her back and padded towards the door. Exhaustion burned in her eyes, stealing herself, she hoped he wasn't back to his surly attitude again. He was hardly her first unpleasant guest, but she always did her best. For some reason, Jordan got under her skin.

He stood in the hallway with his hands tucked into the pockets of the lounge pants. A black t-shirt pulled tight over his muscles. Shadows darkened his eyes. He was hurt and the need to help him tugged her past her impatience.

Goldie barked a warning.

"Shh, girl. It's okay." The dog quieted, but didn't leave her guarding position.

"I came down for a drink and saw your light still on. I wanted to apologize for what happened. I didn't mean to attack you."

"It's fine. I shouldn't have gotten close to you to wake you, but I didn't know what else to do. You were crying out for James."

"I shouldn't have stayed here." He ran his hand over the stubble on his face.

"You didn't have much choice. Your car broke down. There isn't another hotel in miles. What were you going to do, stay out in the blizzard?"

The weight of his gaze gave her an uneasy feeling in the pit of her stomach. "It's better than risking someone's life—your life. I'm unsafe for people to be around."

"I'm sorry." It didn't seem like enough, but there was nothing else she could say. "Have you sought help?"

"Yes, I went to a shrink, but it didn't help. They discharged me because of it. They train you for years to fight, to kill. But when it's your best friend, a guy who's like a brother to you, the guy who went through boot camp and all the training with you, they tell you to forget about it. You can't forget it, and go on like nothing happened. I was there, I should have done something more." His anger turned into pity and remorse.

"Jordan, if there was something you could have done, I am sure you did it. I know this isn't going to help, but maybe it was his time."

"His time?" Anger surged through his voice. "His time? How can you say that? He had a wife and a baby on the way. One he never saw born. It wasn't his time."

"You can't blame yourself."

"Oh yes, I can. It should have been me." He whispered. "I was supposed to be on that watch, but he switched with me because I was sick. He took my shift...he died in my place."

There were no words that could make this better for him. He had to find the forgiveness in himself. She could tell him over and over it wasn't his fault, but until he came to accept the facts, nothing she said would ease his guilt.

She wrapped an arm around him. "Come on, I think you could use a drink."

* * *

She handed him a beer. "I'm sorry I don't have anything stronger."

"It's fine." He said, keeping his gaze on the fireplace.

"Why did you come to Clearwater?"

"I didn't intend to stop here. I was passing through to Idaho. That's where James' wife lives. I promised him I would stop in and see her and the baby once I made it back to the States. I don't know if I'm making the right choice. I'm sure she blames me. But a promise is a promise, and I plan to keep it."

"I'm sure she doesn't blame you, and you need to stop blaming yourself."

"There's no one else to blame." He sat his bottle on the coffee table.

"What about the people who killed him? Shouldn't they be blamed?"

He didn't say anything. Instead, he leaned back on the couch and closed his eyes.

"I know I don't know you, but I know guilt eats a person alive. Your friend wouldn't want you to live like this."

"You, the counselors, the military, everyone thinks I should just get over it. But I can't. I don't know how." He sighed. "They want me to talk it out, be rational—embrace the fact that people die in a war. Marines die—soldiers die—I get that. But this was different…James wasn't just a Marine or just people…he was my friend."

"I'm not a counselor. I don't know all the right things to say, but when my grandmother died. Everyone said—'you know things happen for a reason'. It doesn't matter if it happens for a reason, it just matters that it hurts. It's okay to hurt and to miss him. It's not okay to beat yourself up. You have to talk to someone, do something. I'll help you in any way I can." Maybe she pushed it, but she laid a hand on his leg. Comfort came in different forms.

He opened his eyes and looked at her. "Why would you help me? Like you said, you don't even know me."

"Because I can feel your pain. I can see it in your eyes. Your anger is getting the best of you. I'm sure you are a wonderful man. You need to let your pain and anger go so you can live. If not, your friend's death was for nothing."

Chapter Five

Why would she want to help him? He stared at the ceiling. The sun would be up soon, but sleep eluded him. *I could have killed her.*

Questions ran around in his head. What did he have to do to make the dreams stop? The shrink did nothing, but make them worse. Did he have other options besides another counselor? Would he ever be able to sleep without the visions of that night being played out repeatedly? It wasn't like he could do anything to change it, so why did his mind keep replaying it, forcing him to relive those horrible moments over and over again.

Sick of feeling sorry for himself, he levered himself off the bed. She mentioned wanting to redo the other two rooms. Maybe he could give her some suggestions. He needed something to do, something to keep his mind on other than his pilgrimage to see James' family.

He dressed in his blue jeans and threw on a black long sleeve sweater. He needed a shave but that could wait until later. Running water might wake Chloe. She was up late with him, and he didn't want to disturb her…again.

Across the hall was one of the rooms she wanted remodeled. She mentioned it was one of the larger rooms in the bed and breakfast. There was a king size four-poster bed in the center of the room, a small office to the left, and a three-piece bathroom. This was one of two guest rooms with its own bathroom. The other three had to share the hall bath. He saw potential. It would depend on what Chloe wanted to do, but he could easily draw some designs.

The second room was smaller. It would be better suited for a short stay or someone spending only a little time in the room. A queen bed sat by the windows, and a small sitting area arrayed around the door. He explored the other three remolded bedrooms and the hall bathroom and retreated to his room to draw up a few ideas for Chloe to look over. For the first time since leaving the Marines, he felt useful. Instead of destruction, he saw potential…

That's something…

Chloe tugged the turtleneck sweater up, making sure to cover the fingermark bruises on each side of her throat. She believed him when he said he hadn't meant to hurt her, but she didn't want to show him the evidence.

He hadn't shown up for breakfast. She didn't dare go inside—not after last night—but she wanted him to eat, too.

"Come in." He called.

She opened the door to find him sitting at the small desk. "I made breakfast and thought you might be hungry."

"Oh...I didn't realize it was so late." He looked up and blinked as though noticing the sun shining in the window. "What time is it?"

"A little after eight."

"Oh." He dragged his hand over his face. "Give me a minute and I'll be down."

* * *

Jordan joined her downstairs a few minutes later. She set a platter of pancakes on the table.

"I'm sorry. I didn't realize it was so late."

"Don't worry about it. Sit down and start. I'll grab the coffee." Joining him at the table, she nodded to the papers beside him. "What are you working on?"

His lips curled into a smile and he shoved another bite of pancake into his mouth. "I couldn't sleep and you mentioned drawing up plans for the other two guest bedrooms. I hope you don't mind, but I drew up some ideas for you to look at."

"You did?"

"Yeah, don't look so surprised. I had nothing else to do and didn't want to wake you. I used to work at my father's construction business before I enlisted. I worked with him all through high school, and when I was on leave. If you don't like them, you don't have to use it. It was just my way of trying to pay you back—make up for what I did last night. Plus it got my mind off...things. I forgot how much I loved doing that."

"I'd love to see."

He wiped his hands on his napkin and handed her the papers.

She looked over the documents, the designs were more than she imagined. The ideas looked so warm and welcoming. *Beautiful...*

"Wow, they're perfect. I love this one." She tapped the larger bedroom design. "The ideas for all of it is wonderful, but I especially like the idea of adding a large window to that room and taking advantage of the views." She nudged her plate aside, spreading the design out in front of her. "I didn't mention a design for the bathroom, but thank you. I planned to do that later. Why did you take out the tub?"

"Winterbloom is a bed and breakfast, and three of the rooms share that bathroom. I don't think the guests would appreciate it if another guest took a long bath while they waited to shower. The guest room you finished already has a bathroom, and if they really have to have a bath when they come, they should book that room. If you don't like it, I can change the design to allow for a tub."

"No, you're right—we've had that problem before. I love it and the large walk in the glass shower. It makes me want to redo my quarters." She smiled at him.

"If you want, I can look at it and give you some pointers on the best use for your space."

A forbidden thrill raced through her at the idea of him in her bedroom. "Thank you. But that isn't in the budget at this time. I would love for you to look over the cabin if we can get to them before you leave. With all this snow, I don't know if it will be something we can do. If not, I can get a local to come in and look at it. But I have to say, you seem to have eye for detail. These designs are wonderful. Have you thought about getting back into that?"

"Yeah, this morning while I drew these up. I loved doing it and it was always my plan after the Marines but then the service became my life and I forgot about it. Dad sold his business a few years ago because Mom wanted to travel, but that doesn't mean I couldn't start my own business." A glimmer of hope peeked from beneath his fatigue.

Chapter Six

"I noticed you have a lot of the supplies already that I would need in one guest room. I could get started on it." He loaded the last of the dishes into the dishwasher.

"Oh no, I couldn't."

"I offered. It's not like there's anything else for me to do. You want the place in order so when the official papers come through you can reopen. Let me do this." He dried his hands on the dishtowel. "I'm not one for sitting around doing nothing. I'm going stir crazy. Let me do this for you."

"I don't know. You're my guest, and I don't want to impose."

"You're not. I'd actually consider it a favor…doing something useful. Come on. Let's go upstairs and see what you have, and go over the designs."

Her grandmother always talked about redoing the house to give it more character, but it wasn't until right before she died that they finally started her dream. Carrying it out, and making Winterbloom special, meant the world to her.

Jordan led her into the first room on the left. It wasn't a homey room, but she wanted to make it a retreat for her guest. "This room appeals more to business professionals, and authors who need to get away to finish their book…"

"How did you know?" she asked, surprised.

He pointed to the desk. "I saw a few books over there by Melissa Edwards. The dedication mentions Winterbloom."

She loved that book and the author. During her many visits, she and Melissa had become close friends. "Yes. Melissa comes here often. She finds this place very inspirational."

"She stays in this room, correct?" Not giving her time to answer, he continued. "She's the idea behind this design. I think if you tore down this wall, putting in a half wall would give it a more open concept. I also would like to open up the exterior wall and put in a window facing the pond. New furniture and paint, and this room will be a whole new place." He paused stepping around her to open the bathroom door. "Now for the bathroom, I think gutting it, is the best choice. There's enough room in here to do a stand-alone glass shower, and a whirlpool tub for the guest to relax in. I think your female guests would especially enjoy that."

"I like that. But adding a window to the office area, I'm not sure about."

"Trust me. In the end, you're going to love it. Natural light enhances a mood. I'm sure Melissa would find it motivating to look out onto the lake while she's writing."

"But it's the middle of winter. I don't want a hole in the side of my house."

A smile curved his mouth, a real honest grin. It was the first one he shared with her and her heart skipped. "Now that's a very reasonable complaint. However, I would only take a day, two at most, if we ran into problems to do it. Or you can wait until the other work is done."

"You sound so sure that I'm going to let you blow a hole in my house." She lifted an eyebrow at him, and chuckled. *Knock out a wall in the middle of winter. That's crazy.*

He touched the side of her face, rubbing a finger across her cheek. "That's because you can't see the final project. Doing this would make this one of your most sought after rooms. You could charge more for it."

Gazing into his eyes, she wanted him to kiss her. The touch between them was intimate and she longed for more. "Kiss me," she whispered, throwing aside her caution.

He didn't hesitate. He leaned in close, placing his warm lips on hers. They tasted sweet, like maple syrup. She couldn't get enough. She laid a hand on his chest; and wanted to throw him on the bed.

He pulled back. "I'm sorry."

She stared at him. *He has got to be kidding.* "What?"

"I shouldn't have done that." He stepped back running a hand over his face.

"I asked for it, and I wasn't finished." Finding her confidence, she hooked her fingers in the front of his jeans, pulling him closer.

"I...we...can't. You're beautiful, and I want you. But I can't." He broke her hold and walked away. The door to his room closed moments later.

Leaning against the wall, she tried to figure out what she did wrong. She had never been the aggressor before but something about him called out to her. He wanted her as much as she wanted him.

The ringing of her cell phone brought her back from her thoughts. She wanted to ignore it, but pulled it out of her pocket. The caller ID said Ryan, and if she didn't answer, he would be at her door in no time flat.

She hit talk. "Hello Ryan."

"Is everything okay? I called Winterbloom's number but you didn't answer." She could hear Ryan's police radio in the background.

"Everything is fine. I was upstairs looking over the work I wanted to do in the guest rooms. I didn't hear it."

"I was heading your way. I thought something happened. I don't like you out there alone with your mystery guest. Is your guest giving you any problems?"

"Ryan, everything's fine. The guest is in his room watching television, and I needed something to do with my time. Goldie is right here with me. Stop worrying about me and get back to work."

"Chloe, I ran a check on the license plate. His name is Jordan Sheppard. Since being discharged from the Marines he's dropped off the grid. Something's not right about it. What would he be doing in Clearwater?"

"Stop worrying. He's just passing through. Once the storm passes, he'll be on his way. Now get back to work." She hung up. She wanted to tell him that Jordan was no threat to her, but he was a threat to her heart.

"Goldie, Ryan is going to send himself into an early grave if he doesn't stop worrying about everyone." Goldie just looked up at her with big dog eyes.

Walking over to the bed, she decided to strip the sheets. No one stayed in this room. If she moved the furnishings out, they could get started.

"Don't just lay there girl. Come help strip the bed. Then you can put them in the washer." The dog just looked at her like she was from another planet. "Fine. I'll do all the work and you just rest." She laughed at herself. *I can't wait for Winterbloom to be back open. I'm talking to a dog.*

Chapter Seven

Jordan laid on the bed listening to Chloe work in the other room. He felt awful about what happened. The last thing he should have done was kiss her—no matter what she asked. Chloe deserved someone better, someone not damaged like he was.

He would give anything to have met her *before*. "Oh, what am I talking about, I would have broken her heart," he said to the empty room.

He didn't want to watch television, but he turned it on for company. He wanted to be with Chloe. She deserved someone that could give her the world, not some out of work, broken Marine, with PTSD.

His cell phone rang on the dresser. The caller ID display read MOM.

"Hi, Mom. How's Florida?"

"Florida's great. When are you going to join us? I miss you."

Her voice made him homesick. She always had the right words to put things into perspective. If she said it would be 'okay,' then it would be. Unwilling to worry her, he kept his tone upbeat and cheerful as he could manage. "I miss you too Mom, but I'm glad you are enjoying Florida. Yes, I'll come visit once I do a few things."

"When? You've been saying that for weeks. Now that you're out of the Marines I think you need to come home. Being around family is what you need. You don't need to be out there on the road. Come home." He could hear her nails clicking on the kitchen counter, waiting an answer.

"I don't know, Mom. I'm stuck here in a blizzard. Once the weather lets up, I will get back on the road again. I suspect a few weeks before I can come down. I'll be there soon."

"Not soon enough." She was silent for a long moment. "I love you, Son. Come home soon."

All the years in the Marines and never once had he been homesick. He used to laugh at his unit mates when they complained. How odd to finally understand what they went through, odd and humbling. It had to be worse for those with a wife and children waiting for them.

* * *

Opening his bedroom door, he hoped to find Chloe across the hall but the room was empty. She'd stripped the bed and removed most of the small furniture and decorations. Even the bookshelf was bare.

Downstairs, music hummed softly and the dog played with a squeaky toy. He followed the tunes, but couldn't find Chloe. He poured himself a cup of coffee, and froze. Barely visible from the window, she stood by the wood stack in a heavy coat.

Jerking the door open, he winced at the cold assaulting him. "Chloe, are you crazy? Get inside."

She shot him an angry look and continued to gather wood.

"Come in, I'll get the wood." He glanced around for his coat.

She waded through the snow, and stamped her feet by the door. She brushed past him with her arms full of wood, still not speaking to him.

I screwed up.

Her eyes were full of anger; her shoulders were squared tightly ready for a fight. He darted out into the snow, grabbed an arm full of wood and followed after her.

Her wood sat stacked nicely by the fireplace, along with her coat to dry. Chloe curled up on the couch with her book.

"I'm sorry."

She didn't look up from her book, seemingly refusing to acknowledge him, and he didn't blame her. He'd acted like a first class jerk earlier.

"I don't know what to say to make this better. But honestly, I am very sorry. I was a jerk."

"Dang right you were. You kissed me and then act like it is the biggest mistake of your life. That's fine. Once the storm has passed, you'll be on your way. We'll never have to see each other again." She shot up from the couch and headed out of the room.

"Chloe, please." But she didn't stop. He learned from his mother sometimes it made things worse to follow a woman. Sometimes the best thing was to let her cool off.

"Looks like I really messed up this time." He leaned down to pet the dog. But even Goldie didn't want to be around him and followed her owner out of the room.

Chapter Eight

Unable to fume for long, she stopped hiding in her room. She found Jordan asleep on the couch. He waited for her. She knew he suffered and her heart hurt for him. She wanted to help him, but didn't know how.

Tiptoeing away, so as not to wake him, she led Goldie into the kitchen and heated the roast from the previous night's dinner, and made sandwiches. She was just finishing the preparations when she turned to find him standing by the counter.

"The aroma woke my stomach. I'm starving."

"I thought you would be. There's more where that came from. Go ahead, get started. I'll grab drinks."

He grabbed the plates and headed for the dining room table. "Anything but beer, please."

She grabbed two cans of cola. In the dining room, she found candles lit and the lights turned down low.

"I wanted to make it up to you. I planned on cooking dinner for you when you decided to come out. Sorry I fell asleep."

"You know how to cook?" She couldn't keep the surprise from filling her voice.

"My mother thought a man should know how to cook, and clean. She even taught me how to sew, well mostly how to sew a button on. I was always playing with my shirt buttons as a kid until they would fall off. She got tired of me doing that and as punishment, I had to sew the button back on. Threading a needle is hard work."

"It sounds like your mother is a great woman. She tried to turn you into the perfect husband." Granny would approve. She believed in self-sufficiency. "So why didn't you ever settle down?"

"Mom's been on my case for years now. She wants grandbabies. But the military is hard enough, and harder with a family. I was always deployed. I guess in the end, I never wanted someone stuck at home worrying about me, wondering if I would make it home, or if a man in uniform would show up at her door telling her the bad news."

"Instead, that would happen to your mother."

"I know." Regret colored his voice. "My dad was a Marine, she's a Marine wife. She's damn tough."

"She might be used to it, but that doesn't mean she wants her son doing it. But I understand why you did it. You're a hero…"

"I'm no hero!" He shook his head. "I let my best friend die in my place."

"Jordan, it wasn't your fault. There was no way for you to know what would happen."

"I heard the dryer buzz, why don't you handle that? I'll clean up." He grabbed the dishes and escaped to the kitchen, shutting her down. Again.

On her way to the laundry room, the cell phone on the coffee table vibrated. She didn't remember leaving her phone out and grabbed it to answer. If Ryan called and she didn't answer, he'd show up.

"Hello."

"Umm…I'm calling Jordan. Do I have the wrong number?" A woman on the other end asked.

"Umm." She pulled the phone away from her ear and looked at it. It wasn't until she really looked at it. That she realized it wasn't hers. It was the same phone, but hers had a jeweled cased that clipped onto the back. *Shit!* "If you hold a moment I can get him."

"Wait, who am I speaking with?"

"Chloe, I own the bed and breakfast he stumbled upon."

"Stumbled upon?"

"It's a long story, but a snowstorm has him stuck here. He was heading to Idaho. To…umm…sorry I'm not sure the name of the person he's visiting there."

"Megan O'Malley." Sadness darkened her voice. "He feels it's his duty."

Everything was clicking for her. "You're…"

"James' wife. But I'm surprised he told you."

She would have never answered the phone if she realized it was his, but now that she had and someone was on the line that might be able to help him. She couldn't let the opportunity pass. She sat on the couch and let out a short laugh. "I wouldn't say told me is the correct words. But yes I know."

"Then you know he blames himself?"

"Yes. He thinks you blame him too." It wasn't her place, the woman was a widow...but her husband was dead and Jordan was here.

"But I don't. I tried to tell him that. No matter how many times I tried, he just doesn't listen. It was war, things like this happen. There was nothing he could do." Megan sounded desperate on the other end. Her tone said she wanted to help Jordan but didn't know how. "He needs to forgive himself, or he'll never be able to move on."

"I know." It was all Chloe could say, but it wasn't enough.

"Have you known him long? You seem to care about him."

Before Chloe could answer, Jordan walked into the room. "Ahh."

"Is that my phone...?" He moved closer to her. "Who's on the phone?" Jordan snatched the phone from her.

She mumbled an apology and slipped away to deal with the laundry.

* * *

"Who's this?" Jordan asked, as he watched Chloe slip out of the room. He should be angry with her instead he found his gaze lingering on her swaying hips as she rushed away. He fought the urge to call her back, to wrap his arms around her.

"Jordan, it's Megan. I was worried when you didn't arrive, and this storm. I thought you might still be out in it."

"Megan." The weight of the world landed on his shoulders with a hard thump. "I'm sorry. The car broke down and I'm stuck in Clearwater, Wyoming. I found a little bed and breakfast to wait out the storm."

"I'm glad you're safe. I was worried about you. Jordan..."

When she failed to continue and the silence dragged across his nerves, he asked, "What?"

"Don't mess this up. I can tell from her voice she cares for you."

Before he could tell her that she misunderstood the situation, and Chloe was the owner, she ended the call. Instead of calling her back, he stood by the fire wondering if Megan was right. *Does Chloe really care or is she just being friendly?*

Chapter Nine

Chloe took her time in the laundry room. She folded the bedding and straightened things up, anything she could do to avoid facing Jordan. She didn't know how to explain what happened without sounding intrusive and guilty. She wasn't used to guest just leaving things lying about, especially something that closely resembled her own phone. She'd invaded his privacy and she barely knew him. She had no right to answer his phone, but at the same time she was glad she did. Knowing Megan O'Malley didn't blame Jordan might have been fate's way of helping her help Jordan. It might be the key that would help him let go of his guilt. If she could only figure out how to help him.

"Chloe, are you hiding?" Jordan called from the top of the steps.

"No." She hollered, but she was sure he could hear her guilt, just like her Granny always knew when she was lying. "Just dealing with the laundry."

He descended the stairs and watched her from the bottom step. "I haven't done laundry in a while, but I'm pretty sure it never took me this long to fold things from the dryer."

"Okay, fine. I'm hiding." She turned to face him, certain she had guilty stamped all over her face. "I'm sorry. I didn't realize it was your phone. I saw it there, and it looked like mine. I just grabbed it."

"I'll forget about it if you forgive me for being such a jerk since I walked through your door."

"I was never angry at you...well okay, I was earlier. But you deserved that." *Way to make an apology.*

"You're right, I did." He grinned, letting her off the hook. "Come upstairs and let me make it up to you."

* * *

After his conversation with Megan, he realized he could face his pain and fear or he could let it continue to cripple him. Maybe he'd just met Chloe, but she could quite possibly be the best thing in his life. He found some spare blankets and took pillows from the bedrooms upstairs to make a bed up in front of the fire. He lit candles around the living room and added wood, stoking the flames.

Tonight he was going to show Chloe the affection he felt for her. He would make tonight count, and live like there wouldn't be a tomorrow. *You never know when your number's up. James always said that...*

Tonight, for the first time in a long time, he wanted to reap the benefit of being alive. He wanted to live.

Leading Chloe into the living room with her eyes closed, reminded him of Christmas morning as a kid. When she opened her eyes, he could tell she was surprised.

"Chloe, I made a mistake earlier. But I hope you will give me the chance to correct my ways."

"What do you have in mind?" A playful smile softened her face.

He answered with a kiss. "You're beautiful. Come." He pulled her towards the fireplace.

Easing down next to her on the blankets, he faced her so he could stare into her eyes. "Since I walked through that door, I wanted to protect you from me, but I can't keep myself away from you. I'm a protector; it's what I do. But I can't protect you from myself. If you want me to stop just say so. You deserve so much more than I can give you, but I want you. You scare the hell out of me, because I've never wanted a woman the way I want you—like a lit match in a powder magazine."

"Jordan, you're what I want."

He placed a hand on the side of her face. "I hope I can live up to it." He kissed her. Their lips met with passion and desire. The air sizzled around them.

He broke their kiss to lift her sweater over her head. "You have too many clothes on."

"You too." She grabbed the waist of his sweater and pulled it over his head.

He laid her back to rest against the pillows before pulling her jeans down her legs. Her cute pink panties called to him, grabbing them with his teeth and pulled them. She laughed at him. "You're beautiful." He kissed his way back up, taking time to kiss her flat stomach. Moving her pink and white bra aside he trailed wet, teasing kisses to each of her hard dusky pink nipples. He wanted to linger, but the faint shadow of bruises on her neck stilled him.

"I'm sorry." He whispered, throat tight.

"Shh…it's okay. You didn't hurt me. You stopped. I'm right here." She tugged him upwards and fused her mouth to his, silencing his objections.

Never again. I'll never hurt her again. He pulled away long enough to shed his clothes. Her gaze scorched as it swept over him.

"Do you like what you see, beautiful?"

"Maybe" she said coyly.

"Just maybe, huh? Let's see what we can do about that." Confidence and cockiness surged through him.

He slid on top of her, taking hold of her nipple with his mouth. Teasing it with his tongue, causing her to arch her back under him. He caressed each inch of her body. "I want you."

"You have me. All of me."

"Good." He lowered himself to draw her dusky pink nipple into his mouth. His eyes never left hers as he sucked and played, before kissing across the valley to her other nipple. Letting her nipple slip between his lips, he gazed up at her. "I don't have condoms. I wasn't expecting…"

"I'm on the pill."

He didn't want to rush, not when he could savor the moments. Her unabashed reactions to his touch were a miracle.

"Please Jordan, I want you now."

"We have all night."

"Then give it to me now, and we can have another round or two." There was a twinkle in her eye as she spoke those words.

"Your wish is my command, beautiful." He placed his hands gently on her knees, spreading them, giving him the access that he desired. Teasing her sensitive flesh with his fingers before finally sliding himself in to her warm wet core. A cry of desire and need escaped her lips. Her body arched, she licked the side of his neck.

Her moans of pleasure spurred him faster. Their bodies, bound together, found rhythm and passion vibrated through him desperate for release. He fought the ecstasy, fought to hang on and drive her to her climax. Digging her nails into his back, she writhed. Their lips meet again and again. She screamed against his mouth and he held on for another few seconds, prolonging the beautiful agony until his release burst free.

He knew he wanted more of her, doubted he would ever get enough. Collapsing next to her, legs still entwined, their energy spent for the moment. She curled her body into his, her hand resting on his chest.

"Looks as though you enjoyed that, beautiful." He wrapped his arms around her.

"Oh yes." She lazily ran a hand up and down his chest. "Ready for another round?"

He snickered. "I might have been a Marine. Always ready to go at a moment's notice, but I do need a little recovery time."

* * *

The sun was coming up when they finally had enough of each other. The fire flickered low, and the candles were long out. Propped on her arm, she watched him doze and traced the tattoo of the globe, anchor and eagle on his arm. Sleep beckoned, but she didn't want the moment to end.

"Jordan, you know Megan doesn't blame you, don't you?"

His eyes remained half closed. "Yes, she told me at the funeral. But if you were in her place, wouldn't you blame me?"

"No."

"Come on, Chloe. Somewhere deep down, you would have to blame me. I took away her husband, the father to her daughter."

"No. It was war. You didn't deliver the killing blow. When Megan married him, she knew the risks. There was nothing you could have done. You need to be grateful you're alive. Live in the here and now. I'm so grateful you're alive."

Chapter Ten

The next few days passed in the blink of an eye. They started working on the guest room, referring to it as the writer's retreat. They could handle most of the interior renovations and save the external for after the storm.

Every day they worked side-by-side, then spent the evening in each other's arms. But in the back of her mind, she knew their time together was coming to a close. She wanted the storm to stay, but it was moving past their little town the sun once again came out. The promised ten feet of snow blanketed the landscape, drifting twelve and fifteen foot deep in places. The road crews worked overtime to dig them out. Soon Jordan would be leaving to see Megan, and her heart was breaking.

Jordan cooked dinner while she looked through the new J.C. Penny catalog to find items for the bedroom. Having colors for the bedspread and curtains would make picking a color for the walls easier. The domestic intimacy created a blissful bubble—and made her sad at the same time.

"What's wrong?" He kept an eye on the chicken breasts grilling on the stove.

"Nothing."

"Chloe, I have come to know you better than that in the last few days. I can tell something's on your mind. What's wrong?"

The tears glistened in her eyes. "You'll be leaving soon."

"I'm glad you brought that up." He sat the tongs aside, turning down the chicken he came to the table. "I don't want to leave. What we have is special. Marry me?"

"What?" she asked. *Marriage?* She didn't expect that.

"You heard me. Marry me. Make me the happiest man on earth. I know this isn't the romantic way, and I don't even have a ring. But we can take care of that after the storm." He got down on one knee. "Chloe Frost, marry me."

"Yes."

Epilogue

Six Months later…

The whole town gathered at the pond behind Winterbloom. She wanted to wait until the rooms were finished to allow guest to stay.

"Chloe?" A woman called from behind her.

"Yes?" she said without turning around.

"I'm Megan."

Chloe turned around and was face to face with the woman and her little girl that helped bring them together. "Wow. Sorry, Jordan said you wouldn't be able to make it."

"I know. I told him Stella here was sick. She was, but she made a full recovery. Plus I really wanted to surprise Jordan. I'm so happy for him…for both of you."

"Thank you. Have you seen him yet?"

"Yes. I talked him downstairs. He's come a long way. I think he finally believes it wasn't his fault, and that I don't blame him. I wanted to ask if you'd both consent to being Stella's Godparents. He accepted, and I hope you will also. The last few months…he's become a brother to me, it only seems right that we'll be like sisters. I want Stella to have a strong family around her. What do you say?"

"Yes. She's adorable. Jordan has shown me all kinds of pictures of her. I can't believe she's already a year old."

A knock at the door interrupted their bonding moment.

Jennifer poked her head in the door. "It's almost time. Are you ready?"

"Jennifer, come met Megan and my Goddaughter Stella. Megan, this is Jennifer, my best friend and Maid of Honor."

"Oh yes, I have heard a lot about you. You were the one who talked Jordan into redoing your coffee shop." Megan said as Stella bounced happily in her arms.

"Guilty. It needs something fresh, and he did such a wonderful job here. I don't think it will be long before the whole town is bugging him for different jobs. I know Ryan already asked him to come on as a deputy, at least part time. We don't get a lot of problems here, but Ryan deserves a break from time to time, and they're sometimes called to help up at Jackson Hole." The sheriff's turnaround where her "visitor" was concerned surprised her at first, but the men seemed to connect on a level that didn't include her. A storm drove Jordan into her life…and the promise of so much more kept him there. She was grateful for little miracles…and the snow.

A holler from outside made them return to the present. "Well, are you going to get married or not?" Megan asked.

Chloe gazed around the beautiful yard. The sounds of laughter and people talking filled the air. The butterflies filled her stomach and she grasped Jennifer's hand for friendly support. Goldie waited next to Jordan.

"Let's have a wedding. I'm sure Jordan's a bundle of nerves by now."

Unexpected Forever

Pregnant...

The stick turned blue and Tessa Bradley's world fell apart. But unplanned turns out to be the best thing that ever happened to her. Add a marriage of convenience to her best friend and unplanned just might give her the happily ever after with the man she's always loved.

Deployment...

Gunny Cameron White devoted his life to God, country and the Corps. Marriage has never been a blip on his radar. When his best friend—a woman he's always loved—turns up pregnant and alone, he throws out the rule book and commits to her like a Marine.

Marriage...

Can two people overcome the choices of their past when an unplanned baby gives them the chance of an unexpected forever?

Chapter One

Pregnant? Tessa Bradley's hand slid across her abdomen, was there really a little person growing inside her? Her doctor's voice droned on, but she couldn't hear him. She was twelve weeks pregnant without a father for her baby, and after today's shift—an unemployed mother-to-be.

It can't be...I was so careful.

She hit the end button on her cell phone, and slipped it back into her pocket. During the last nine weeks, she'd worked as the secretary for a law firm in town, while their permanent one was on maternity leave—talk about irony.

How was she supposed to be a mom when she didn't even know how to take care of herself?

"Tessa, there you are." Mr. Jacob smiled as he stepped into the office. "I wanted to give this to you before you left. It's just a token of my appreciation for stepping into Bev's shoes while she was on leave. I thought this might turn into a permanent position when I hired you, but Bev obviously has other plans. She wants to come back. If things change, you'll be my first call." He offered her a plain white envelope.

"Thank you. I appreciate it." She accepted it with a small, honest smile. Mr. Jacob was a wonderful boss and a good lawyer. He truly cared about his clients and did everything he could to fight for them both inside and out of the courtroom.

"Very well, it's Friday and we have no more clients booked for today. Why don't you take off and enjoy your weekend?"

She grasped at the generous offer, especially after the doctor's call. She needed to get out; maybe a walk in the park would help her clear her thoughts. Maybe then, she would have a better idea what to do about her situation. In a daze, she moved around the office and gathered her things.

"Thank you again for the job Mr. Jacob." She called to him from the door as she slipped her purse over her shoulder, and let herself out for the last time.

The air felt cool against her flushed skin, and the wind tugged her long brown hair, but she didn't care. Heading into the park, she made her way past the children's playground.

One day I'll be one of those frantic mothers watching from the bench praying my child doesn't get injured.

The countdown to 'one day' ticked faster than she'd ever imagined.

"Tess?" He looped his arm around hers, startling her out of her reverie and pulling her to a stop. "Aren't you supposed to be working?"

Cameron White stood before her in his breath-stealing, damn-isn't-he-good-looking crisp blue Marine uniform. The medals on his chest made her proud—and served as the steel fence between the future she'd wanted and the life he'd chosen fifteen years ago. He was a fine specimen of manhood—over six feet, muscular from his military training and hours in the gym, and shoulders wide enough to carry the world.

Over the years, she'd nursed a long-standing fascination and attraction for Cameron, one he refused to acknowledge after he joined the Marines. She tried to supplant the desire, redirect it to someone else, but even Brian didn't measure up to the yardstick she judged all men by. They weren't Cameron.

Young Marines spoke of him with respect, edged with fear. She knew he was strict, and expected only the best from his men, but he was also fair. Whenever someone needed a helping hand he was there, helping, guiding, but he expected his men to learn from their mistakes—to pay for their mistakes with pushups, loss of leave, whatever it took to drill the message home. He pushed his men to the breaking point, making them the finest Marines he could and he wouldn't stand for them to give less than one hundred and ten percent.

"Why are you in your dress blues?"

"I just left John's wedding, they pushed it up so they could be married before he ships out. It was a nice ceremony by the lake."

She heard him but it was as if his words came through a haze, distant and she couldn't focus. Her legs felt heavy, and her head swam.

"What's wrong Tessa? Are you feeling okay?" He cupped a hand under her arm and guided her over to a bench.

"I'm fine…I just need to go home." God help her it was good to see him. He was like a port for a ship lost at sea but she needed to wrap her mind around what she was going to do—and how could she tell him? She didn't think she could bear his disappointment.

"Come on, I'll take you home." Arm around her waist, he pivoted neatly and guided her toward the street.

"I'm fine. My apartment isn't that far, I can walk. I'm sure you have other things you need to do before you have to go." Even to her, the words sounded flat and they wouldn't convince him, but it was all she had left.

"You're all that matters today. I was coming over once you got off work."

Even if he didn't believe her, he didn't force the subject. Maybe all the years they had known each other had enlightened him to the fact that if he pushed she'd only shut down more. *What am I going to tell him?* She tried to think of something, anything as he led her towards his car. They only had a few days left together before his upcoming deployment. She didn't want to ruin the time she had left with him by bringing up her mistakes.

Just the thought of another deployment was enough to send her into panic mode. Yes, he was career military and that was part of his job, but it scared the hell out of her every, single time. In truth, he married the Marines from the day he enlisted. He wouldn't be there for their weekly movie date, or nightly chats. Selfish? Yes, but he was such a large part of her life, she didn't know how to give it up—even for only a short time—without her heart breaking.

If she were honest with herself, she'd admit she was in love with him, and had been since they were sixteen. Fifteen years later nothing had changed, at least not for her. For Cameron, he'd chosen the Marines, and that loyalty was absolute. He left no part of himself free for a girlfriend, let alone a wife. No matter how much she'd always wished otherwise, Tessa had accepted they would never be anything more than friends. Cameron wouldn't allow anything more. He said something else, but she didn't really understand it, the world around her tilted and she swayed. Blackness swamped her vision and everything faded.

* * *

Awareness returned with a jerk and she recognized the sterile surroundings, and bleach-like odors. *Why am I at a hospital?*

Her gaze fell on Cameron, sitting in one of the hardback hospital chairs. Even with the slight disheveled state of his uniform, he still managed to look powerful and authoritative. They'd been walking to his car when she...she what?

Oh, I fainted. Embarrassment flooded under her confusion. *How long have I been out?*

"Hey beautiful, you're awake. You gave me quite a shock." He pressed a kiss to her cheek. The closest they had come since he joined the Marines. Oh before the Marines, things were different. They were young and in love, but the day he gave his commitment to the Marines everything changed.

Even in her present condition the memory of the day he joined the Marines came flooding back. They'd grabbed a bite at Pete's Burgers when he turned to her all serious. "I joined the Marines..."

Unsure what she was supposed to have said, she'd sat there in silence, her burger held mid motion and just stared across the booth at him. The icy chill of fear had raced through her.

"I leave for boot camp in two weeks...Tessa I want you to find someone else. Don't wait for me."

"What?" She'd asked, unable to believe what he'd said. Two years together and just like that, he'd decided to end it.

"I won't do to you what my dad did to Mom. I won't leave a widow behind if I'm killed." He tossed his burger back into the basket, as if he'd been disgusted by the thought of it. "I don't want you sitting around here worrying about me."

He'd closed the door to what was between them, and pushed her away. His protection had hurt her and what he failed to understand was that together as a couple or not, she'd still worried about him. It didn't matter if she wouldn't be his widow, if he died she'd still grieve just the same. Understanding his reason didn't break her heart any less—then or now.

She tried to swallow the lump that formed in her throat. "What happened?" Speaking irritated her dry and scratchy throat.

"You passed out." He handed her a glass of water, and watched her as she took a sip. "I knew something was wrong with you, why didn't you tell me you weren't feeling well?"

"I'm fine. Just tired. It must be all the long hours I was putting in for Mr. Jacob, but the job ended. I'll catch up on my sleep. Don't worry about me." She tried to soothe him, to dispel the worry that clouded his eyes. "Will you get me more to drink?" She asked handing him the empty cup back.

He looked for a pitcher, but there wasn't one. "Sure."

She could tell by the way he lingered he didn't want to leave her alone. "Thanks Cam I've got dry mouth and I'm really thirsty."

With him gone she let her eyelids drift close. The screech of the curtain being pulled back snapped her eyes open. "That was qui…oh sorry Doctor."

An older man in a white coat stood before her. "Ms. Bradley, you're awake. I have your test results back." He flipped open the chart in his hand. "I'm assuming your doctor already called you with the lab work he drew yesterday and you know you're pregnant."

Cameron stood behind the doctor, the cup of water in his hand, his eyes wide with shock. He heard the doctor tell her that she was pregnant. As her mother used to say the cat was out of the bag now, and there was nothing she could do to shield him from her mistake.

As if the doctor realized someone was behind him, he turned. "If you could please go back to the waiting room so I can talk to the patient I'll send a nurse to get you when I'm done."

"No, doctor it's fine. He can stay." With the damage already done she gave the doctor the authorization he needed to talk in front of Cameron. As if satisfied the doctor turned back to her. "You passed out today because your iron level is very low. I have spoken with your doctor—a close colleague of mine—and he has ordered light modified bed rest for the next week as well as start you on an iron supplement and a prenatal supplement. If you want your baby to be healthy, you're going to have to start taking better care of yourself, and remain on very light duty for the remainder of your pregnancy, resting as much as possible. Your doctor would like you to follow up with him in a week. Any questions?"

"No. Thank you, doctor."

The doctor flipped the folder shut, not bothering to look back at her, he moved the curtain aside. "I'll finish the paperwork and a nurse will be in to discharge you shortly."

She wrapped her arms around her stomach, as thoughts of how she would manage plagued her. She was barely getting by herself, how was she going to raise a child on her own? Even with the anxiety and dread of the uphill battle that waited for her, love for her unborn child towered all. She'd do right by her child. She wanted her child to have everything she didn't. Including a real family, with two parents, but she didn't see how that would happen now.

Cameron's hand fell away from hers, and he rose. "Pregnant?" He sounded so surprised. She'd expected anger, but not surprise. "How?"

She scooted up in the hospital bed trying to find a comfortable position. "Cameron, you're old enough to know how…" She tried to make light of the situation, he didn't need to know—she didn't want him to know how terrified she really was. If her doctor required her to continue the bed rest longer than a week, that invited a whole host of fresh problems. She had no one she could turn to. Her mother died years ago and her father—no, her father wasn't an option. Cameron was the only one she had and he was about to leave, too.

"Damn it Tess, you know what I mean." He spun back. "You haven't been out with anyone in weeks, does *he* know?"

"I don't want to discuss this…not here." Her words hung in the air until the nurse pulled back the curtain.

"Here's the first dose of the iron and prenatal supplements the doctor prescribed. You'll need to drink a lot of orange juice while you take the supplements, so that it will help you absorb the iron." The nurse handed her one of the little white cups, with two small red pills along with one oblong white one inside.

Tessa turned to grab her cup of water, but Cameron was already there, handing it to her. She tipped the cup back tossing the pills in her mouth before following it with a drink of water.

"Ms. Bradley, if you could sign your discharge paperwork you'll be ready to leave."

Tessa signed the paperwork, desperate to get out of there, even if it meant having to face Cameron. She slid her legs off the side of the bed, rising to stand on her feet before the nurse scolded her like a child.

"Oh no you don't, the doctor ordered bed rest. I've got a wheelchair on the other side of the curtain, just stay there while I drop this paperwork off at the door and I'll wheel you out."

Cameron helped her into the wheelchair, and gave her hand a little squeeze as if trying to reassure her that everything would be fine.

She sat there surrounded by her thoughts for a moment. *How am I going to manage the bed rest alone? There's no one I can rely on to manage the mundane tasks, let alone anything else. I'll never be able to stay off my feet, completely. There's household chores, grocery shopping, laundry, the list went on and on.*

As the nurse wheeled her out to the car, Cameron walked beside her. All of his unasked questions hummed between them. Was he disappointed in her? She suspected that to be the case, but it was her life. It wasn't as if she had planned to get pregnant, especially by a man that wouldn't be around to help her raise their child, but it happened. *No, my baby, my responsibility. I can do this.*

In the car, Tessa rested her head against the back of the stiff leather seat. She fought to keep her eyes open. Her stomach still lurched and she wasn't sure if it was from the pregnancy or nerves. "Where are we going?" She asked when he drove past the exit to her apartment.

Cameron shot her a quick side-glance. "You're on bed rest, that means you shouldn't be alone, and no steps. I'm taking you to my place. You can stay with me for now, tomorrow I'll go over and gather some of your stuff."

"I can't..."

"Tess, don't." He took his hand from the steering wheel, and placed his hand on her thigh. "You need someone, let me be that someone, at least for tonight. We'll take tomorrow when it comes."

His confidence let her relax and she knew it was silly to lean on him, but Cameron always had that effect on her. He took charge and tonight—tonight she wanted to let him. Tomorrow held just as many questions, but at least this day would be behind her. She could begin to figure out how she was going to make a life for her and her child.

Chapter Two

Not wanting to wake her, Cameron carried an exhausted Tessa into his apartment. Her body fit against his chest almost as if she belonged. Love and family should never be in the plans for a Marine. If they'd wanted him to have a family he'd have been issued one when he enlisted. Sweat, hard work, and loyal dedication had earned him the title of Gunnery Sergeant. He'd never wanted to commit himself to a wife, a family, not with his job, a job that gave no certainties. Infantry life only left the unknown, especially whether he'd make it back from any mission. Not the type of life he wanted to give a wife—not the life he wanted to give Tessa.

His mother lost her husband, leaving her alone to raise him and she'd never been the same without him. The day he gave his commitment to the Marines he vowed he'd never do that to a woman he loved, yet here he stood looking down at Tessa and thinking that very thing.

Before he lifted her from the car he made sure he had the key ready, he didn't want to have to set her down if he didn't have to. Slipping the key into the lock, he pushed it opened, and stepped inside. Kicking the door closed behind him, he didn't turn on any lights. He knew the layout of his apartment.

In his bedroom, he laid her on the bed. He wanted to do something to ease the tension he could feel in her body. He slipped her shoes off before pulling her dress slacks down, baring the creamy white skin. He pulled the covers up from the bottom of the bed, covering her to her waist, before lifting her gently and tugging the sweater off. He grabbed a t-shirt from the edge of the bed and slipped it on her. If he couldn't remove the anxiety, he could at least make her comfortable.

Her eyelids fluttered opened, giving him a glimpse of her beautiful blue eyes. The eyes that kept him company through every mission he had been on, the one woman he always came home to. He never told her, determined to let her go because it was best for her. But he was in love with her, and had been since they were sixteen. He realized it years ago, on one of the missions that nearly got him killed. He thought he'd never make it back to her, but he did. Still he couldn't let his love cloud his judgment, he couldn't be a Marine and a good husband, not with the possibility of leaving his wife a widow.

"I didn't mean to fall asleep." Sleep coated her voice and her eyes closed again.

"It's okay. You need to rest."

"I'm sorry, Cam. I didn't mean to drag you into this. I'll be a single parent but I'll do right by my child, he or she will have everything I didn't have and be surrounded by love." She mumbled, sleep trying to reclaim her, but she fought.

"Shh, it's okay." He repeated, and tucked the blanket around her.

"I should have known better than to get involved with him, but I swear I didn't know he was married…"

He'd suspected who the father was. No way would that self-centered asshole admit any responsibility for the child, and he knew Tess would rather struggle than take him to court for child support. She wouldn't want to give any rights to her child to that bastard. "Tess, it's okay, just sleep." He smoothed her hair away from her face, and she opened her eyes again. "I've got duty in a few hours. Stay in bed except for bathroom and meals. I'll be back at four."

"I'll be fine. Don't worry…" Her words were cut off as sleep dragged her under again.

Holding her hand, he stared at her, surprised by the regret that filled him. Regret that it wasn't his child growing within her now, that it was someone else's. Someone who'd never cherish Tessa the way he would. He almost lost his chance with her, because he couldn't see past his career. He wouldn't let that happen again. He had six days before his deployment and he vowed to convince Tessa she deserved more than what she had. She didn't deserve to struggle as his mother had being a single mother, especially when he could provide for her, even if it was in name alone. *This is my fault…all those years I've denied what is clearly still alive between us. Did my resolve of not wanting to leave a wife a widow drive her to these decisions? Maybe it's time to retire from the Marines and man up for her.*

With fresh determination, he kissed her forehead. "I won't let you down. I'll always be here for you and your child."

Tessa woke to the sun peeking around the curtains. She laid there a long moment, a hand on her stomach. A small padding flesh where just below her child grew. *Her child.* She still couldn't get over that in six short months she'd be a mother, a single mother.

She wanted to roll back over, and go back to sleep but her stomach had other plans. It rolled with each move she made. Taking a deep breath, as if that helped the nausea, she twisted to her side, letting her feet drop to the floor. The warm carpet tickled the underside of her feet.

On the nightstand, she found a folded piece of paper with her name on it, and the filled prescription that the doctor provided.

Tess,

Follow the doctor's orders and rest. There's food in the fridge. I'll be back around four with dinner...your favorite.

That was her Cameron, all orders. Even if he could be a strict pain in the ass, she didn't want to think of her life without him. He'd always been her rock. Somehow, he'd always known when she needed him, it didn't matter if he was deployed to another country or just around the corner, he'd provided the support she needed to get through some of the toughest patches of her life.

She grabbed one of those little red iron supplements the doctor prescribed and the prenatal vitamin, before she padded her way to the kitchen for a glass of water. The kitchen was one of the best parts of the apartment, they'd spent many hours there, her cooking while he sat at the bar watching her.

Opening the double doors of the refrigerator, she found a plate with food, and a small note on top. *Don't forget to eat.* As late as they'd gotten in, he couldn't have managed more than three hours of sleep before reporting for duty. Yet he still found time to get her prescription filled, and prepared her a plate with food. Suddenly hungry she grabbed it, stripped off the clear wrap, and popped it in the microwave.

Minutes later she sat at the bar with her heated meal, her thoughts turning back to the issue before her. Uncertainties weighed heavily on her shoulders, but she had to come up with some solution, the baby growing inside of her depended on it. Each bite of food felt like lead in her stomach. Still, she managed to eat half of the chicken breast, and all of the steamed broccoli before pushing the plate aside.

Maybe I can find a job where I can work at home, resting. She grabbed the newspaper that Cameron must have tossed on the end table on his way out the door, and slowly made her way back to the bedroom. Fatigue already weighing down her limbs, each step harder than the last, she prayed her whole pregnancy wouldn't be an uphill battle.

* * *

After depositing the takeout containers on the counter, Cameron went in search of Tessa. He found her in the middle of his king size bed fast sleep. He tossed the duffle bag he packed from her apartment on the floor and slipped out of his jacket, before closing the distance between them. He sat on the edge of the bed, slid the newspaper in her hands away. "Tess, wake up."

Her eyes fluttered open and confusion clouded her gaze, it seemed to take her a moment to realize where she was. "I'm sorry; I didn't mean to fall asleep."

"Don't. There's no need to apologize you need the rest. Hungry? I brought food." She nodded. "Let me just change and I'll bring it in to you."

"No, not in bed. I'll come out. You change; I'll see you out there." She didn't bother to put on other clothes, the t-shirt he slipped onto her still in place as she slipped out the other side of bed.

He watched her walk out of the bedroom, the gentle sway of her hips acted as a hypnotist chain drawing him in. *Damn she looks good in my shirt.*

A changed occurred between them last night, and he couldn't keep her out of his thoughts, and not all of them were strictly platonic. He wanted her—wanted to touch her, but he couldn't—no wouldn't—she meant too much to him.

He needed to change before their food grew cold. He tried to pack away the thoughts of her naked under him. But the tautness in his body rebelled, and they wouldn't fit back into that tiny box he kept them in. Swearing under his breath, he stripped out of his uniform. No, wanting Tessa filled him and wouldn't be denied, because of his unrealistic beliefs.

"Cam, are you coming?" Tessa called.

"In a minute, go ahead and start." He didn't know why he even wasted his breath, he knew her better than he knew himself and there wasn't a chance in hell she'd eat without him. She could be dying of starvation and still she'd wait for him to join her before she dug into the food.

She was amazing, and deserved so much better than what he had to offer. For years he had half-hoped, half-despised the idea that she'd find someone and start the family she always wanted. Now, she'd get part of that wish, but he had wanted to see her with a safe man, a man that would love her and protect her as she deserved.

He found Tessa sitting at his small dining table, their meals already dished out. "I would have got that, you're supposed to be resting."

"I didn't have to do much, just grabbed the plates, and silverware. I sat down to dish the stuff out. Even in my condition I think that's on the approved list of things to do." She chuckled. "Next you'll want to spoon feed me...don't you dare get any ideas."

"I'd never think of it." His lips curled up into a smile. "Come on let's eat while it's still warm." He sat down next to her and dug into his sweet and sour chicken and white rice. Chinese food was one of their favorites for an evening in. He looked over at her until she started to eat her chicken and broccoli.

He stalled on small talk as they ate the rest of their dinner; he wasn't sure what she would think of his plan. He spent most of the night and the day preoccupied, going over the possibilities of what the best way to deal with her situation. Finally, he decided on straightforward plan. *She has to agree. It's logical. It's safe.* He'd already put the necessary wheels in motion.

"Since you're done, why don't you rest on the couch for a bit? We can put in a movie." He cleared away the dishes, putting them in the dishwasher.

"I know you have a lot to attend to before you deploy. If you just take me home I'll be out of your hair."

"Just go rest on the couch. I'll grab you a pillow and blanket so you're comfortable, I'll only be a second." When she continued to stand by the table looking at him, he pointed to the couch. "Go."

Everything cleaned up, he returned with a pillow and the blue and white quilt his grandmother made him. He got her settled on the couch, tucked in and comfortable before he grabbed a beer and sat on the recliner facing her.

"So what are we going to watch?" She snuggled down under the quilt.

"Actually I want to discuss something with you first." Never in his life had he been so nervous, not even in the worst battle moments of his career. His stomach protested the food. "Just hear me out before you answer."

"Okay." Hesitation tightened her expression and her knuckles turned white where she fisted the quilt.

"Marry me—"

"What?" Her voice climbed and she stared at him.

"I thought you said you'd hear me out." He raised an eyebrow at her. When she remained quiet, he continued. "You're going to need support over the next coming months. Right now, you're unemployed, without benefits. The military provides great benefits for us and our families. You can use it to make sure you and your child are healthy. You can also take the time to go back to school, like you always wanted, and build a stable future for both of you." Even saying the words he hated how they sounded, so cold and uncaring when everything in him burned. He wanted to help her, to see that they were both cared for, not out of some duty but out of love. He loved her, yet he couldn't tell her that.

Chapter Three

Tessa leaned forward as if that would make the words clearer. She couldn't believe what she was hearing. Cameron wanted to *marry* her. *Is he out of his mind? I'm pregnant; everyone would think it's his baby.* "What?"

"Tess, just what I said. My job is dangerous, I can't change that and I can't provide you with the security you deserve, I deploy, I'm gone...I can't promise I'll be back, but I can help you in other ways." He caught her hand in his much larger one. "I'd like to tell you to take all the time you need, but I can't. I deploy in a few days. We'll need to do this quickly."

She tried to digest the words but it was like trying to swallow a brick. Cameron offered her a marriage of convenience, not something she ever wanted to hear from him. "Even if I were to say yes, you're missing a key point. You're about to deploy and I'm supposed to be on bed rest. That doesn't change that part of the situation."

"Actually I've thought of that already. Do you remember Jordan Sheppard? We went to his wedding a few months ago." She nodded, and he continued. "They have a bed and breakfast in Clearwater, Wyoming. As well as a couple beautiful cabins that sit behind it, lots of privacy to anyone who needs it. I've arranged for you to have one of the cabins until I'm home. There's someone that comes in twice a week to clean, and Chloe cooks all the meals for the guests. You'll have someone to help you while I'm away. I spoke with a friend of mine that's a doctor at the base and under the circumstances, he believes you'd be safe to travel as long as you're resting, but he wants to look you over, or we can visit your obstetrician if you'd prefer. Chloe has recommended a doctor in Clearwater, to see to you and the baby." He rambled on, explaining all the arrangements he'd made in the last few hours.

He squeezed her hand until she met his gaze again. "Just stay in Clearwater until the birth, then you can come back and stay here. You'll be close to the military base, where there's childcare, and support. But while I can't watch over you let me know you're in safe hands. Jordan was a fine Marine, I'd trust him with my life in battle, and I'd trust him and Chloe with you. They'll be able to help you in ways I won't be able to during your pregnancy. Tess you know neither one of us have anyone else, and you need someone right now. I'd give anything to be here, to help you through this time, but I can't. I'm sorry."

She cupped his check, the five o'clock stubble rough against her fingertips. "I…I don't know Cam. I wanted a marriage built on love, not out of convenience. This is my mess, I got myself into…you deserve better than this." Tears filmed her vision, but she didn't care. It was the truth, Cameron deserved better than to be tangled up in a mess she created. One day he'd see that he did want a wife and children of his own. She had always hoped he'd want her when that time came, but not like this. Not out of duty, or friendship.

"My sweet Tess, I wanted so much more for you too. I wanted you to have the family that you always wanted, with the house and white picket fence, but right now, you must take the situation at hand. You need to provide for your unborn child and I can help…I want to help. If you want a divorce once the child's born and you're on your feet, I'll give it to you. No questions asked but let me help you." When she didn't answer, he added. "You don't have to answer now. Sleep on it."

Sleep, how does he expect me to sleep after that? She let her head fall back against the pillow, her thoughts running in circles. He put in a movie, before he relaxed back into his recliner with his beer in hand. She watched him out of the corner of her eye more than she watched the movie.

Could she marry him if love wasn't involved? If she had been asked that before she found out she was pregnant she would have said no. But now if it meant saving her unborn baby she would. Maybe this was an opportunity—to prove to him they could have a real relationship again. To prove to him that marriage wasn't out of the question. He could have his career and her, too.

* * *

A movie and two beers later, Cameron sat watching Tessa sleep. Even in sleep, her face held a worried look, one he wished he could wipe away. He was still on edge, waiting for her answer. He hoped the answer would be yes, not because he didn't see another option for her and her unborn baby, but because he wanted her as his. It was selfish and he knew it, but he had almost lost her and if the father had been anyone but that married son of a bitch, he might have.

Damn it, I'm a selfish asshole. I want her all to myself, yet I can't be the husband she deserves, or the father the baby needs. He hated himself for it, but the Marines were his life, and even if he wanted to turn into a family man the Marines owned his ass for another year. Could he really give up his career, the adventure and adrenaline? He never thought so before, but if anyone could convince him to become a civilian again it's Tessa.

He pushed the legs down on the recliner, quietly as not to wake her. He'd rather carry her into bed and feel her body against his, it was the closest he would allow himself to get. If they married, he'd need to keep himself in line more than ever. Bury his feelings and make sure they remained a tightly guarded secret.

She looked up at him, the blue eyes drawing him down like the sea wanting to swallow its next victim. "What time is it?"

"Almost midnight, I was going to carry you into bed so you could rest comfortably."

"I can walk." She pushed back the quilt and rose. "There's nothing wrong with my legs, I'm only pregnant."

"I didn't want to wake you." Against his better judgment, he followed her, and cupped her cheek. Her pale pink lips called to him, he wanted to kiss her but his restraint was better than to give into the calls of flesh. He let his hand drop away from her, and stepped back. "Get some rest. I don't have duty tomorrow, so I'll make us breakfast when you get up."

She nodded and walked away from him, down the hall to the master bedroom that he gave her. He'd crash on the couch again, instead of making up the guest bed. His gaze followed her, need hitting him like a sucker punch. His body demanded he follow her. Instead, he ordered himself to take a cold shower, hoping it would chase away the images of her naked against him, his shaft buried deep within her core.

Chapter Four

Tessa spent most of the night awake, tossing and turning as decisions plagued her. She stared at the warm grey walls for hours, snuggled deep under the comforter. Cameron's scent surrounded her and offered comfort. It was sometime in the early morning hours when she made her decision. She slipped out of bed and made it across the room before there was a knock at the door.

"Tess, may I come in?" Cameron asked from the other side of the door.

"Yes." When he opened the door and stepped in, authority poured off him even in blue jeans, and a grey t-shirt that strained over the bulging muscles of his biceps. "I swear you have super human hearing."

He gave her a grin that made her weak in the knees. "You know I'm a light sleeper. I wanted to see if you wanted me to start breakfast."

"Umm give me twenty minutes, I want to shower first, and then I'll help." She headed towards the adjoining bathroom.

"The doctor said only baths for the next week. He doesn't want you standing for a shower while you're supposed to be on bed rest." He reminded her. "And don't forget—can't be too hot, so just a warm bath."

Damn it. He was right and she planned to follow the doctor's orders completely. She wanted to make sure her child would be healthy. She hated baths, but she'd deal with it for as long as necessary. "Damn. Okay, I'll take it later, baths always make me sleepy. Let me help with breakfast."

"Not happening. You can sit at the bar and keep me company, but no helping." He turned on his heels and headed back to the kitchen, with her following.

"Before, you start, let's talk." She grabbed his hand and tugged him toward the couch. Sitting she pulled her legs close to her, and wrapped her arms around them. *Soon I won't be able to do this, my stomach will get in the way.* She smiled at the thought; still unable to believe in just a little over six months she'd be a mother. With her gaze glued to the floor, she broached the subject that was hanging in the air. "I considered your proposal…Cam I'm not sure this is fair to you…but if you're serious then yes. Yes, I'll marry you. You can help me give my child things I can't otherwise, but most importantly it will give me a healthy baby. Somehow I'll find a way to pay you back."

She felt the weight shift on the couch. He nudged her chin up and kissed her. The strong spicy hint of coffee overwhelmed her for a moment before she tasted him, pure and full of life. This was not like the kisses she shared with him all those years ago, no that boy had been replaced by a man. The stroke of his mouth on hers held a promise of desire. Enough to give her hope.

He broke away, and their gazes locked. Desire heated his eyes for a moment before his shields pushed back into place and he pulled away. She longed for his touch again, to feel his lips on hers, his hands on her body. She craved his touch like a diabetic craved sweets.

"We'll make arrangements to get the marriage license today and see the doctor. I'm done with duties until the day of deployment, once we have the doctor's okay we can make flight reservations." He rose, and grabbed his cell from the coffee table. "Rest, let me make the appointments and then I'll start breakfast."

Cameron loved to be in charge and she'd just given him permission to take over. Her stomach twisted and her heart pounded against her ribs.

I can't believe I'm doing this.

* * *

The café was quiet at this time of day, giving them privacy. In just an hour both of their lives would change. Scary as it all seemed, she embraced the potential for her, but she wasn't sure about Cameron. Would he regret it? End up hating her? Or worse—simply be her friend only until she was on her feet? Doubt plagued her.

The doctor gave her permission to travel, because of her circumstances. He insisted that as long as she rested and took care of herself, she'd have a healthy pregnancy. It did very little to ease her concern. All her life she had been carefree, but now her stomach churned with worry.

Tessa sat there watching a young couple very much in love sitting two tables over. She wished that Cameron would look at her the same way the guy looked at his woman. She missed sharing a real connection with Cameron, she treasured their friendship, but she wanted more. Soon there would be paperwork saying they were married, even if it wasn't heart and body. Somehow, she had to make it enough.

He dug into his turkey sandwich while she barely picked at hers. "Tess, you need to eat."

"Sorry." She smiled at him. "Nerves." She picked up her sandwich, taking another bite before looking back at the couple, and then to him. He looked so calm. "Cam, are you positive you want to do this?"

"Sweet Tess, are you getting cold feet?" He put his sandwich down and stared at her with uncertain eyes. "You know me better than this. If I wasn't sure, I'd never have asked. You've never doubted me before don't start now." He shoved the last bit of his sandwich into his mouth, and looked up at her. "If you're not going to finish eating, we have another appointment."

"Appointment?" They had another hour before they had to be at the justice of the peace in the park behind the courthouse. "Where are we going?"

"I told you an appointment." He took hold of her hand, gently pulling her to her feet. "Come on." He wrapped his arm around her waist, and tucked her close to his side on their way out of the café.

Unless she imagined it because she longed for it, there was more to his touch than just the friendship he claimed. Oh how she wanted there to be more. He led her down the street towards the shops. "Where...?" Her voice failed, when he stopped in front of a small dress shop.

"Just because it won't be the wedding of your dreams doesn't mean you shouldn't have a pretty dress to get married in." His hand slid down to rest on her hip. "Come on. You deserve it."

"I can't..."

"Don't argue. You can't be married in jeans. Now come on, we don't have a lot of time." He opened the door and ushered her inside.

An older woman, her brown hair greying at the temples, stepped forward. "Mr. White, you're right on time. I'm Lisa, your personal shopper."

Cameron offered his hand to Lisa. "Lisa, thank you. This is Tessa, we're getting married in an hour. Can you help her find the perfect dress?"

Lisa looked Tessa over, taking her in as if she was a stock of meat before nodding. "It doesn't leave us much time, but we'll find something suitable. Come along dear."

"Go ahead. My uniform is at the cleaners down the street. I'm going to go retrieve it and change. I'll be back shortly." He kissed her cheek, before turning on his heels and leaving her alone.

She'd never been a girly girl, always one for jeans, and t-shirts or if the weather called for it sweaters. She could count on one hand how many times she wore a dress. Cameron knew this and still he insisted, not as some weird sense of torture but because it was the wedding rituals. He wanted her to have the whole experience even if they were rushed.

* * *

Tessa stood next to the large oak tree, her creamy white dress flowed around her body. Even though she hated dresses, she felt like a princess. One who—in a way—was getting her prince. All her life she had wanted to be in this very place with him. She only wished they were getting married because they loved each other. Still even if for a short while, she would be Mrs. Cameron White, the wife of Gunnery Sergeant White.

He was not only the best Marine she knew—willing to lay his life down for his country without a second thought—but he was also the greatest man to ever touch her life. Look at him—marrying her, no questions asked—to provide her with security. He was her hero.

"With the power vested in me by the state of North Carolina, I now pronounce you husband and wife. You may kiss your bride."

Her heart leaped, as he leaned towards her. His breath feathered a caress across her mouth and then he kissed her. Adrenaline flooded through her veins, as she opened her lips allowing him entry to her mouth. His tongue slipped between her lips, the kiss devouring her until he suddenly jerked away, as if his control snapped back into place like a rubber band stretched to its limit.

He gave her one final brush to her lips before pulling back. The passion evaporated or maybe she'd only imagined it. They were married, but he seemed even more unattainable than ever.

Chapter Five

Tessa's first day of married life, seemed to speed past in a blink. She'd convinced Cameron she needed to gather things from her apartment before they left for Clearwater. Unsurprisingly, he wouldn't agree without the condition he carried her up the steps to her apartment citing the fact that she was on strict orders no steps.

It was the only time he had touched her since their wedding ceremony. She ached for his touch, and that did little to alleviate the demand. After the wedding, a part of her wished he'd complete the claim. She wanted to be his wife in more than just name. She promised herself in time she would be, but for now she wouldn't let it ruin the limited time she had left with him.

She lay curled in bed with a cup of tea as he packed the last of her things. Of all the things they were taking, very little were his. He'd packed a small bag to keep at the cabin for when he was on leave. That way he could fly straight to her without the delay of coming by his apartment.

Her eyes began to grow heavy, but she fought it with all she was. She had such limited time with him that she wanted to cherish each and every second. Sleep could wait until she was alone.

"You're getting tired, why don't you sleep?" He added the last of the stuff on the bed to the suitcase and zippered it.

"Sleep can wait." She wrinkled her nose, but when he raised an eyebrow and his jaw flexed, she sighed. He got points for not parroting the doctor's orders, but she conceded defeat and took the final sip of her tea. "Fine. Will you lay with me?"

"I don't think..." He shook his head, lifting the suitcase from the bed and sitting it next to the door.

"Don't think, just do. Please...you're leaving soon. I just want to feel your arms around me." She hated that her voice sounded weak, with a touch of begging, but she couldn't help it. She felt so alone, and it would only grow worse when he left. She was desperate for his touch, wanting to have it before it was too late.

He nodded, coming around the bed, to get in beside her. He didn't bother to undress, and probably planned to humor her until she slept and then head to the sofa. "Okay. You need to sleep; we have a long day tomorrow. Jordan's going to pick us up at the Jackson Hole airport to take us to Clearwater."

Setting her empty tea mug aside she curled her body into his, and rested her head against his shoulder. Holding him tight, she tried to memorize every part of the experience—the way his body felt, the smell of his cologne, the thump of his heartbeat drumming steadily beneath her hand. She completely supported his career—it made him who he was—and she'd never ask him to give it up, not even for her, but she wished he could stay with her. Being a military wife took strength and sacrifice, and she never realized just how much—and they hadn't even been married twenty-four hours. Maybe it wasn't something everyone could do, but she'd go to the moon and back for him.

"Is everything okay?" He ran his fingers lazily over her shoulder, rubbing in small circles.

She tilted her head up meeting his gaze, and gave him a smile but she knew it didn't go to her eyes. Her stomach was in too many knots. "I'm fine, still reeling from the last few days."

He kissed the top of her forehead. "You know I'll do everything in my power to come back to you." A hint of anxiety thickened his voice.

She knew that and she knew it wouldn't stop her from worrying either. The look on his face said he was thinking about his parents. He always said he never wanted to widow a woman, not after watching his mother grieve. But she doubted he realized that was his own grief talking—because he lost his dad, too.

"I know you will. What happened with your parents isn't going to happen to you. You'll come back to me…to us."

"I just don't want you worrying about me." Anxiety filled his gaze, as if memories of his past were coming to light and he felt doomed to have them played out again, but this time instead of with his parents they would be with her.

"Cam, I've always worried about you. This deployment will be no different. But in the end—in a few short months—you'll be back home. Everything's going to be fine…" She brushed her fingers along his jaw. "I have no doubts you'll come home to me."

As long as Tessa was in his arms, he didn't want to move. It was almost as though she was the missing piece to him. Her body fit snug against his as if she belonged there.

If things had turned out differently for his parents, maybe he would have made her his years ago. The worry of leaving her a widow was too much for him to bear. He still despised the idea, but she needed him and her immediate problems trumped other possibilities. His Tess deserved the world and more than he could give her.

His wife.

In just seventy-two hours she'd be in Clearwater alone and he'd be about to deploy. For the first time in his military career, he seriously regretted his orders. He didn't want to leave her, not in her condition. When he deployed this time, he would be leaving behind family.

Chapter Six

Tessa relaxed against Cameron's tight body, his arm around her shoulders and his fingers gliding along her collarbone. His friend Jordan drove while Jordan's wife, Chloe played tour guide, pointing out different aspects of Clearwater. It had been a long day. All she wanted was to get to the cabin, and be alone with Cameron. In two days, he'd be gone again and while she should be used to his deployments—it felt different this time.

"I'm sorry Tessa. You had a long trip and here I'm rambling on about our town. It may seem like there's not much here, but it's a nice small town. I'll do my best to see that you enjoy your time here." Chloe explained.

"It's fine Chloe. It's a beautiful town, thank you for having me." She wanted to be friendlier, but she didn't have it in her. The sun might just be setting, but for her it was two hours later, and they had been on the go since early that morning. Between arriving at the airport two hours early to go through security, and three plane transfers she was exhausted.

"We're almost there, and you can rest. We've already stocked your cabin with supplies you'll need." Jordan announced, glancing in the rear view mirror at them.

"Thank you." Cameron told him. "We really appreciate it."

She watched out the window as the small town went by, the rod iron light posts were just springing to life as they drove towards Winterbloom Bed and Breakfast. Shops were beginning to close for the night, but one in particular caught her eye, Tiny Treasure Baby Store. She'd have to make a trip there once she was off bed rest. She couldn't wait to begin shopping for baby clothes. For the first time since finding out she was pregnant, real excitement thrummed within her. What would she have? A son or a daughter?

Deep in thought, she didn't even realize they pulled in front of a cozy cabin. A warm light glowed inside, making the place inviting and the lake view was stunning especially with the sun sinking low in the sky. The building even had an ATV parked alongside the walkway to the cabin.

"Welcome to your temporary sanctuary. The ATV is so you won't have to walk to the main house if you wish to come over. For now, until you're off bed rest, and unless it's an emergency Tessa please use the phone and call us. I also wrote down our cell numbers, they're inside on the table. Add them to yours and keep it with you at all times. You never know when you might need us." Chloe explained while Jordan helped Cameron with the luggage.

"Thank you for everything." She gave Chloe a smile, truly grateful for all she was doing, and then turned towards the cabin.

The men dealt with the luggage quickly enough and Cameron came to her, wrapping his arm around her waist. "Thank you both for everything. I'm going to get her settled, we'll see you tomorrow." He led her inside, and she heard Jordan start the SUV, back up and drive away.

The inside of the cabin had a homey feeling to it. The warm brown couch dominated the living room, with a large flat screen television hanging on the wall, and a small fireplace catty-corner to the sofa. A creamy white shaggy throw rug covered cherry wood floors to designating the section as the living room. A small table set further in, and just beyond that, a galley style kitchen, and a hallway that she assumed lead to the bedroom.

"Come on. Let's get you in bed, I'll unpack." With his arm around her waist, she was left with no choice but to go with him. The bedroom was done in a warm gold, the fluffy white comforter that contrasted beautifully with the dark walnut furniture. "Get out of those clothes, and into bed."

She did as he asked, too tired to argue. She folded her clothes and set them on the chest at the edge of the bed, and crawled in between the sheets. "You must be as exhausted as I am. Leave the stuff, come lay with me."

"I'm fine." He told her, but she could see the traces of weariness around his eyes.

"Cameron, we don't have much time left together before you have to leave, please…" She hated that there was a hint of begging in her voice. She shouldn't have to beg her husband to come to her, to lay with her. They were married, even if he didn't love her, she still wanted him. For the time being just feeling his body against hers was enough. She didn't know how long that would be enough, but while it was she wanted to take advantage of each opportunity she could to enjoy it.

"I know…" He sat on the edge of the bed, watching her. "You've been quiet today, do you regret this?"

"Regret what? Getting pregnant? Marrying you? Coming to Clearwater?" She shook her head. "I regret none of it. My unborn child will be healthy because of you. I've always believed everything happens for a reason…maybe *us* is the reason."

* * *

The movie ended and Tessa was surprised to find herself still awake. Neither of them had slept much the night before, and neither of them seemed in a hurry to sleep now. They cuddled together in bed, their empty popcorn bowl had been pushed to the side. Their time together was ending much too quickly. In the early morning hours, he'd catch his flight back to North Carolina and report for duty.

Her heart beat frantically with the thought of him leaving. She hated herself for being weak, for thinking she needed him to get through it. She might not *need* him, but she wanted him. They were very different things, but both left her body crying out for his touch.

He nudged her chin up, his eyes dark and thoughtful as he studied her. Her breath caught in her throat when she thought he'd kiss her. "My Tess, I've never seen such apprehension in your eyes as I do tonight."

"I'm going to miss you." She tried to smile when all she wanted to do was cry. She went through this with each deployment to a degree, but normally he wasn't there to see it. He was always so busy attending to last minute preparations that she only got a portion of his time. It was made worse because after the arduous trip to get here, he refused to let her see him off at the airport. She never missed a deployment or a welcome home. "When you board that plane, you'll have no one there to say goodbye."

"I'll know you're safe. Plus I've always liked our private goodbyes better." He lowered his head, their lips met and desire coursed through her. He pulled her lower lip into his mouth, sucking on it, before letting it go and sliding his tongue deep within her mouth. His hand moving from her chin gliding up the side of her face to tangle in her hair, drawing her closer to him. She could almost taste his reluctance even as he ended the kiss. He rested his forehead to hers and their noses brushed. "If it helps when I walk out the door tomorrow just picture me boarding the plane instead. Yours is the only goodbye that matters to me."

"I'm coming with you…to the airport." She leaned forward pressing her lips to his again, unwilling to waste their last few hours together. Her hand slipped under his shirt, running up his rock hard chest, feeling every toned muscle with her fingertips, as she tried to pull it up and over his head.

A knock sounded on the cabin door.

"I'll get it." Cameron told her pulling away from her. He rolled off the bed, and paced over to the door. Pausing, he glanced back. "You're not coming to the airport, you're on bed rest."

She rose up on her elbow meeting his gaze head on. She was going, even if he didn't like it. "The short drive will be fine. I won't be driving, I can rest in the backseat. I need to see you off."

He didn't reply, just walked out to answer the door. Moments later Chloe entered, bringing a tray with what looked like chocolate cake. Tessa looked beyond Chloe expecting Cameron to be right behind her, but he wasn't there.

"I brought you chocolate cake." She smiled holding up the tray. "Don't worry he'll be back soon. There was a call for him at the main house…one of his men. I guess he couldn't get through to Cameron's cell phone."

Weird. Tessa reached for his cell phone that lay on the side of the bed with her own, and low and behold, it was off. In all the time she had known him she never knew him to turn his phone completely off. Vibrate yes, but never off. She turned her attention back to Chloe. "Thank you. Sorry I can't get up, I promised Cam I would stay in bed. I better keep my promise if I want him to not fight me going to the airport with you guys in the morning."

Chloe stepped towards the bed, setting the tray on the nightstand. "Are you sure…about tomorrow?"

Tessa didn't even try to keep the frown from showing. She didn't know Chloe very well, but she thought if anyone she'd have Chloe on her side. "I have to…"

Why can't anyone understand that I need to see him off? I've always seen him off and just because I'm pregnant isn't going to be the reason I don't this time.

* * *

Cameron stepped out of the small office at Winterbloom to find Jordan in front of the television with a beer in hand. Jordan seemed to be adjusting well to civilian life, and for the second time since he found out Tessa was pregnant, he questioned his career.

"Everything okay?" Jordan muted the television.

"Seems one of my men has gone AWOL I've alerted the MP's that if he's found to detain him until I've returned tomorrow." He frowned. The kid was young, but it was a stupid Marine who ruined their career. "How do you like civilian life?"

Jordan eyed Cameron before answering. "At first I was lost, my whole life was the Marines. It wasn't my choice to leave, and I was bitter, but now I have Chloe, and I'm happier than I've ever been. Are you thinking about it?"

It was clear that by *it* Jordan meant civilian life. "I don't know…maybe. A wife, a child, they don't go well with our line of work. I don't want to make her a widow. I might not even make it back for the birth." He was treating Tessa's child as if it were his own, and he wanted to be there for the birth. He hadn't told anyone she wasn't pregnant with his child, not even Jordan and Chloe. As far as anyone knew, she carried his baby, that is why they married so quickly.

"I know what you're going through. You were one of the few that shared my beliefs, about family and the Marines, but Tessa's a strong woman, she's going to be fine. If you stay in, she'll make an excellent Marine wife, you won't have to worry about her. She's got the strength, and backbone to handle it."

"I better get back to her. See you at oh six hundred." Outside he took off in a steady jog, around the lake, his mind on the uncertain future. Would he really be willing to give up his career as a Marine? After fifteen years of devoted military service, maybe it was time to give it up for Tess.

Chapter Seven

The Jackson Hole airport was small and not busy at this time of year with the ski resort closed for the season. Getting through security wouldn't be a challenge, and he delayed as long as possible for the extra time with Tessa. Jordan and Chloe waited by the doors, giving them privacy. Cameron sat near the security line, his arm tightly around Tessa, dreading the moment that he had to leave. He never experienced the emotions he'd been going through the last few days with Tessa.

"My sweet Tess, it's almost time." He ran his hand down her arm. He wanted to pull her closer to him, but he didn't want to hold her too tight.

"I know." Tears glistened in her eyes, and she squeezed him tighter.

"I'll be back…" He almost told her he promised that he'd come back to her, but at the last second, he caught himself. He was a man of his word, and he would never let anyone down, especially not his Tess. "Before you know it I'll be back, and we can give our baby everything they ever wanted. If you'll let me I want to be the father to your child…I want to be more than just a name on a piece of paper to both of you." His free hand went to her stomach. He wouldn't have even known she showed at all if he hadn't changed her clothes the night after the hospital. A small bump formed in the concave of her abdomen, just the faintest swelling and her hips seemed fuller and her breasts lusher.

"You'll always be more to me…to us…then just a name. Our child couldn't be luckier than to have you as their father." The tears rolled down her cheeks.

The intercom system overhead crackled to life. "We will begin boarding, flight 718 to…"

He had already said his goodbyes to Jordan and Chloe leaving the hardest one—Tessa's for last. He rose taking her with him. "Tessa, may the days go quickly until we can be together again. Take care of yourself and our child. Do as the doctor orders, and let Chloe and Jordan help you. You're not superwoman, take it easy for the sake of him."

"Or her…" She let out a gentle tear-cloaked laugh.

He tilted her head back so he could look into her eyes. "Either way I'll love our baby as if he or she is my own. You know that don't you?"

She nodded a split second before his lips crushed hers. The damn loudspeaker called his flight number again, and he knew he couldn't put off the inevitable any longer. He broke the kiss, his mouth hovered over her lips for another second before he kissed her a final time. "I'll be back, I promise."

He promised and he would deliver. When he got back, he would make his claim crystal clear. He should have done it now that they were married, but he let the guilt of his father's death rule his life. They were different people and he didn't have to live his father's mistakes. He'd always made it back home to her and didn't plan to stop now. He wouldn't leave his Tess and their child alone.

"I know you will." She cupped his cheek, gaze locked on him. "Stay safe."

He bent over, grabbed his small carry on, and slipped it over his shoulder before pulling her back into his arms. "I'll see you soon." It wouldn't be the last time he held her close to him. Still reluctant, but determined he walked through security to catch his plane.

* * *

Tessa wasn't sure how long after he left that she sat there, tears freely falling down her face. She was lost in her heartache. He just left and already she missed his touch. She had no sense of time, or the people moving around her, until Chloe came to her, laying her hand gently on her shoulder.

"Tessa, we should get you home." Chloe squeezed her shoulder when she didn't look up or move.

Jordan knelt down to her, taking her hand in his. "Cameron's the best Marine I know. He's a damn good Gunny, he'll be okay."

She smiled at Jordan, and then up at Chloe. They barely knew her yet they opened up their home and hearts to her because of Cameron. She had nothing but gratitude for them, without them she wasn't sure how she'd make it through the pregnancy if this bed rest continued more than a week.

Blinking to clear the fog of his departure, she nodded. "I'm sorry. Yes let's go." She started to rise from the bench, but Jordan didn't move from his kneeling position in front of her. Unless she was prepared to knock him over, she'd have to wait until he got out of the way.

"Just wait here with Chloe for a few minutes. I'll go get the SUV, and come around to the main doors to pick you ladies up." He squeezed her hand and rose.

"Jordan's right. You need to stay strong for your child and for Cameron." Chloe came around to sit with her. "You don't want him to worry that you're not taking care of yourself."

"I know. It's not my first deployment—well my first one as his wife—but you know what I mean. My emotions are haywire lately, I guess its pregnancy hormones." She rose from the chair, she swayed on her feet, the world tilting on its axis.

"Whoa there." Chloe shot to her feet, and steadied her. "Maybe you should sit back down."

"I'm okay." She closed her eyes briefly, when she opened them again the world no longer spun. The doctor explained when her iron level returned to normal the dizzy spells would cease. She couldn't wait for that, the dizzy spells were getting old quickly.

Chloe caught sight of an SUV pulling upfront of the airport. "There's Jordan. Are you okay to walk to the SUV?"

She had to pull it together, if Cameron found out about this incident he'd worry more about her then he already did. She didn't want his mind on anything but the missions he had to deal with. A distracted mind could get him killed. "Yeah, I'm fine. I'm just tired."

Chloe nodded, and slipped her arm around Tessa's waist, but when Tessa would have protested, Chloe quelled her with a look. "Precaution...I'd rather be close and you not need me then to not be there and you pass out, and fall to the floor. No fighting, I gave Cameron my word that I'd make sure you were safe."

Tessa didn't fight. She wanted a healthy child and had already taken too many risks the last few days. It was time to really follow the doctor's orders. She'd go back to her little cabin, and to bed. Bed rest was what the doctor ordered, and that's what she would do, but damn it would be boring without Cameron to keep her company. *What the heck am I going to do on bed rest all alone?*

Chapter Eight

Tessa arrived back at the cabin from the airport, exhausted, and lonely. She fell into the bed, buried her face in his pillow, and the scent of his cologne, crying until she fell into a deep sleep. She missed him like an amputee misses their limb.

Over the years, she had been through a number of deployments and none hit her like this one had. Each one left her missing him, but none of them left her feeling as if her heart had been torn from her chest. It wasn't because she was his wife now, or that he wouldn't come back to her, no it had to be the pregnancy.

Through the curtains, she could see the afternoon sun setting over the lake. A white piece of paper on the nightstand caught her eye. *Tessa.* Cameron's handwriting. A fresh spate of tears in her eyes, she reached for it.

My dear Tess,

Though I can't be with you in person at this time, I'm with you in spirit. My every waking thought will be with you while I'm away. Don't worry, I'll be back to you, soon. Until then take care of yourself, and our unborn child. I'll see you soon.

Cam

She read the note repeatedly, until her tears stained the paper. It was painfully clear he didn't mention anything about love in the note. *In time, I'll get him to see he loves me, and I'm already in love with him.*

"I brought you dinner."

Tessa turned to find Chloe in her doorway, her heart beating frantically against her chest. She told Chloe to let herself in whenever she came over, so she didn't have to get up. *See, I'm taking this bed rest seriously.*

"I apologize I didn't mean to startle you. I just thought you'd be hungry." She held up the tray with her dinner. "Doctor Bowman called, he wants to see you the day after tomorrow. He wants you to come in for a checkup."

The talk of the doctor instantly made her hand go to her stomach. Six months and she'd have her beautiful baby in her arms.

Just the thought of it eased her loneliness. Her child would get her through the deployment, the loneliness. She took the tray from Chloe, the grilled chicken, and pasta smelled heavenly.

* * *

It was late when Cameron finally staggered into his apartment, between the day of traveling, and then stopping by the base to see to the situation of his missing Marine, he was exhausted. When he finally landed, he sent Tessa a text message letting her know he arrived, he planned to call her long before then but time got away from him.

Standing in his apartment, he was truly lonely. She had only been a part of his life day and night for a few days, yet his apartment smelled of her perfume. He walked into the bedroom half expecting to see her, but she wasn't there. He pulled out his cell phone, tempted to call her but it was after two in the morning there.

His temptation won out over his practical side. He wanted—no needed—to hear her voice again, and since he was set to deploy in just a few short hours, it might be his only chance for a while. He hit the number two button, bringing up his first favorite saved number—her cell phone number. He stared at it for a moment, before swallowing the lump in his throat and, hitting the talk button. It only had to ring twice, like she had been expecting his call.

"Hello?" Her sleepy voice filled the line. Never in his entire career had he been so split on his loyalties. He made a commitment to the Marines what seemed like a lifetime ago, and only days since he committed to Tess as her husband yet the devotion of his heart clearly laid with her.

"I'm sorry to wake you…I meant to call hours ago…" To his own ears, his voice sounded weak, and pitiful. Damn it, he was a trained Marine, and could kill with his bare hands, but Tessa brought him to his knees.

"I was hoping you'd call." He heard ruffling of the covers, as she readjusted in bed. He could picture her lying in bed, her spaghetti strap tank top and those cute little boy shorts she preferred.

He pictured stripping them off her, pulling the shorts down with his teeth watching her arch under him as he took his time unwrapping her. His shaft grew, standing at full attention for a woman it would be months before he could touch again. He shook his head trying to clear the thoughts, his hands clenched in fists, until he had little half-moon shapes from his fingernails, pressed into his palms.

"I shouldn't have woke you but it will be early for you when I leave…it was my last chance. I wanted to make sure you're okay."

"Please don't worry about me, I'm fine, and because of you our baby is going to be fine too. You need to keep your head in the game, stay safe and come back to us."

Visions of that horrible day filled his mind. He was out playing with some of the other kids on base, when a familiar car drove down the lane. A hush came over the block as everyone stopped to watch, praying the Marines weren't coming to their house. Everyone, even the children, knew what that car was, they understood someone wasn't going to be returning home, and soon the family would be leaving their quiet little street.

Two Marines in their dress blues stepped out of the car, they put their hats back into place, straightened their uniforms, and everyone held their breaths, praying they weren't about to be informed their husband wasn't coming home. Cameron remembered how heavy the ball felt in his hands as they moved around their sleek black car, heading…heading to his house.

Daddy!

His young screams filled his mind as he'd run to the house, back to his mother who'd crumbled on the porch steps sobbing. That was the day his whole world changed, the day he had to step up and care for his mother, to be the man of the house.

"My sweet Tess, I know you'll be fine. You're a survivor, just like me. We wouldn't have gotten through everything in our past otherwise." He sat down on the bed, her scent surrounding him like a warm blanket. "I miss you."

"Me too." The sadness in her voice pulled at him. "But we'll be together soon, with our child."

"You take care of *my* baby. Next time you go to the doctor's make sure you tell him I want a bouncing baby boy." As those words flowed from his lips, he realized the truth in them. He wanted a son that he could play ball with in the back yard, to teach him all the things his father never had time to teach him.

"A son, huh? Well I'll see what I can do about that." She let out a soft laugh. "Chloe mentioned this evening Doctor Bowman wants to see me the day after tomorrow…to follow up because of the trip, and everything."

"Your pregnancy will be fine as long as you take care of yourself." The glaring numbers on the bedside clock reminded him he had to be up in four short hours. "I'll call when I can, but I'll be able to check my email more than call you, especially with the time difference. I left you my laptop, so make sure you email me. I want to know everything the doctor says, and each step of the pregnancy."

"Yes, sir." She teased. "It's not my first rodeo. I'll email you, but if you have a chance to call anytime, don't worry about the time. I'll let you know what the doctor says."

"Good. Now get some rest. I'll see you soon." Not knowing when he'd get to hear her voice again he hated to say goodbye, but they both needed to get some sleep. Especially since after arriving in Clearwater they barely slept, they laid in bed watching movies, talking, but sleep was the furthest thing from their minds. Neither of them wanted their time to end.

"One last thing, Cam…" There was a long pause. "I'm so proud of you. Our child couldn't be blessed with a better father. Stay safe."

"I promise." He ended the conversation and collapsed back onto the bed. *What the hell was I thinking? I went from my job is too dangerous and I want no commitment, to a wife and child on the way in a matter of days. A wife is one thing but one I'm in love with, and have been for more than half my life complicates things a bit.*

* * *

Long after they ended the conversation, Tessa wished she'd told him she loved him, but that would only serve to complicate matters further. He didn't need to leave for this deployment with any more strain then he already had. To tell him she loved him would only serve to make things tense between them.

She could feel there was still a strong connection between them, and he still had feelings for her. But were those feelings love or merely obligation, she wasn't sure. His kisses, his touches, they made it seem like love, but it could be lust on his part. She couldn't tell him her feelings until she was sure about his.

Chapter Nine

The four walls of the cabin were beginning to close in around Tessa, and no matter how nice the bed, she couldn't get comfortable. The small cabin was beginning to feel like a prison instead of a retreat. She needed company and though Chloe tried she still had a bed and breakfast to run, leaving her alone most of the time. She was going stir crazy but today was her doctor's appointment and with any luck, he'd give her permission for light activity instead of bed rest. Her sanity depended on it.

She sat on the edge of the bed and pulled her hair into a ponytail when she heard Chloe come in. She opened her mouth to say something, but closed it when she felt the first flutter in her stomach. She stilled hoping to feel it again. *Is that my baby?* When it didn't happen immediately she was about to write it off as a nervous stomach.

"Tessa, you okay? You seem a little pale." Chloe quickly closed the distance to her, taking Tessa's hand in hers.

"I think…" The flutter interrupted her again. *That's my baby!* Tears swelled in her eyes, and she wished Cameron were there with her to share this moment. "My baby…I felt her." She laid her hand on her stomach, a small bump protruding. Until that moment she thought it might have been some mistake, but feeling her child move under her hand she couldn't deny it.

"That's wonderful." Chloe squeezed her hand. "We should be going."

Tessa grabbed a tissue from the bedside table, using it to dab the tears, before checking her make-up. "Okay. Let's go." With more determination to do right by her child—even if that meant bed rest for the entire pregnancy, and therefore her sanity—she rose ready to meet the doctor that would bring her child into this world.

* * *

Cameron,

By now you've arrived, and have started your deployment, and I'm sitting here counting down the days until I'll see you again. Today while I was getting ready for my first appointment with Doctor Bowman, I felt our baby move for the first time. It was just a little flutter, almost like butterfly wings expanding, but it's amazing. It seemed to make this whole pregnancy real. In less than six months, we're going to be parents. How scary is that? (Cam, if it's too much...or if you've changed your mind...I'll understand.)

I had my first ultrasound and everything looks fine. Our sweet child has a strong healthy heartbeat, but we were unable to find out the sex. I had hoped I'd be able to let you know you were having that bouncing boy you wanted. I'll have another one at twenty weeks, so you'll have to wait seven more weeks.

The doctor says things are going all right, but tomorrow I'm going to the hospital for an IV iron infusion to bring up my levels. The iron supplements aren't working as quickly as the doctor would like, and this will be the faster way to bring it to the level he'd like to see for pregnancy. He assures me it's safe for the baby.

The best part of it...I'll be off bed rest. I'm only allowed to do light duty and resting frequently but it's better than sitting in bed all the time. The walls were beginning to close in around me without you here to keep me entertained. I promise I'll take it easy.

Stay safe,
Tessa

* * *

It was a long grueling night when Cameron was finally able to get back to their temporary base. The dry desert air made the heat worse, but as he logged into his email his day began to have a ray of hope. An email from Tessa shined like a lighthouse to a sailor lost a sea. He felt his shoulders relax as he clicked to open it.

He read the email twice, letting the words sink in. *She felt my son move.* It pained him that he wasn't there with her, to share in the excitement. *Does she doubt my commitment to her and the baby because of the distance that separates us?* He hated the thought that she questioned him. After all these years, he would have thought she'd known him better than that. He wouldn't have committed himself to them if he weren't sure. *Maybe now, is the time to tell her I love her? No, not until I'm safe at home with her. Then I'll tell her. Telling her now will only make her worry more.*

Tess,

I know oceans, and more miles then I care to remember separate us, but please don't start doubting me—doubting us—now. You, our child (read son) and I are meant to be.

That's wonderful news. Don't worry I have faith that in a few weeks you'll know that we're having a son. With all kidding aside, son or daughter, it doesn't matter to me, as long as he or she is healthy.

Don't forget what we talked about...call the school. See about enrolling in the last two classes you need for your legal studies degree. If you do it now and you'll be done before the baby is born. You won't be working once the baby is born, but I know the degree means a lot to you and I want to see you finish it. You're too close to give up now. You're on my accounts, checkbook, credit cards, and everything you need is in the top nightstand draw. It will give you something to keep you busy while you're resting. Do it...

Take care of our child,

Cam

He closed the laptop, and made his way back to his bunk. Tiredness wore at every muscle in his body, but his thoughts were on Tess.

* * *

Tessa relaxed in the recliner, the IV dripping slowly, while her thoughts turned back to Cameron's email. Going back to school was a big decision, but after the baby was born when would she have the time? It was time she stood on her own two feet, she needed to be able to provide a life for her child, and she didn't want to have to rely on Cameron.

Going back to school would give her something to focus herself on while she waited for Cameron to come home. With only two classes left, it shouldn't be too difficult, especially since all her classes would be online. She unlocked her cell phone, pulling up the Internet and searched her email for the number. She'd make a life for her and her child, if Cameron stayed with her or if he didn't mattered only to her heart. She wanted the degree whether she stayed married or not, it was something her mother thought she'd never accomplish and she would prove her wrong yet again.

Chapter Ten

Tessa thumbed through one of the law books for her class, the sun was beginning to set over the lake, and she'd have to go in soon. She preferred to be outdoors, sitting by the lake, especially while the weather was so welcoming.

She had been here three weeks, her stomach growing quicker than the time was passing. She longed for Cameron to be home, she ached to hold her child in her arms. Things were changing faster than she could keep up with, turning into something, she never expected her life to be—turning out to be exactly what she wanted. She let the pages of the book fall shut, her gaze drifting skywards and she let her mind wander.

Her cell phone that lay discarded beside her on the bench vibrated. *Cameron?* Her heart skipped a beat, with hope it was him. When she grabbed her phone, her stomach plummeted. *Tony.* Her hand went to her stomach. The biological father of her child was the last one she wanted to hear from. She was tempted to not answer it but he'd only call back.

She took a deep breath and answered the phone. "Hello?"

"Tessa, my love." His voice was ingratiatingly sweet, making her sick to her stomach. "I've gone by your apartment the last two nights, but you're never home. Where are you sugar?"

"Tony, we made it clear we were done weeks ago, why are you calling now?" She expected hurt—or even disappointment—after all she devoted the last year of her life to this man before she found out he was married. But all she felt was impatience. She was tired of his lies.

"I miss you. Let me come over tonight and you won't doubt my love for you any longer." His husky voice clawed along her skin, but he left her cold. She wanted nothing to do with Tony.

"We're done. We would have never started if I knew you were married. I'm not into married men Tony. So go back to your wife and leave me alone."

"It's that Marine of yours, isn't it? Carmen? I heard you were kissing him. Damn it, you're mine! Come back to me and we'll let your cheating fall by the way side."

A red robin landed on the path around the lake, catching her attention. "His name is Cameron. Cheating? Isn't that like the pot calling the kettle black? You've been cheating on your *wife* for over a year now. Nonetheless, it no longer matters. Tony, we're finished. I'm not some possession that you can claim, I'm a person and have needs and wants of my own. I won't be the second woman. Don't go by my apartment again, I've taken a job out of town for the time being." With that, she ended the call. She wouldn't tell Tony she was pregnant, not that he'd want anything to do with the child, but because her son or daughter deserved better than him as a father.

If Cameron never offered to help, it still wouldn't have changed things. She'd never let that man use her child as a weapon. Her anger spiked. She couldn't believe he had the audacity to ask her if she was with Cameron. Who she was with was none of his business, Tony was the cheater.

A four-wheeler powered down the path in her direction, jarring her from her thoughts. She tilted her head and spotted Jordan and Chloe. *Dinner time.* She rose, grabbing her things, before crossing the path to the cabin.

"Hey Tessa, we thought we'd have dinner with you tonight at the picnic table if that's okay?" Chloe climbed off the four-wheeler with a large tray of covered dishes.

"That will be great. Thank you. Shall I grab drinks?" She sat her stuff down on the table, and took a step towards the door.

Jordan came around the four-wheeler towards them, he held up a cloth bag. "I've got that covered."

Chloe took the lid off the plates to reveal spaghetti and meatballs, and set up the table. "Just what you asked for..." She smiled at Tessa.

"Thank you, Chloe. When Cameron comes home he won't recognize me if you keep giving in to all my cravings." Tessa teased, sitting down on the bench, swinging her leg under the table.

"I have strict orders to see to all your needs." Chloe shot her a quick smile before taking a bite.

As they ate, they made small chit chat, talking about the bed and breakfast, her pregnancy, anything except the white elephant in the middle of the table, Cameron and his deployment. It was the one thing that seemed to consume Tessa's every waking thought.

"If you ladies will excuse me I promised Sheriff Ryder I'd meet him, we've got to discuss the plans for that upcoming conference." Jordan rose, and added the gathered plates onto the tray before kissing his wife. "Don't rush, Ryan and I will be awhile. I'll leave the four-wheeler for you."

When Jordan was out of hearing range Chloe turned back to Tessa, her eyebrows rose in question. "What's going on today? You seem upset. Feeling okay?"

"I'm fine." Tessa didn't want to tell Chloe all the details, especially since she and everyone else, believed Cameron was the father. "I just heard from an old acquaintance, and it brought up some bad memories. That's all."

Bad memories…that's how she described a year of her life wasted. The only good thing to come from that relationship was her pregnancy, and the possibility to explore what had been in hibernation between she and Cameron for years. *I guess the saying, all bad things happen for a reason is true.*

* * *

Cameron,

Chloe and I are getting along better than I could have expected. She's truly an amazing woman, and she seems to bring out the best of everyone around her. I don't know how she manages to stay sane running Winterbloom day after day, but at least now, she has Jordan. Aww, what a sweet couple they make, so much in love.

I started back to school, turns out, I have enough credits that I only have to take a couple tests for one class and I'll graduate. This means I'll be finished long before our child's born. I've even started taking on some freelance legal projects…don't worry I'm not taking on too much. It gives me something to do while I'm taking it easy.

Tony called…guess my landlord told him we were together. He suspects I've been with you… Nevermind none of that matters, I only brought it up because I didn't tell him he's the father. I don't plan to either. I won't let him use this child the way he used me. If you decide you don't want to be a surrogate father, then I'll raise him or her on my own. I just thought you should know…I don't want anyone besides us to know his role. Our child deserves the world, she doesn't need to know I'm a complete screw-up.

Our child is active in the evenings, fluttering around like a small butterfly. She seems to find peace in our evening stroll by the lake. Clearwater is such a peaceful place, in the city you never hear the birds chirping as you do here. I thought I would go crazy with the lack of noise, but I've found peace in it.

Stay safe. Missing you,

Tessa

Setting the laptop aside, she rose from the couch, and she rubbed the small of her back trying to ease some of the tension that resided there. Doubts plagued her as she went for her evening stroll. In all the years she had known Cameron, she had never known him to commit himself to something he didn't believe in. Yet still she couldn't help but question if he stepped up as a father to her unborn child out of some duty rather than his commitment to her. She wanted him to be a father and husband because he loved her.

Why do feelings always have to get in the middle of a good relationship? Why can't I be satisfied with our friendship? Instead, I need him to return the love I have for him. Things are always so damn complicated.

* * *

Cameron winced as the coldness of the icepack on his bare shoulder, the heat of the air and his body made the icepack a mixture of relief and torture. The damn IED explosion rocked his team but at least no one died. He sent a broken man home to his family, his leg nearly gone, but the important part was he'd live. His bruised shoulder was the worst of his injuries, and he'd be sore for a few days but the Marines taught him to work past that. There was no room for sissies in the Marines.

He opened his email knowing there'd be another message from Tessa. She had been emailing him daily, giving him a touch of home through the many miles that separated them.

My Tess, always the worrier, when I get back I'll wipe all the doubt from your mind. He hated there was nothing but words he could give her now to try to relieve her doubt that he wanted to be a father to her child. With time, he'd prove he could be the father, and husband she wanted. Realization dawned on him, like the sun coming over the hills, he'd always wanted to marry her, to be the one man in her life. The thought of her needing something he couldn't give—a man that was there, with a safe career—was the only thing that held him back. He had always loved her.

Tess,

Your daily emails are the connection I need to make this deployment not seem as lonely. Especially today, when I had to make the notification that one of my men would be returning stateside due to injuries he sustained. Damn IED's.

I only have words to tell you I'm committed to our child. I'll be home soon and I'll prove just that. Until then think of me as our child moves within you, and know the secret is safe with me. He will only know us as his parents, and he'll be a happy bouncing boy. Which if you notice I keep referring to our child as he while your email mentions she. Know this, boy or girl, I don't care as long as our child and you are healthy. Two weeks until we know the sex...two weeks until I'm proven right.

Clearwater is a beautiful place. The small town is so different then where we were raised. It's a safe town, with residents who bond together in a time of need. Downside, it gets snow, and I mean lots of snow.

Cam

Before hitting the send button, he stared at the last paragraph, and wondered if he was serious about giving up his military career and settling down. This deployment was one of the worst since his first, his thoughts turning to Tess each chance it had, and he longed to be home. He knew he was leaning towards giving it all up, setting down and living the life Jordan seemed to love so much.

If he did, Clearwater would be a perfect place to start over. They had no ties anywhere else, and she already seemed to be forming a close friendship with Chloe.

Chapter Eleven

Tessa sank into the couch and put her feet up, she couldn't believe the day she'd had. Her feet ached, but in a good way it had been too long since she had some girl shopping time. Before her appointment, Chloe took her into Jackson Hole to do a little maternity shopping, it had been one thing she had been dreading thinking she'd been stuck in elastic waistband pants, and too girly shirts for her tastes. Chloe surprised her by taking her to a small shop that catered to young pregnant woman, with clothes that would bring out the pregnancy glow.

She found so many different outfits that she just adored, and in doing so she found out Chloe and her had a lot in common, besides shopping. When Cameron returned from his deployment, it would be hard to leave behind the first female friendship she had formed in years.

"I put the last of the bags in the bedroom. You email your sweetie and let him know the good news, while I go check on Winterbloom then I'll be back to help put the stuff away. I'll talk to Jordan and see what he has planned for next Friday, and we can go do some baby shopping." Chloe's hand rested on the doorknob as she turned towards Tessa one final time. "This is so much fun. I can't wait until I'm pregnant. Maybe it's time to start nagging Jordan to build our cabin, he's only been planning it for months. I think it's time he breaks ground. Then we'll have our own privacy and can start a family, can't have screaming babies all night in a bed and breakfast."

Tessa laughed, at the thought, and powered on the laptop. Chloe had such excitement about Tessa's pregnancy, she was sure it wouldn't be long before she too was expecting. Chloe and Jordan would be good parents, their love was strong and true, and they both had hearts of gold, or they wouldn't have opened up their lives and home to her. There was no doubt in her mind they'd be excellent parents.

Cam,

The email you've been waiting for is finally here...maybe I should draw this out, teasing you, but I won't. The reason isn't that I'm too good to tease you, no it's more selfish than that. I want to rub it in I was right...we're having a baby girl. Yeah that's right, I was right. Seriously, though, I know you wanted a son, I hope you're not too upset about it.

Chloe was there with me when I found out, but I couldn't stop myself from wishing you were there.

She looked up from the email and pulled out his extra set of dog tags that she wore around her neck. They were normally hidden beneath her shirt, next to her heart, giving her a senses of comfort. She fiddled with them for a moment. *In a way, you were there.* She kissed the tags, praying he was safe.

She's beautiful. I've attached the sonogram picture. I can't believe I still have four more months before I can hold her in my arms. That's not as bad as thinking of how long until you're home.

I apologize to cut off quickly but Chloe just returned. We've got to put away my new clothes. Yes, we went maternity clothes shopping today, and had a girl's day out. So unlike me I know, but it was fun. We're going to do it again Friday, but this time shopping for little girl clothes. Finally, I'm going to have my own little princess to dress up.

Stay safe. Missing you,

Tessa

She reclined on the bed folding the last of the clothes, while Chloe made use of the closet space. "I still can't believe I'm having a girl, a daughter."

"It's exciting." Chloe hung up the last item and stepped back to the bed, sitting down on the edge. "Jordan can handle things at Winterbloom Friday after breakfast so we can go shopping. I just have to be back in time to cook dinner. That was the little catch that he threw in, but we won't be gone that long. You're still supposed to be taking it easy."

"It's really great to have a friend like you. Thank you for all you're doing for me."

"There's no need to thank me. I'm glad to help, I'm enjoying it." Chloe patted Tessa's leg and rose. "I better get back before Jordan thinks I've run off shopping again. I'll see you in the morning."

Tessa was debating about calling it an early night when her cell phone rang. Each time it rang, she hoped it would be Cameron, he called once so far but it seemed so long ago. Her soul longed to hear his voice again, while her body longed to feel his touch, to feel his lips pressed against hers. Even with all that, she didn't have to look at the caller id to know it wasn't him, something inside her told her she didn't want to answer the phone yet she had to.

She picked it up, pushing the talk button as she raised it to her ear. "Hello?"

"Damn it Tessa. Where the hell are you?" There was so much anger and hostility in Tony's voice, it sent chills up her spine.

Even with the miles that separated them, she couldn't forget the temper Tony had. She chose her words carefully, as she had done many times before, to not make him angrier. He never physically harmed her but the temper was always something that seemed to boil under the surface. "Tony, there's nothing left for us any longer."

"You had no right to marry him. You're mine! I want you back here now. I'll start the paperwork to get it annulled."

Shit, how did he find out? "I don't want it annulled. Even if I did, I wouldn't come back to you. You're married. I won't be the second woman. It's time for us both to move on. If you're not happy with your wife you can find someone else, but as for us it's over."

"Tessa, if I have to come and find you, you'll regret it." Venom dripped from every syllable.

"Things are over between us, if you come near me I'll call the police. Goodbye Tony." She moved the phone away from her ear but she could hear his screaming. *You're mine, I'll find you!* She refused to give in and have the last word. She would no longer be his doormat. If he called again she'd get a new cell phone number.

She tossed the phone beside her on the comforter, and got up. Rubbing her hand over her growing stomach, she was pleased how much she had changed in a few weeks. Opening her dresser drawer wanting comfort, she pulled out one of Cameron's t-shirts instead of the normal tank tops she favored to sleep in.

Quickly she changed out of her clothes, tossing them in the hamper for the laundry woman, and slipped into the t-shirt. Her stomach was growing so quickly the shirt was beginning to become snug around her body, giving her the feeling of being wrapped in his arms, his cologne still clung to the shirt, making her only miss him more.

Crawling back into bed, ready to sleep her cell phone rang again. She grabbed it without looking at the screen. *This is his last warning.* "If you call me again I'll get a restraining order…"

"Tess, what's going on?" Cameron's voice was full of concern.

Damn it! She mentally kicked herself for not checking the phone screen before she answered. "Cam…it's so good to hear from you. Did you get my email?" She tried to pretend she didn't start the conversation off on the wrong foot.

"We'll get to that in a moment. Tell me what's going on? Who did you expect to be calling?"

She let out a deep sign, her shoulders sinking with the knowledge she was adding to his worries, but not telling him would only serve to make him more concerned for her. "Tony…he found out we got married. He must have read it in the paper. None of that matters…"

"It matters to me. I knew he had a temper but you always said he never touched you and I believed you. But I won't have him threatening you. He's dangerous." Sorrow touched his voice. "He's a lawyer so he could have the connections to find out where you're at. I doubt he'll go through the trouble, but just in case I want you to let Jordan know, he'll protect you until I can. Also if he calls again I want you to get the restraining order."

"Cam, don't worry. I was just overreacting…"

"Don't argue with me. I want you safe, I'm sorry I can't be there to protect you myself." There was a deep sigh, before he continued. "I got the email. I called to tell you those three words I know you're dying to hear…you were right. We're having a baby girl." The happiness now replaced the sorrow she heard in his voice only seconds before. The emotions in his voice changed so quickly she had a hard time keeping up with them.

"I know you wanted a son, you're not upset?" She curled into bed, cupping her stomach.

"No, we can have a son later. We'll need to set down some ground rules, such as no dating until she's thirty." He teased.

"You're going to be one of those dads who scares off all her suitors, aren't you?"

"Until the perfect man comes along for her, yes." He laughed. "I wanted to call and tell you not to worry. I'm happy to be having a daughter, and she's beautiful."

Under her fingertips, her little girl was active, doing summersaults and kicking. "She's being very active this evening. She must know I'm talking to her daddy."

"What does it feel like?"

She thought about it for a moment, trying to put the sensation into words. "At first it felt like butterflies expanding their wings for the first time, but as the time goes by it gets stronger. Now, it's almost like popcorn popping, especially when she kicks." There was some movement on the other end, Cameron said something to someone but she couldn't make it out.

"Sweetheart, I'm sorry I've got to go, a mission dropped on us. Get some rest and take care of my daughter. Start thinking of names."

"Stay safe."

"Don't worry. I will, I have something to come home to." With that, the line went dead.

She kept telling herself he was a trained Marine one who had fifteen years of experience. He'd be fine. It did very little to calm her nerves.

Chapter Twelve

Tessa was adding a touch of lipstick when Chloe hollered from the front of the cabin. "You ready?" Their baby-shopping trip was about to start, and she couldn't wait. Now that she knew she was having a little girl she could pick out all the cute little outfits she had been looking at online. Whatever she didn't find locally, she could always order online.

She took one final look in the mirror, the pale blue cotton sweater hugged her stomach, emphasizing her pregnancy without making her appear fat. She found her hand went to her stomach often, always searching for her daughter's movements, and it brought her comfort. It was becoming an unconscious gesture. "Coming." She called, slipping her feet into the ballerina shoes.

"Jordan has asked us to stay in town, to be on the safe side with Tony's threats. Jennifer Anderson—she's the owner of Express-Ohh's the local coffee shop—is going to watch Winterbloom for us on Wednesday and we can do some more shopping in Jackson Hole if you're up to it." Chloe explained when Tessa came out of the bedroom.

"It's fine. I'm sure we'll find plenty of great stuff at Tiny Treasure Baby Store, and I can order whatever else I need online."

"It's up to you, but we have to go to Jackson Hole anyways. Jordan's got to pick up supplies to finish remolding the last cabin." Chloe spun around to head back outside, her red curly hair twirling around her in the breeze.

"Okay." Tessa grabbed her purse and followed Chloe out. "Thanks for taking me shopping. I sold my car a year ago, because living in the city you don't really need it. I can catch a cab if I have to and my apartment was centrally located that I could walk anywhere I needed to go. It seemed pointless to keep the car when I rarely used it." She climbed into the passenger side of Chloe's SUV. "Here you have to have one. I feel like such a burden."

"You're not. It's great going shopping with you, to have something to do besides run Winterbloom. Jennifer and I are close, we talk on the phone almost every day but we rarely get to go out and do things together. Both of our schedules are too busy, and she's single. It's nice to have a married friend." Chloe spoke as she drove the SUV around the lake, and onto the tree lined driveway that lead to Main Street.

"Winterbloom takes a lot of your time, it's surprising you have the energy to do anything else."

"It does, but I love it. I helped Gram run it for many years, and when she passed, it just seemed right I would continue on the legacy. Having Jordan there to help is wonderful, and we always hire someone to help out during winter—our busy season." Suddenly there was excitement sparking in her eyes. "Jordan's going to break ground for our new cabin, in two weeks. That will give him time to finish the last guest cabin. That means we can work on starting our own family, and we discussed hiring someone full time as an innkeeper. Winterbloom is very successful and it's time I stepped back a little from doing everything myself."

"That's wonderful. You and Jordan are going to make wonderful parents. I hope you'll let me have the honor of shopping with you in return, it will be fun to be on the other side." Tessa couldn't suppress her frown. She hated the idea of being on the other side of the country when Chloe got pregnant. She'd miss seeing her every day and going shopping together—and the routine they'd fallen into and loved. Returning to North Carolina meant someday she might have to face Tony. It was a large area, but she had a feeling he wouldn't give up without a fight.

Chloe slid the SUV into a parking space on Queen Street in front of Tiny Treasure Baby Store. Stepping out of the SUV Tessa took in the small shops lining the street, she hadn't been on Queen Street but she knew it was the main road out of Clearwater, heading towards Montana. Across the street was An Intimate Fit, clearly a lingerie store from the mannequins in the window. *Guess you can shop for your child, and then go across the street and get something sexy for your husband.* She laughed at the thought of wearing lingerie with her ever-growing stomach.

"Want to go there next?" Chloe asked, coming around the stand next to her. "The Intimate Fit...they have the best stuff there. We can find you something sexy for when Cameron comes home for leave."

"I can't..." She started to say she couldn't wear something like that in front of Cameron, their relationship hadn't progressed to that level yet, but she kept her mouth shut. Chloe thought her unborn child was his and she wasn't about to explain it wasn't. "Not in my condition. I look like I've swallowed half a basketball."

"Pregnancy makes you glow, and if Cameron is anything like Jordan he'll love you no matter what you're wearing. I say when he comes home you wear only the natural glow of your pregnancy, forget all the silk and lace of lingerie until he's home for good. Your time will be too limited during leave."

If only...

* * *

It had just started to rain when Chloe parked in front of her cabin. "Go ahead in, put your feet up, I'll grab the bags."

Tessa nodded, and slipped out of the SUV, reaching around to rub her back. Her back was sore, and only grew worse as the day went on. She needed to sit, with the back massager that Chloe brought her a few days ago. It was pure heaven to her sore body.

Inside she found Jordan leaning against the kitchen counter taking a long swig from the beer bottle in his hand. "Everything okay?" She asked wondering why he was there waiting for them.

"Yeah. Chloe and I have a surprise for you. Where's she?" He sat his beer down on the counter.

"I'm here." Chloe sat the bags next to the door. "I've been anxious about this all day. Let's show her."

"What are you two talking about?" Tessa's forehead knitted in confusion.

"You'll understand in a moment." Chloe slipped her arm through Tessa's and led the way back to the bedroom.

The open window let the cool breeze in, making the bedroom feel cool. She wanted to crawl into the bed, and let the cool wind drift over her body. *The bed?* There were wrapped packages covering it, her gaze drifted over the packages before something larger caught her attention. The beautiful stained black crib stood near the far side of the bed.

"Jordan made the crib for you. He's almost finished with the changing table and matching dresser for her clothes...it's why we're going to Jackson Hole on Wednesday. He needs more stain to match the crib and you can pick out the handles you'd like." Chloe grinned, but Tessa was only half listening.

"You shouldn't have…" She walked around the bed to touch it. There was so much thought and work put into it, the design in the woodwork appeared to be hand carved, adding to its beauty. She ran her hand over the wood; taking her fingertip, she slid it along the carved flowers in the design. "It's beautiful."

"The flower design matches the nursery bed set you showed Chloe you wanted if you were having a girl. Once you knew what you were having I was able to add them." Jordan explained.

"The stuff…" Chloe nodded towards the packages on the bed. "I had specific instructions from Cameron before he left. They're from him. There's a note from him with them. I think you'll want to do that alone. Jordan and I will be outside, when you're ready, I'll help put everything away. Take your time."

They left her, and the silence filled the room, Cameron was many miles away yet he found a way to give her something, to be a part of the pregnancy. She'd never truly be alone with a man like that. He'd always be there for her, even when he physically wasn't.

She slipped her finger under the seal of the envelope, opening it carefully. The sentiment filled her, spilling her tears down her cheeks.

My Tess,

I'm sorry I can't be there now, but I hope this gives you some comfort as you prepare for our child. I've left Chloe with instructions to find the perfect thing for you and our child, on my behalf. This is just a small token of the love I feel already for our child.

Thank you for letting me be a part of this journey with you. I'll be home to you both soon.

Cam

Cameron had always been a man of action, instead of words but when it mattered, somehow he always found the right thing to say— or write. She tucked the note into the nightstand drawer, wanting it close to her. She'd save it and add it to her daughter's scrapbook, but for now her attention turned back to the remaining things on the bed.

She opened the largest package that sat next to her, letting the paper fall to the floor, she found the crib set she had planned if she had a daughter. The white background had large black swirls through it with pink roses, and the edges had vibrant pink trim. It was beautiful, and the silky feel would bring a soothing comfort to her daughter.

She'd surround her in girly things, giving her the true girl experience, the one thing Tessa never had. Tessa's dad hadn't left room for the feminine in their house. It wasn't until she was out on her own that she was able to purchase nice clothes. Before that all she knew had been denim jeans and t-shirts. And she still dressed in them regularly, but when the occasion called for something dressy, she liked to go all out. She did have a fascination with heels, especially boots with heels.

Before she realized it, she had all the packages open, and spread out on the bed. There was everything she'd need for the crib, a beautiful mobile with pink and white roses dangling from it, along with baby blankets, a few small toys, and her favorite a matching diaper bag.

Chloe went through all the trouble to order this stuff so Cameron could be a part of it, which made it more extraordinary. Her fingers went to his dog tags again, as she thought about him, before she rose off the bed and went to find Chloe.

"Oh sweetie, none of this was meant to make you cry…" Chloe rose from the picnic table and came to her when she came out of the house.

"They're good tears. Thank you." She hugged Chloe, before turning to Jordan. "Thank you. I love the crib. It's everything I wanted and more."

"You're welcome." Jordan stayed sitting on top of the picnic table, watching the women.

"Come on, let's go organize your room while Jordan starts dinner." Chloe turned them around and started walking towards the cabin.

"Wait a moment…I thought you said you were cooking tonight?" Jordan rose from the cabin eyeing his wife with question.

"Oh love, but the steaks taste so much better when you do it. Won't you do them? They're already marinated, and the veggies and potatoes for the grill are on the counter."

"Fine." He acted like he was upset that he had to cook, but everyone knew Jordan loved his grill almost as much as he loved Chloe. "Tessa, why don't you come over to the house for dinner? It will do you good to mingle with the guests."

"Okay." Tessa nodded, before she followed Chloe into the cabin.

"We're going to need to wash the clothes and bedding before we put them away, but we can at least start setting up the other things we bought." Chloe explained as they entered the bedroom again. "Things are going to be snug with the baby furniture in here, but you'll make it work. Once the baby is born you won't have long before you…"

Tessa knew she was about to say before she was gone. They both knew the close friendship they had formed would soon be strained by distance.

"I'll visit…" Tessa told Chloe when sadness filled the silence, but they both knew visits would be far between. They both had their lives, and commitments. She'd be busy with her daughter, and Chloe with Winterbloom and soon her own family.

"I know." Chloe smiled trying to lighten the mood. "Don't worry we have a lot of time left still."

Chapter Thirteen

Alone again in her cabin, she was surrounded by reminders that soon her daughter would be born—not that the protruding stomach, and movements weren't to enough let her know she'd soon have a little life depending on her—she couldn't help but be sad, too. She seemed to be stuck always losing someone. First, it was Cameron to his deployment and soon it would be Chloe. Loss kept following her and she only hoped that the new life forming within her would change all that.

In her favorite spot, snuggled deep within the covers of the bed, she pulled open the laptop again. It had become her nightly routine to email Cameron before going to sleep.

Cam,

Thank you doesn't seem like enough but it's all I can say. Today after shopping for baby clothes, I came back to a surprise. Jordan made our daughter a beautiful crib, it has hand carved flowers into the design. It's striking, and matches the crib set I wanted. That leads me to the surprises Chloe had laid out on the bed from you. It means so much that you did that, our daughter is going to have a beautiful nursery when we return to North Carolina, until then everything in crammed into the cabins bedroom.

Today for the first time I felt a true kick from our little girl. Wow, she has a power kick. It's like she's playing soccer in my stomach with my organs. She's going to make her daddy proud. Oh, but it's wonderful. I can't believe I'm almost six months pregnant now. Soon our daughter will be here.

Stay safe. I miss you,

Tessa

P.S. I think we should name her Rosalie after your mother. She seems to have the same fighting spirit your mom had. I can't think of a name better for our little girl.

* * *

Rosalie? She wants to name our girl after my mother...I can't believe it. Cameron sat there at the computer looking at the pictures of Tessa's growing stomach that she shared. He yearned to be there to feel the kicks of his daughter. He clicked the reply button, with anticipation of telling her of his plans.

My Tess,

Rosalie is perfect. Mom was an amazing woman; she made us the people we are. It would be an honor to have you name our daughter after her. Thank you.

Today I put in the paperwork for my leave. I planned it for the end of your pregnancy, with any luck I'll be there for the birth of Rosalie. I know you were hoping I'd be home sooner, but this way I have a better chance to be there for the birth. I wouldn't want to miss being there when our Rosalie made her grand entrance. Just three months…

Cam

He signed out of his email, beyond ready to get some sleep, to be with Tess if only it was in his dreams.

* * *

Cam,

Though it means we'll be apart longer, I understand. To have you there with me when I bring our daughter into this world means more to me than having you here now. Rosalie will be here soon.

Until I see you again stay safe. Missing you,

Tessa

Chapter Fourteen

The months passed quicker than she would have guessed, but the biggest surprise was how her stomach grew, extending to give Rosalie room to grow. Now with just six weeks until her due date, her nerves stretched taut, as hard as her stomach. She wasn't sure if she was more anxious about her upcoming due date or for Cameron's leave.

She curled on the couch while Chloe knelt near the coffee table, packing the last of the care package for Cameron when her cell phone rang. After two tries, she was able to scoot forward enough to grab her cell. "Hello?"

"Mrs. White?" An official sounding voice filled the line making her heart beat faster.

"This is her. Who's this?" She rubbed her stomach, doing her best to calm Rosalie, who was picking up on her unease.

"I'm Second Lieutenant River. I'm calling to inform you, your husband has had an accident." There was a pause as if he was letting it sink in. "The injuries he has sustained are not life threatening but they are required to transport him stateside. He'll arrive at Camp Lejeune in North Carolina tomorrow, you can see him after twelve hundred hours."

No, not my Cameron. "Injuries?"

"They are not life threatening, he's busted up, but he'll heal." His voice was calm as if he was telling her the weather. Only serving to upset her more, this was her husband they were talking about. She wanted to know what happened to her husband. "There was an attack on the compound, his leg was broken in two places, and he's banged up—bumps and bruises."

"Is there a way for me to get in touch with him?" Her voice sounded weak to her own ears, but she needed to hear his voice, to know he was okay.

"I apologize, Mrs. White. Your husband has undergone surgery to repair his leg, he's stable and is to be transported shortly. During surgery to repair the damage to his leg they had to put in two screws to keep the bones in place, he'll need physical therapy, but he'll heal with time. They will be transporting him back to North Carolina where you can see him tomorrow afternoon." She heard a ruffle of papers; it sent the distinct feeling that she was another assignment to him.

"I'll make arrangements." She hit the end button and turned to Chloe, sobs wracking her body. "I've got to go…" She pressed a hand over her mouth, trying to stifle the sobs. There was so much she needed to do but her mind couldn't wrap itself around any one thing. She stood there at a loss as to what to do. *Reservation…pack…* Her thoughts were all over the place.

"What happened?" Chloe came to her, laying her hand on Tessa's arm.

"Cameron…" She fell into Chloe's embrace, and sobbed. Tears coating her throat making it hard to breath, let alone talk. Chloe held her, rubbing her back, as she tried to pull herself together. When she was finally able to speak, she told Chloe what happened. "I've got to go to him…he'll be in North Carolina tomorrow."

"Shhh…I'll make us reservations. Just sit down, and breathe. Cameron's going to be okay." Chloe pulled her cell phone from the pocket of her shorts. "Jordan, I need you over here."

Chloe had just powered up Tessa's laptop to make the reservations when she heard the sound of a four-wheeler squealing to a stop in front of the cabin.

Jordan didn't bother to knock he came rushing into the cabin, looking around to see what the emergency was. "What happened?"

Tessa's tears returned with a vengeance as Chloe explained the situation. Part of her knew she was overreacting, according to the Marine that called, Cameron's injuries weren't life threatening but she wouldn't be convinced until she saw him. Right now, she couldn't convince herself that he wasn't on his deathbed, and until she knew, her emotions were uncontrollable.

"Go pack for her, I'll make the reservations." Jordan came and knelt in front of Tessa, taking her hand in his. "Words mean little comfort in a time like this, but whatever comforts they can give you, know the Marine that called wouldn't give you false hope. If he said Cameron would be okay, he will."

Tessa knew his words were true yet she found little peace in them. She held tightly to the dog tags around her neck, praying he would be okay. "I'm going to lie down, if you could book me on the first plane out I'd appreciate it."

She went to the bedroom, and lay on top of the covers, pressing his shirt to her nose. She wished his smell that clung to the shirt was stronger but it was fading quickly. Chloe moved around her, packing her a small suitcase but Tessa didn't pay attention. Her thoughts occupied with concerns for Cameron.

* * *

Dusk was beginning to set over Clearwater when Tessa woke to Chloe gently shaking her arm. She let out a soft moan, and rubbed her sore eyes. Dried tears coated her cheeks, making her face feel stiff. "I'm sorry, I must have fallen asleep."

"You needed the rest." Tessa could see the sadness in Chloe's eyes, reminding her all over again, of what happened. "We need to be leaving for the airport shortly, if you want to freshen up. I've got your suitcase in the car, but if you need something from it…"

Tessa shook her head. "It's fine. I'll just put on pants, the airplane might be too chilly for shorts." She didn't care about changing or freshening up, all she wanted to do was to be on her way to Cameron. Each minute ticked by like an hour, making her stir crazy.

Jordan poked his head in the bedroom door and when he saw that she was awake, he came in. "Hope's here." He told Chloe.

"Great. I'll bring her up to speed, if you want to…" She nodded towards Tessa, as if she meant for Jordan to keep an eye on her and rose from the bed. She strolled out of the bedroom, leaving them alone.

"Who's Hope?" She swung her legs off the bed and used her hands to push herself off the bed. Rubbing the small of her back, she walked to the dresser, and grabbed out a pair of gray yoga pants, with pale pink trim at the top. If she was going to have to travel most of the night, she might as well do it in comfort.

Jordan leaned casually in the doorway, watching her. "She's normally our winter help. She's going to take over for a few days while we're away."

"I'm fine to go on my own. You guys don't have…"

He took two quick strides to her, and took hold of her hand. "Tessa, we're not going to let you go on your own. He asked us to watch over you until he could do it himself, and that's what we're doing. Plus you've become like family in the last few months, we wouldn't want you to be alone in a time like this." When she started to protest he added. "Save your strength, you're not going to be able to sway me. Winterbloom only has a few guests, and Hope will manage. She's used to doing it when the place is full, she can manage two guests. Go ahead and get changed, we'll be leaving in ten minutes."

Chapter Fifteen

Tessa rushed through the halls of the hospital, trying to find Cameron. Reception sent her to one area, only to find out when they got there that he had been moved. *Damn it, where is he?* She wanted to scream at the nurses, at anyone that would listen but she knew it would get her nowhere.

"Third door on the right, down that hall..." Jordan explained. After the third nurses' station she let Jordan deal with it or her temper that was hanging by a threat might break.

She didn't wait for him to finish; she took off down the hall towards him. *Cameron, I'm coming.* In the dim light of the room, she could see Cameron asleep in the bed. Her strong, handsome man looked fragile, breaking her heart. His normally tanned skin was pale and drawn, the white hospital gown and linens seemed to make it worse.

She sank into a chair by the bedside, watching her husband's sleeping form. She wanted to take his hand in hers, but didn't dare to disturb him. Sleep was the best thing for him, in his condition. She did her best to push the tears that were welling in her eyes, there was no way she wanted him to wake to find a weeping wife by his side.

Chloe stepped into the room, walking quietly to Tessa. "I just wanted to let you know that we'll give you privacy. We'll be down the hall in the waiting room, whenever you're done, or need a break." She squeezed Tessa's shoulder and then left.

Alone with Cameron she couldn't stop herself from wrapping her hand over his, he slept so peacefully she had to watch his chest to know he was still breathing. She kept reminding herself it was the pain medication but it did little to calm her nerves. "Oh Cameron." Tears running down her face, she whispered more to herself then him.

She must have fallen asleep waiting for him to wake up because the next thing she knew she woke to his hand stroking through her hair. "Cam..." Their gazes met, and she had to blink the tears away again.

Pain shot across his face as he moved to the far side of the bed. "Come here, love." He patted the space he'd made. She didn't have to be asked twice, she rose from the chair, stretching out her muscles before squeezing in next to him. Lying next to him, she wrapped her arm around his chest, and held him close to her.

"Shh, love, I'm okay." He used the hand that was around her and gently rubbed small circles down her back. "It's only a broken leg. I'll be back on my feet and my old grouchy self in about twelve weeks. I know it's bad timing with Rosalie due in six weeks. I'm sorry."

"You big dope…" She lightly hit his chest, and instantly regretted it when the same pained look shot across his face again. His teeth set and his eyes snapped shut. "I'm just glad you're okay. A cast and crutches don't matter to me as long as you're all right." She gently lifted her hand, not wanting to hurt him more than she already did. "I saw the look, besides your leg, what other injures do you have? What's wrong with your chest?" She tugged the blanket down, her hand diving under his hospital gown.

"Hey, I'm naked under there." He teased, and grabbed her hand. "I'm fine."

"Cam…"

"Bumps, bruises…"

"Don't forget the burns." The doctor stood by the door watching them. When she saw him, Tessa, moved to get out of the bed. "Don't get up on my behalf. I just wanted to see if the patient was awake. The surgery went well, we had to put two screws in your leg to join the bone back together. You'll be in the cast for twelve weeks, and physical therapy, but you'll be good as new in a matter of months. It's been over seventy-two hours since your surgery, if you were going to show an infection you'd have done it. As long as things continue on track you'll be released the day after tomorrow. Depending on your mobility after you're healed, your military career might be over."

"No worry Doc. I decided to retire…I have a family now, a daughter on the way." He raised the arm that wasn't around Tessa and ran his hand over her swollen stomach.

After the doctor left Tessa turned back to Cameron, surprise still coursing through her. "I never intended for you to give up your career. You don't have to do this…"

"I know...this is what I want. I want to make a home with you and our daughter, and I was thinking of doing it in Clearwater. It's the perfect place to raise a family." He slipped a strand of hair behind her ear. "Tess, I fell in love with you years ago, and all these years I've been stuffing it into a box, using the excuses that Marines and family don't mix. It was stupid and I wasted all those years...now I want to make up for that. I love you."

"Oh Cam, I love you too. I've always loved you." She pressed her lips to his, kissing him deeply, trying to make up for all those lost years.

He pulled back from her, his eyes wide. "Was that..."

"You felt that?" From the look on his face, she knew he did. "That is our daughter...Rosalie is letting Daddy know she's there. I can't believe you felt that, she refuses to do it when Chloe touches my stomach." He moved his arm down her body until his hand was on her stomach. Rosalie took it as an invitation to become active. She kicked against Tessa's stomach as if to say hello.

"Is she always so active?"

"Yes. She's full of spirit. Right now she's showing off." Tessa lowered her hand to her stomach. "Shh, baby girl. Daddy's not going anywhere. You have plenty of time to show off." She had read a lot of different pregnancy and parenting books and they all said different things. A rare few say a child can't hear you in the womb but she tended to disagree. When she talked to Rosalie, her baby listened. Now was the perfect example.

She stayed curled in his embrace for a few moments, enjoying the warm security his arms offered, before she moved away.

"Where are you going?" Cameron protested.

"The bed's not big enough for you to have enough room with my pregnant stomach pressed against you." She ran her hand down the length of her stomach, as if he couldn't see just how big she was before.

"Stay, it's fine. I've waited too long to hold you in my arms, to feel your body pressed against mine. I don't want to let you go now." He ran his hand over her stomach, exploring the curves of her stomach. "You have a glow about you that I've never noticed before. You're beautiful."

He raised his arm from her stomach, and used the back of his hand to rub his fingers down her cheek. "I was serious about settling down in Clearwater…we have nothing to keep us tied here, no family, or job. We can start over, make a new life for our daughter and us. You've grown close to Chloe and Jordan and I are good friends. It seems like a good place to start over. What do you say?"

Raising a family in Clearwater. I'll be able to have the best of both. What's the catch? You always have to choose, you don't get to have everything. She had a hard time wrapping her mind around it. "What about your friends, your life, apartment? You don't want to leave everything behind for me…"

"My dear Tess how can I make you understand that you're the woman I love, the one I want to spend my life with. I'm not giving up anything as long as I have you next to me. My life doesn't matter unless you're with me." He ran his hand down her cheek. "If Clearwater isn't what you want we can go anywhere. I love you."

"I love Clearwater, it's the small town I've always wanted to raise a family in. Everyone is so sweet—Jennifer Anderson, the owner of Express-Ohh's had become a good friend as well. I'm not sure if you remember her from Chloe's wedding but you'll like her. All the cute little shops, it's just how I've always pictured a small town, and they have this adorable little baby store—Tiny Treasure Baby Store is owned by Zoe Noble. I bought so many cute baby outfits I don't have any more room." She smiled up at him. "I'm sorry I'm rambling. Clearwater is fine with me or anywhere as long as you're by my side."

"Then it's settled. When I'm discharged, we'll go back to Clearwater. We can look for a house and settle in before Rosalie is born. We'll give our Rosalie the complete family you always wanted." He pulled her snug against his body. "How's Chloe and Jordan? Glad to get rid of you for a few days?" He teased.

"Oh…" She started to rise from his embrace. "They're here…down the hall in the waiting room. They wouldn't let me come alone. I should go let them know you're awake."

His grip on her tightened, keeping her snug against him, as if he was scared to let her go. "Call her. I'm not letting you out of my sight, not even for a moment. It's our time now, nothing will separate us."

Chapter Sixteen

"I don't want to leave you." Tessa sat on the edge of the bed, her hand in Cameron's, as he fought sleep, but the antiseptic smell of the hospital was getting to her. Chloe and Jordan stood on the other side of the bed watching them.

"Love, you need to get some rest. Go take a nap in a comfortable bed and gather some of my clothes so we can leave straight from here." Cameron's voice was laced with sleep. "All of you need to rest. I'll be fine."

"Tessa he's right you need some sleep. I'll go with you and Jordan can stay with Cameron, if there's any change, he'll call us." Chloe stepped forward and grabbed her purse off the bedside table where she tossed it.

"No…" Jordan took hold of his wife's arm. "You stay here, and I'll go with Tessa. Just because she hasn't heard from Tony in a while doesn't mean he isn't still a threat. Being back in his city, we need to be on guard."

"All of you go…" Cameron's eyes where shut, the pain pill threatening to pull him under at any moment.

"No…"

Chloe held up her hand, silencing the argument. "It's okay Tessa. Jordan's right, I'll stay. Go get some rest and pack, I'll call you if anything changes."

Unhappily Tessa agreed to the plan, she leaned over and kissed Cameron. "I'll be back before you wake. Rest." With a heavy heart, she followed Jordan out. In the hall, the medical staff moved about, checking on the patients, she couldn't help thinking that some families weren't as lucky as she was. Many others had loved ones in worse condition than Cameron, and more than she wanted to think about would never see their loved ones again.

There was a woman by the nurses' station tears pouring down her face, an older woman who appeared to be her mother had her arm around her. There was so much grief written across their faces, she expected they received news their loved one didn't make it.

Reminding her of the news report, she heard on their way from the airport. *Protestors.* The poor families that lose love ones in the line of duty had enough grief to deal with they didn't need protestors at the funerals protesting the war. To Tessa there was a time and place for things and a funeral of a young military soldier was not it.

She had always been supportive of the soldiers who fought for their freedom. They rose to the call of duty while others ran for shelter, and gave them the freedoms they loved so much. One of those being the freedom of speech, but in her opinion some took that liberty too far. Protest the war, fine, but not at the gravesite of someone who just gave their life for their country.

For a moment she thought of the worst case, if Cameron had come home in a casket instead of injured. To have these protestors at his grave would have been too much. After everything he'd given to his country, to have them repay him that way would have been as heartbreaking as his loss.

Jordan left her to her thoughts, as they drove across the city. Even Rosalie seemed subdued.

* * *

Tessa sat on the bed holding a picture of them she found on his nightstand, taken just a week before he joined the Marines. The love that they felt for each other all those years ago was apparent in the picture. Young love, blossomed into an undeniable love that she had for him now.

"Is that everything?" Jordan asked after returning from putting the suitcase she packed of Cameron's stuff in the car.

"Yes." She stood, slipping her purse over her shoulder, taking the picture with her. She wanted it to be one of the first things in their new home, a reminder of where they came from. She took one last look around the apartment before turning back to Jordan. "I'm ready."

Outside she went to slip the picture frame into her purse while he locked the door when someone came moving towards them. There was such speed and anger in the movements it caught her attention.

"There you are! I've been looking everywhere for you since I heard you arrived..."

Tony barreled towards her. She took a step back but it was too late...Tony's fist came flying at her and impacted with the side of her head. The blow sent her stumbling back into the wall, and the frame fell. Jordan was there, moving between them, shoving Tony away from Tessa. Tony kept yelling at her but she only caught a few words.

"You stupid bitch...think I'd really let you get away...you're mine! You're pregnant..."

She wasn't sure if she lost consciousness but the next thing that she focused on was Jordan leaning over her, and holding an ice pack to her temple. "Tessa...Tessa can you hear me?"

"I'm sorry...what?" She raised her arm, bringing her hand to her spinning head.

"You're pressing charges against him...the police need your statement."

"Okay." She moved as if to get off the floor, but Jordan's hand on her shoulder kept her from getting up.

"Not until the paramedic checks you out." He nodded to the nearby medic who was waiting. "Hold this to your temple I'll get the officer to take your statement and we can get you out of here."

She noticed the picture she had been holding a few feet away, covered in shards of glass and for some reason that was the final straw. Tears shook her. Every time her life went right, something else went wrong. Her life was like the broken picture frame, in so many pieces and no matter how many times she tried to put it back together it always seemed to fall apart again.

* * *

Cameron woke to Chloe speaking quietly into her phone. Only catching the odd word he could tell just from the way Chloe's shoulder sagged that something was wrong. *Tess?* Forgetting about his leg, he started to get up, to find out what was going on. The agony from his leg didn't let him get far. "Chloe?" He called to her, drawing her attention.

"He's awake, I'll let him know." Chloe ended the call and walked towards the bed.

"What is it? Is Tessa okay?"

"Tony was waiting outside your apartment when they were leaving..."

"Damn it! Is she all right?" Anger roared through him. *She should have never come back here. This is entirely my fault.*

"She's going to be fine. She'll have a black eye, the paramedic looked her over and everything else is fine with both her and the baby." She laid her hand on his chest, pushing him back into the bed, when Cameron started to get up. "She's giving her statement to the police officer now and Jordan will bring her here when they're done."

"I've got to go to her."

"Jordan's with her and there's nothing you can do. Just stay in bed. They'll be here shortly." She didn't take her hand off his chest even once he stopped fighting against it.

"She needs me." He explained.

"You're right she'll need you, which is why you're not going to her now. She'll need your comfort, and you can't give that to her if you're doped up on pain pills because you got out of that bed and went to her." She sank into the chair beside the bed closely watching him. "You get out of bed now you're going to do more damage to your leg. You have a daughter on her way; you're going to need to be at your best, which means there's no time to go screwing up the healing process. So just lay there and wait, they'll be here soon."

He knew she was right but it killed him not to go to Tessa when she needed him. Being laid up was not something he did well. He was a man of action. "Tony?"

"He's in custody."

Now that he knows she is pregnant, will he figure out it's his child? If he does, Rosalie will only consider me her stepfather. Damn it. He'd do whatever it takes to hide the fact she was Tony's biological daughter, even if that meant forging a paternity test. There was no way he'd let Tony use Rosalie as a pawn against Tessa.

Chapter Seventeen

The black eye was already beginning to take color when they finally made it to the hospital. Drums beating loudly away in her head replaced the dizziness, but thankfully besides the headache and black eye she was okay. More importantly, Rosalie was okay.

When she entered Cameron was sitting up in bed, concern creased his angelic face. "My Tess…" He tried to get out of bed, but the pain stopped him, instead he held out his hand and she went to him. She wanted to be in his arms, she felt safe there. "Jordan, call and find out the first reservations you can get us. If we can leave tonight, I want to. Tony's a lawyer; he'll be able to make bail. I want her out of town before then."

"There's no reason to rush you from your hospital bed, I'll have to face him eventually." She curled into his embrace, feeling safe and protected, even Rosalie who had been subdued since she left the hospital hours before seemed to notice the excitement.

"You can face him in court if it comes to that. Ryan, the Sheriff from Clearwater, checked the temporary restraining order was served and is on file here too, Tony will have that violation as well. Right now I just want you out of town, and safe." Cameron kissed the top of her forehead, and looked over at Jordan. "Thank you."

Jordan nodded. "I just wish I could have protected her better. I was locking the door when he attacked. He must have been lying in wait for us to come out…I didn't see him before when I was out there."

"It would have been worse if you weren't there. Thank you Jordan." Tessa explained.

"Just rest, I'll see about reservations. Chloe, you want to get a cup of coffee with me while I do?" It was clear Jordan was making an excuse for them both to step away for a few minutes, giving Tessa and Cameron some privacy.

When they left, Cameron raised his hand to her chin, tipping it back gently so she was looking at him. "Did you ice it?" His eyes were dark with anger, yet he kept his temper in check, even his voice was calm.

"It's fine." She nodded. "I should have been looking, but I was slipping the picture of us from your bedside in my purse. I didn't see him coming."

"None of this is your fault." He ran his hand over the dimple in her chin. "I've always loved that picture."

"The glass is broke…" She slipped her hand into her purse and pulled out the picture frame minus the glass, and tears slid down her cheeks before she quickly wiped them away. "Sorry pregnancy hormones, seems like I'm always crying."

"Shh love. It's okay. We'll get another picture frame." He rubbed small circles down her back, trying to calm her. "Everything's going to be fine, I promise. Close your eyes and rest, you've been through a lot the last few days."

* * *

Cameron watched Tessa sleep peaceful in his arms, while his thoughts tormented him. He never expected to marry and settle down, yet he was doing just that, and he wouldn't change it for the world. He loved Tessa, and for reasons beyond him, she saw goodness in him and loved him too. It was almost too much to ask for, yet he wanted more. He hoped like he never did before that Tony would never find out of Rosalie. The thought of losing his daughter, or her being used as a pawn in his games sent him swirling towards the breaking point. Hatred and fury coursed through his veins like the roaring fires of hell, when Chloe and Jordan returned carrying a tray of food.

"Tessa needs to eat." Chloe nodded to the tray. "Jordan said she refused to get some on their way back because she wanted to get back to you."

"Okay. We'll wake her in a moment. What about reservations?" Cameron asked.

"First flight back is at ten tonight. I have us booked, but it means flying throughout the night. I'm not sure, in her state that it's the best to…" Jordan set the drinks on the hospital bed table.

"She'll be fine. She needs to be somewhere safe. I can't protect her here." He ran his hand through her long brown hair. "I'll protect her at all costs…"

"The cost being your child?" Chloe asked almost slamming down the tray.

"Chloe, even though I haven't been here for each step of the pregnancy, I know her OBGYN told her that both the baby and she are healthy. Traveling isn't going to change that. She can sleep on the plane." He looked down at the sleeping Tess before returning his gaze back to Chloe. "You have to realize that staying here puts her in more danger then flying through the night. Tony is a nasty man, he'll get out of jail and he will come for her."

He refused to let Tessa stay in danger longer than necessary. Once she was safe in Clearwater, he'd make sure Tony received the message loud and clear to stay away from her. Too long he'd stayed out of it, not wanting to interfere in case he was wrong, but he couldn't keep his opinions quiet once he knew, and now it was time Tony found out you couldn't treat people like he had spent too long doing to Tessa.

Chapter Eighteen

The night was long and grueling, and exhaustion hung heavily on Tessa when she collapsed into bed next to Cameron. The trip back from North Carolina was hard on everyone, they traveled in silence, none of them able to sleep. Cameron took the worst of it, his leg up on a pillow, his teeth clenched in pain.

"There's no need to be macho, why don't you take a pain pill?" She ran her hand over his chest, careful to avoid the burns.

"I'm fine. Sleep is what we need." He wrapped his arm around her, drawing her close to him. His dog tags around her neck caught his attention. "Why?"

She raised her hand to them, fingering it. "Don't laugh, they made me feel closer to you." She reached under her pillow and grabbed his shirt that she put there before they left. "I even wore your shirt until my stomach got too big. I really missed you."

"I'm home now and not going anywhere."

She couldn't believe he was there next to her. Too afraid to close her eyes, worried that when she opened them again he'd be gone, she just watched him sleep. She thought the time would never come when she was able to lie in his arms, or if he did, he'd have changed his mind about their marriage. Now that it was here, she knew the wait was worth it.

* * *

Cameron woke covered in sweat, his heart racing, images of the incident that landed him in a cast vivid in his mind. Wounded soldiers surrounding him, as he laid there broken and bleeding. There was nothing he could do for most of them, his attention focused on the youngest Marine under his command who lay clinging to life next to him. He wouldn't let Juan Carlos die. He was too young...with so many people depending on him.

He held that young Marine's hand until they were loaded into the helicopter, giving him the encouragement he needed. The images filled his vision making him feel like he was back there again. J.C's honey-golden skin paled with the loss of blood, and his deep blue eyes held pain and fear. *Damn it, J.C, you're a Marine we don't give up.* Cameron kept telling him, refusing to let one of his men give up.

J.C never should have been there! He volunteered for the deployment to help with his family financially. At twenty-one he was the oldest of nine children, the man of the family since his father took off five years before. Losing his leg meant a long hard recovery road in front of him, and worse yet when he couldn't find work.

If he died, his family would have had the insurance... Cameron hated himself for even thinking it. Having him in their life meant more than money ever would. He met J.C's family and they might not have much but they had love that got them through. *They'll find a way.*

It was damn lucky they didn't lose anyone. Many men would never be the same but at least no one lost their lives. For that, he was grateful.

"What are you thinking about?" Tessa's soft and sexy voice went straight to his shaft.

He looked down to find her watching him. "How long have you been awake?" He cupped the side of her face.

"Long enough to know you've been lost in thought. You were distant, and I didn't want to disturb you." She ran her hand down his chest.

"You're beautiful." He lowered his head to hers, bringing their foreheads together, their gazes locked together. He kissed her. Their lips met with passion and desire. The air sizzled around them. Their kiss broke apart, but his lips hovered just over hers. "I've waited for so long, I want you."

"Me too, but your leg..."

"It's fine." He slipped his hand under the loose silk nightshirt that she wore, and pulled it up her body. "You have too many clothes on."

She leaned up allowing him to slip the shirt over her head. "You too." She grabbed the waist of his shorts.

"Then help me resolve that." He told her before lowering his head to her neck, kissing gently. His tongue trailing soft lines down her neck, teasing her and nibbling against her smooth skin, bringing the desire coursing through them.

She broke the kiss, and rose to her knees. With agonizing care, she pulled down his shorts. "Are you sure you are up to this?"

"I think *it* speaks for itself." He raised his eyebrows suggestively. He leaned up, and caught her dusky pink nipple into his mouth. He knew pregnancy had made her nipples extra sensitive; so he laved it in a lazy, tender circle with his tongue. Her sharp gasp coupled with the clasp of her hand on his head was all the encouragement he needed. Gliding a hand down her body, he explored the gorgeous curves. She really had never been more beautiful. And he promised patience in the future, but he'd missed her for far too long. Teasing her sensitive flesh, he lifted his head to catch the soft cry with a long, satisfying kiss.

"You'll have to be on top." He murmured against her mouth.

She rose, moving to straddle his body, her hands running along his chest, careful to avoid the white bandage covering his burns. "If you'd been hurt worse..."

"Shh." He gave her hips a light squeeze. "No more of that. I'm here. We're together."

For the barest moment, her lower lip trembled and she seemed to be caught between tears and a smile. The utter vulnerability tore him in two. . "Cameron, I need you."

"I'm here. I'll always be here." It was a solemn oath, one he should have given her a long time ago. She deserved long stroking touches, teasing caresses, and languid kisses until she screamed—but rose carefully and he helped her balance as he fisted himself and angled his shaft to help her glide down into place.

She settled around him like a hot, liquid glove and he couldn't stop his own groan. Hell, he didn't want to. They lay there, suspended in that moment and he looked up at her. The unbound length of her hair framed her gorgeous face and she smiled. "You feel good."

Laughing softly, he rubbed a hand up her side and cupped her breast. The angle sucked, but he was creative—he would manage. "Move, sweetheart."

She wrinkled her nose. "Bossy."

"Yes, ma'am." He couldn't arch his hips, it would jerk his leg, but he flexed his arms and helped her rise and she did it with agonizing, exquisite slowness that ripped another pair of long, sighs from both of them. It was like pleasurable torture, a slow, inexorable build. She roamed her hands over him, petting him, teasing him, but always with smooth, strokes that wrapped his shaft, fisting him with her inner muscles.

Need turned him inside out and he slid a hand between them to tease that tight bundle of nerves. Her rhythm faltered and he watched the pleasure break out over her expression, her release clamping down around him and pulling his own. He came with a shout—the slow, sensuous eroticism of it all made perfect because it was Tessa.

It had always been Tessa.

He helped her ease down on the bed next to him. And caught her lips for another long, breathless kiss. "I love you, Tessa."

It would always be her.

Chapter Nineteen

Cameron leaned against his new truck, looking at the house they just bought. He just brought a load of their belongings over while Tessa and Chloe were busy packing at the cabin. Moving from North Carolina they decided to start over, selling everything, so the first thing they had to do after they bought the house was decorate it. All the furniture new, and fit their style contemporary and comfortable, representing the new lease they both had on life. His life had done a one eighty in only a few months. Clearwater was something he never thought he wanted, the small quiet life but he couldn't be happier now. Lost in thought he didn't turn around to the vehicle coming up the drive, suspecting it was Jordan.

A truck door shut behind him, jarring him back to the presence. "Hey Cameron."

He turned to find Sheriff Ryan Ryder walking towards him. His long legs closing the distance quickly, his hand was on his gun like a character leaping out of the pages of some novel from the old west. It was a natural pose for him. "Afternoon Sheriff, what can I do for you?"

"There's something I've wanted to do for years—but being the only law enforcement in Clearwater time never seems to be enough—but you might be just the person to bring it to Clearwater now that you're sticking around." Ryan took his hat off laying it on the front of Cameron's truck. "We need someone around here to teach self-defense, gun training."

"Sheriff I don't think that's needed here..."

"Hear me out Cameron...self-defense has always been something I support. People need to defend themselves, and their families. Clearwater is a safe town, but we have many people traveling through, so trouble can spring unexpectedly. We have a lot of small shop owners that could be in danger if a patron got out of control." He adjusted his gun belt, looking off to the vacant land that at one time had been used for farming, surrounding the house. "Gun training...damn that's the call I deal with most. Someone out hunting and they don't know how to handle the weapon properly. Many of these hunters were taught by their father, or grandfather, passing it down the line, but guns have changed. They're advancing and if people are going to use them they need to be trained."

"You make a good argument, but I don't know…" Cameron slipped his hand into his pockets.

"I understand." Ryan looked around the ground again before turning his attention back to Cameron. "You have enough land here that you could do it right here. Put up a building for the classes and shooting range, and you could be running within a few weeks." He grabbed his hat off the top of the truck, and slipped it back on. "All I'm asking is think about it."

"I will." Cameron watched Ryan walk back over to the Sheriff truck, and opened the door.

"One last thing, there's a woman in Jackson Hole…she's in a difficult situation…self-defense could make all the difference to her." Ryan got into his truck and drove away.

Damn him! He knows I won't turn away from someone in need. Self-defense…gun training…that could be the answer to what to do with my time. He opened his truck door and climbed in. He needed to talk to Tessa before he made any decision.

Chapter Twenty

Four Months Later...

Tessa was lounging by the lake, her head back with her eyes closed, soaking up the last of the early evening sun rays with Chloe. Rosalie slept peacefully in the bassinet, and the men were grilling. It was a perfect day, making her thankful for all she had. Her life had changed so much in the last few weeks, and everything for the better.

They had moved into their beautiful home only days before, but she already missed the daily connection with Chloe and Jordan. "How's Hope doing managing Winterbloom on a day to day level? Or are you still having problems giving up the control?"

"Hope's doing well. Once Jordan finishes our log home, she'll move into our quarters. It's nice to be able to give over some of the duties to someone else. Winterbloom has been my whole life for so long, it's nice to have a little free time to step back and enjoy life, even better now that I have someone to do it with."

Tessa opened her eyes and looked across the lake, midway between Winterbloom and the cabins where Jordan and a local construction team were building Chloe's new home. The log home was coming along nicely, and would soon be ready for them to move into it.

"How's motherhood and the new business?"

"Amazing. Rosalie is a doll, and she sleeps most of the night. I couldn't ask for a better daughter. Which is great since Cam is busy getting Clearwater Combat and Guns set up." Memories of how lost Cameron was without the schedule of the Marines controlling his day-to-day life flooded back. She had almost begun to think it was a mistake for him to leave his career for her and Rosalie. As much as she loved Clearwater, she'd have followed him anywhere. His leg grew stronger each day, and if he wanted he could have returned to the Marines within a few months, even the limp he had was beginning to fade.

Clearwater Combat and Guns had put the passion back in Cameron that he lost, bringing joy and harmony to their lives. He was doing something they both believed in. Even out of the Marines, he was still being a hero to many. The business was the final piece that completed Cameron, and gave her everything she ever wanted.

"It's becoming larger than we originally expected. There will be a gun shop, and shooting range, but he's also doing different classes for self-defense based on skills, gun training, and other weapons. Cameron also hired another retired Marine to teach karate and martial arts, he'll arrive in August, there's already a number of students from Clearwater School signed up." She looked across the patio to Cameron and then towards Rosalie. "Oh Chloe, everything is just perfect. I love my life and wouldn't want things to be any different."

Losing to Win

The war vet…

Juan Carlos Marquez lost everything he valued in one fateful Marine mission. Now an amputee, trying to put the pieces of his life back together, and to still be a provider for his mother and siblings, might be all he can handle.

The lonely barista…

Rebecca James found a new beginning in Clearwater after running from a disastrous past. As a part-time barista and studying for her business degree, she rarely has time for socializing, let alone a relationship.

The instant connection…

They weren't looking for love, love found them. Will the sparks between Juan Carlos and Rebecca be just what they need to give them both a happy ending?

Chapter One

Juan Carlos Marquez waited for the plane to disembark in Jackson Hole, Wyoming. Within the hour, he'd be in Clearwater where he'd agreed to spend the next six weeks helping his former Gunnery Sergeant, Cameron White, with his new business, Clearwater Combat and Guns. JC had no idea what to expect. He was an amputee now. What could he do to help? Yet, when the man who saved his life asked for help, he couldn't turn his back.

Since returning from deployment, JC felt like a ship lost at sea. He was unsure what to do, and his family treated him differently now. In that one mission, his life changed so dramatically. He went from being the man of his family—caring for his mother and eight younger siblings, to being useless. At twenty-one, he had provided a decent income for his mother and siblings, thanks to the Marines. But he was recently discharged because of his injury, which left him no other choice but to find something else to do.

Just the thought of that fateful mission sent phantom pains where his leg should have been. He rubbed his knee above the prosthesis, hoping to chase away the pain. Nothing helped ease the ache. It was never-ending and exhausted him. When the discomfort crept in, it was unbearable, breaking him down until he had nothing left.

He closed his eyes for a brief second, and that fateful day shot across his memory. Just another normal day of duty, the mission was going smoothly, and everything seemed innocent enough until their Humvee hit an IED. The detonation sent him flying through the air and his leg was in excruciating pain. It wasn't until he landed hard on the ground, fifteen feet from the explosion, that he realized his leg was gone below the knee.

Cameron, the man JC owed everything, was there for him—making sure he held on to reality. Cameron reminded him of his family, refusing to let him give up. Cameron got him through the ordeal, and he owed his life to his former Gunnery Sergeant.

"Sir, excuse me, sir. We've landed."

Opening his eyes, he saw the flight attendant standing next to his seat in the otherwise empty plane. Lost in his thoughts, he hadn't heard her step up beside him.

"I apologize, ma'am."

"It's fine. Do you have someone waiting for you?" She leaned against the seat in front of him.

"No one waiting, but I do have an appointment I need to get to."

"If you're new to the area, why don't I show you around after your appointment? Maybe we can grab some dinner. I don't fly out again until tomorrow afternoon." She bent forward to pick up the tray next to him, giving him a glimpse down the front of her blouse.

"I appreciate the offer, but no thank you." He rose from his seat, grabbing his carry-on. He was ready to get off of the airplane, find a rental car, and make his way to Clearwater.

She reached into her pocket and handed him a business card. "Here's my number if you change your mind. I fly this route a few times a month, so if you ever want to meet, call me."

He shoved her card in his pocket and then headed up the aisle. No woman had approached him since his injury. His air of authority and the uniform were gone, taking away the reason so many women were attracted to him in the first place. Now flirtation from a woman made him uncomfortable. He didn't know what to say.

He walked quickly off the plane, putting distance between him and the flirtatious flight attendant. The ache in his leg slowed his progress. He hadn't been this sore since he was fitted with his prosthesis. As soon as he arrived at Clearwater Combat and Guns, he would take his medication to dull the pain, but he hated the pills because they left him in a haze, unable to feel anything.

Stepping out into the fresh air, he made his way to the rental car. His limp returned, making itself known. He worked so hard to hide it, to pretend he was normal. Though sometimes the limp refused to be hidden.

* * *

JC drove up the long gravel driveway, surprised by the beauty spread out before him. Lush trees bloomed, lining each side of the drive. Ahead, were mountains, more trees, and a deep blue sky with fluffy, white clouds. The only sounds, through his open window, were the birds chirping their happy songs.

This area was so different from the city, which was always busy with blaring horns, people yelling, and the stench of the many different restaurant smells mingling in the open air. He inhaled a deep breath, filling his lungs with the clean mountain air. Rejuvenation eased some of his pain.

No wonder Cameron never returned to North Carolina. This place would be hard to give up.

JC knew what it felt like to live in a city where Marines were stationed. Everything was a daily reminder of what he'd lost. In the three short years the Marines became his life, the routine and discipline reflected in every aspect of his life, even now.

He stepped out of his rental car. Clearwater Combat and Guns was a large building to the right of the driveway. It had to be over three thousand square feet, if not more. The rustic black sign with silver letters had recently been painted. He was impressed with the sheer size of the business, and wouldn't have guessed a small town needed something so large.

"You must be Juan Carlos." A soft female voice called from behind him.

He turned to find a woman with a baby in her arms walking down the porch of a ranch-style log home. The house dominated the other side of the driveway. Red rose bushes decorated the porch's perimeter, drawing his gaze before he could view the rest of the house.

"Yes, ma'am. Please, call me JC. You must be Mrs. White." He held out his hand.

"Tessa, please. I've heard so much about you. It's a pleasure to finally have you here." She placed her delicate hand in his, giving it a gentle shake. "Cameron is in the shop." Her long brown hair swayed over her shoulders as she rocked the baby in her arms. "Come, I'll show you around, unless you prefer to settle in first."

He wanted his pain meds and to sleep for a while, but he came to help Cameron, and he needed to find out why his friend really wanted him to come here.

What does he expect from me?

"No, that's fine. I'd like to see Cameron."

"Very well." She turned in the direction of the shop, walking next to him instead of in front like most people tended to do since his walk was a little slower. "Cam will be glad you're here. With our baby daughter, Rosalie, and the business, he doesn't have time to breathe. Neither of us expected the shop to take off as it has. The other man he hired, Thor, will be teaching most of the hand-to-hand combat, self-defense, karate, and martial art classes, but he doesn't start until August. So everything's falling on Cam now."

"I'll do what I can to take some of the burden from him." JC didn't add that he'd be useless at physical training.

She stopped in front of an open door. "Well, I'll let you two divide the work load. I'll be up at the house. When you're ready, I'll show you to your room."

"Don't think you're going to get away that easy." A deep, raspy voice JC remembered from his days in the Marines, hollered from inside the room. "Bring my little Rosie in here."

JC followed Tessa into the office and found Cameron behind a large cherry wood desk. His hair was a little longer and contentment glistened in his eyes. Pictures of his family filled the walls. Cameron, the man who drilled into JC that marriage and Marines didn't mix, had found the two things he always said weren't for him—happiness and family.

Cameron took the baby from Tessa, hoisted Rosalie in his arms, and then shook JC's hand. "I'm glad you came. Have a seat."

JC couldn't believe his former Gunnery Sergeant, who had dedicated his life to the core, was now a family man. He held the baby like a seasoned father, yet JC couldn't help but think how small the baby seemed to be in the big man's arms.

"Cam, I was going to put Rosie down for a nap." Tessa smiled at her husband cradling their daughter, and then pointed a finger. "If you'd come up to the house before she went to bed at night you'd get to see more of her."

Cameron winked at JC. "Don't let my wife's sweet smile fool you. She's quite a drill sergeant, worse than I was to you and the rest of the men." He leaned to kiss Rosie's head. "I'm hoping with JC here that will all change. I have some stuff to go over with him, and we'll be up shortly. No work tonight. I'm going to throw some steaks on the grill and we'll relax."

"I'll believe that when I see it." She snuggled their daughter in her arm and gave her husband a quick kiss before leaving.

JC sat in the leather chair across from Cameron's desk, waiting for Cameron to explain why he had asked him to come to Clearwater.

When he didn't say anything JC spoke up, he couldn't take the anticipation any longer. "Why did you really ask me to come here?"

"I need help with the shop, and who better than someone I know that has the training and experience. You're like a brother to me. That made the decision easy."

His statement meant a lot to JC, but the obvious still remained. "Cameron, I'm a cripple, I can't run a business." JC rubbed his leg to make a point. "I'm sure there were many others you could've called, why me?"

"You? Because there's no one better. You were an excellent Marine, and just because you lost your leg doesn't mean you lost your life. I asked you here to help me, and you'll soon learn that you still have a lot of life to live. It's a win-win situation." He picked up a file on his desk and tossed it into a drawer. "For all those years, I let the Marines control every aspect of my life, but now I'm a free man, and I couldn't be happier. I never thought life outside of the Marines would ever be something I'd want to explore, let alone enjoy. You'll be surprised at how well you adjust." He smiled. "I know what you're going through. I've seen the same uncertainty in other soldiers. Clearwater is just the place where you can find yourself and your future."

JC frowned. "I'm not the same person. A place doesn't change you. I'll never be whole again no matter what I find here in Clearwater. I'll do whatever I can to help you, but my leg will always be an issue. One I can't move past."

"Your leg doesn't master you. You're in control of your life. If you think of your prosthesis as a hindrance, it will always hold you back. You'll never discover the future. We thrived on schedules, missions, deployments, and danger for years, but there's so much more. Now is your time to discover it." Cameron passed him a folder.

It would have been a waste of time arguing with Cameron. He'd always held strong beliefs, one was the will to overcome anything. So if JC believed in something strong enough, he'd succeed? But being a cripple wasn't something he could will his mind to let go of. "I still don't understand why you want *me*. I can't teach the classes you offer here. What do you want me to do?" He held the folder in his hands, but didn't open it.

"Inside you'll find a list of jobs you can help me with—running the office, signing up clients for the courses, following up phone calls and emails, acquiring gun registration, and so on. You can also oversee the shooting range, assist with the gun training, and I'm sure there's more I'm not thinking of. What do you say, will you at least give it a try?"

"If I wasn't willing to help you, I wouldn't be here. I just don't want to let you down." JC flipped through the pages in the folder. They contained all the basic information about the business he'd need to familiarize with if he was going to be assuming the office duties and allowing Cameron more time with his wife and new daughter. "When do you want me to start?"

Cameron smiled and extended his arm cross the large cherry wood desk. When JC leaned forward to shake his hand, Cameron added. "Welcome aboard. Tomorrow we can start going over the computer system and get everyone registered. It's a great time to learn because it will be slow until the classes begin in August." He pushed the black leather chair back from the desk and stood. "Why don't we head to the house? You can settle in and review the folder. I'll get the steaks on the grill."

Chapter Two

Rebecca James tossed her law book on the counter, and then tied her apron around her waist. The best thing about working the late morning shift at Express-Ohh's was the time it allowed her to study. The café wouldn't pick up until the lunch crowd strolled in, giving her at least another hour to master all she needed to know for her upcoming test on employment regulations.

"Hey Becca, thanks for coming in on short notice." Jennifer, the owner, stepped out of the backroom with a bag of coffee-to-go cups. "I really do appreciate it."

She loved working for Jennifer, but couldn't ward away the sting of jealousy. Jennifer was the girl next door, long brown hair and a slim body that held curves in all the right places. She might only be five-foot-five, but she had real spunk. As if she had downed a dozen espressos, she was always running at full steam no matter the hour, not to mention she always had a sarcastic comment handy. Over the last two years of working for Jennifer, Rebecca wasn't sure she had ever seen her mad.

"No problem, Jennifer. You know anytime you need me I'll be here." She took the cups from Jennifer. "When are you leaving?"

"Since you're here early, I'd like to head out now."

"Go ahead, I have it covered." She stacked the to-go cups on the back counter. Having them close by made them handy for when the orders were pouring in.

"You're a life-saver, thanks." Jennifer grabbed her purse from under the counter, and turned back to Rebecca. "Oh, there's an order for Clearwater Combat and Guns to be picked up at eleven. The sandwiches are already made. You just have to make the coffee. The list is by the phone."

"Got it. Now get out of here. Your mother's plane will be landing soon, and there's no need to come back. I'll close up. Go and enjoy the visit with your mom." Another twinge of jealousy pulled at her heart again. This time, for the relationship Jennifer had with her mother. Their closeness and bond was something Rebecca had wanted for years with her own mother, but that was too much to ask.

Years of trying to compete with the bottle for her mother's attention did nothing for Rebecca's self-esteem. Having a mother who chose booze over her own daughter left her feeling not good enough. During her teenage years, she suffered with extreme depression until she turned eighteen and left home. She found a safe haven in Clearwater, Wyoming.

For the last two years she had divided her time between working at Express-Ohh's and her online college classes. There wasn't a lot of extra time when you were trying to graduate within three years. All of her hard work and dedication was about to pay off. This was the last semester that stood in her way before she'd finish her bachelor's degree in just over two years.

With Jennifer gone, the quietness of the café settled around her. She reopened her law book, sank onto the swirl-stool by the cash register, and pulled her pen from her ponytail. She jotted notes down into her notebook.

"Excuse me." A deep, masculine voice caressed her skin like warm water, forcing her to glance up. Her heart skipped a beat. A tall man loomed in front of her. Slightly over six-feet tall, his blue T-shirt clung to his chest, providing a teasing preview to the six-pack abs that lay snug underneath. His long legs were encased in light blue jeans. With his honey brown skin and deep green eyes, he belonged on the West Coast instead of Clearwater. He resembled a surfer, not a winter snowboarder.

"I'm sorry…I didn't hear the chime of the door. What can I get you?" Rising from the chair, she tossed her pen on the notebook.

"I'm here to pick up an order for Clearwater Combat and Guns. I'm a little early, but things were slow at the shop so Cameron asked me to come over. Would it happen to be ready yet?"

She glanced at the clock behind him. *Ten Thirty.* "Umm, if you could give me a few minutes, I just need to prepare the drinks." She held out her hand. "By the way, I'm Rebecca."

Goose-bumps rose over her skin as he shook her hand. "JC." He released her hand and lowered his bulky frame on one of the bar stools. He then ran his hand through his light, brown hair. The sun's rays, through the windows, highlighted his hair with streaks of gold. "Take your time."

She wanted to run her hands on that fine specimen of a man, to feel his tight muscles taut under her fingers. She turned to review the list Jennifer had left on the counter. "Can I get you something while you wait?"

"A cup of coffee would be great."

She grabbed the pot of coffee and poured it into a cup. "You're new around here, aren't you?"

"Yeah." He paused before sipping the hot coffee. "Ahh, that's good. Cameron and I were in the Marines together. He called me to help him with the shop."

"You're awful young to be retired from the military." Pouring more coffee into a to-go cup, she sneaked a peek at his dark green eyes.

"An injury cut my career short." Was that a hint of disappointment lingering in his voice? "Are you from Clearwater?"

"Naw. I'm from all around. Dad was in the Navy, so I grew up at different ports." She left out the part where her father's job was the reason her mother turned to the booze. Her mother couldn't handle the separation, moving, and everything else that went with a military man. "I moved to Clearwater a little over two years ago, but I love it here. Are you planning to stick around?"

Before he answered, he took another long sip of coffee. He smiled and her knees wobbled. "As long as I'm needed, I'll stay. Cameron has his hands full with the business and a new baby. I'll do what I can to help."

For the next few minutes, she chattered about the weather to fill the awkward silence. She placed the cup holders with the drinks on the counter. "The sandwiches are in the fridge. I'll grab them and help you…"

"I can manage." He swallowed the last mouthful of coffee from his cup and stood. He frowned as if irritated by her offer to help.

Reaching into the fridge she glanced over her shoulder. "I doubt it. Jennifer added a little extra to the order for Tessa. They're very good friends, but Jennifer doesn't get away from the shop much and Tessa just had Rosalie, so to let Tessa know she's thinking of her, Jennifer sends some of Tessa's favorites to her when Cameron places an order." Inside the refrigerator, eight clear plastic sandwich containers were stacked neatly on top of a large square container that contained the sweet goodies. She turned around, holding the boxes. "Why don't you grab the drinks and I'll follow you out."

He shook his head and reached for the tray of cups. "If I knew the order was this large, I'd have brought one of the boys to help."

"Boys?" As she carried the boxes around the counter, his gaze met hers for the first time since he'd entered the café.

"Cameron has a few local high school boys at the shop helping finalize preparations for the classes starting in August. We still have a lot to do before we're ready, but it's coming along exceptionally well." He stepped beside her, grabbing the front door with his free hand. "Let me take those."

"I got them. Where are you parked?"

"Right there." He nodded to the black pickup truck with the company's logo on the door. "I appreciate this."

"It's all in the service you get here at Express-Ohh's." She flashed him her biggest and brightest smile. "Good service keeps our customers coming back." She wanted him to come back. With dedicating the past few years to school and work, she was out of practice when it came to flirting. Not that she ever mastered the art of flirting like most average girls in their early twenties.

"Oh, so it has nothing to do with the fact that you're the only coffee shop in town?" He teased, digging his keys out of his pocket. He pushed the small button to unlock the truck.

She laughed. "You tasted our coffee, do you really think another shop stands a chance?" Sliding the food containers onto the passenger's seat, she could feel his body heat behind her. His cologne teased her senses, imprinting her memories and making her want to turn into his arms.

"Never." He sat the tray on the floor-mat. Turning to her, he dug money out of his pocket. "Thank you."

"You're welcome. I hope to see you around town again." She tucked the money in her apron pocket and strolled back to the door. "Hey, will you be at the town's picnic on Saturday?" Even though she rarely attended the picnics she knew Cameron and Tessa went regularly with Chloe and Jordan, the owners of Winterbloom Bed and Breakfast. Jennifer also planned to close the coffee house early that day. If JC was going then Rebecca would make sure she was there, even to see him from a distance.

"I don't know. Cameron hasn't mentioned it. I'm bunking at their place until the manager's flat is finished above the shop. If they want me to go with them, I guess I'll be there unless there's work to be done. Why?"

Butterflies danced in her stomach, playing havoc with her courage. She nudged a pebble with the tip of her shoe. "I just thought…since you're new in town that I'd introduce you to some of the towns' people. The picnics are a lot of fun." At least that's what Jennifer told her. "You really should come…if you have time."

"If you're going to be there, I'll try to attend, as long as Cameron doesn't have something he needs me to do." He shot her one last smile before sliding into the driver's seat and starting the engine.

Her cheeks filled with heat as she watched him drive away. She was acting like a giddy schoolgirl, but for once in her life, she didn't care, and couldn't wait to see to JC on Saturday.

Chapter Three

Only a week in Clearwater and JC was ready to run for the hills. It was too much of a change in such a short time, especially when he couldn't get his mind off Rebecca. Agreeing to go to the picnic was the biggest mistake of his life, well at least the second biggest one since coming to Clearwater. He was in no emotional shape to have a romantic interest in anyone. Not even adjusted to the loss of his leg, he didn't want to drag a sweet woman into his shit-hole life. The phantom pain returned in his leg.

"Hey, JC is here with the grub." One of the teenage volunteers jogged to the truck, with the other boys only steps behind him.

"It's about time, I'm starving," one of the boys hollered.

"Jake, go inside and get the pitcher of iced tea Tessa brought out earlier. The rest of you gather at the table." Cameron waved the boys aside and assisted JC with the food. "We'll eat in the house with Tessa. After lunch we've got to go up to Jackson Hole. The boys can finish the work today."

"The bottom three trays are ours, and the rest are for the boys." JC pointed to the last tray as Cameron took the sandwich containers from the stack. "Jennifer sent some sweets for Tessa."

Cameron shook his head, his gaze drifting past JC and toward the house. "That woman of mine has a sweet tooth you can't image, and it's only gotten worse since Jennifer's been indulging her." Adding the last of the boys' sandwiches to his stack, he nodded to the house. "You go ahead. I'll give the boys their lunch, and I'll be along shortly."

JC didn't hesitate. Standing around watching Cameron shout out orders only served to remind JC of his military days. He wasn't adjusting to civilian life as quickly as his superior. All he ever wanted to do when he was growing up was to join the Marines. On his eighteenth birthday he signed his name on the dotted line, vowing his life to the core. Two months later, he boarded the bus to boot camp, never looking back.

He had been the man of his family, providing for their needs since he was fourteen. His father was a drunk most of JC's life, but when he was fourteen his father left. He'd return once in a while, and his mother would take him back, but his father never stuck around longer than to get JC's mother pregnant again, and then leave her and the family again. His mother was pregnant with Kelly when his father died.

The core offered a way for him to help his mother support the other eight children. It also forced his next oldest brother, Lee, to step up and be responsible for the family. There was no longer time for Lee to goof-off with his friends, not when he had to make sure his siblings were cared for. JC's mother couldn't do it alone, and when he was in the Marines, the family responsibility fell to Lee and his twin sister, Laya. Laya was like a second mother to their younger siblings, making sure they were washed, fed, and reading them bedtime stories. JC's mother worked two jobs to support her family, so Laya helped with the chores and children.

After the loss of his leg, JC prayed for an infection to take him. At least with his death, his family would receive his death benefits. How was he supposed to support his family with a missing limb? For months he grew hopeless, unable to get out of the bottomless pit of depression that had sucked him in. When he awoke in the hospital after his surgery, he saw his mother crying by his bedside—not for the loss of the body part that he grieved. She was thankful her son survived and made it home to her and the family. She didn't care about money or his missing leg. She had told him that *he* was all she cared about.

It took a while for him to realize it too, but he was thankful to be alive. His mother and siblings needed him. Not for material things, but for love and support. He needed theirs as well. If it wasn't for his family's strong bond, he may have given up.

Thinking of his family made him homesick. Were Lee and Laya managing the younger children okay, or were their grades falling because of their extra duties around the house? Maybe he could convince his family to move to Clearwater. Cameron was paying him a hefty salary to run the shop, and he was sure his mother could find work in Clearwater or Jackson Hole. With his family closer, it would allow him to help with his younger siblings, *and* still repay the man who saved his life.

"JC, do you want help with those?" The screen door banged shut behind Tessa, pulling him from his thoughts.

He made a mental promise to check into housing for his family, and to find out if any shops were hiring in town before he approached his mother with the possibility of moving. "I've got it, but I sure could use a glass of your heavenly sun-brewed tea." Stepping onto the deck, he smiled and winked.

"Like you even have to ask. I have a glass poured and sitting on the table inside for you." She opened the screen door, letting him pass with the boxes.

"You're amazing. If Cameron didn't snatch you up first, I would have fought him for you." He teased. There was something about Tessa that made him forget his worries. She had a calming vibe that put him at ease.

"If he doesn't start getting up with his daughter in the middle of the night, you might not have a hard fight." She teased back, while suppressing a yawn.

"Maybe Daddy should be on duty tonight?"

The screen door opened. "Hey man. I leave you alone with my wife for two minutes and you're trying to convince her I should have baby duty all night." Cameron stood just inside the kitchen, his arms crossed over his chest, and smiling at JC.

"Anything for you, buddy. I'm here to give you more time with your family and that's exactly what I'm going to do." JC sat the boxes on the counter and grabbed the tea Tessa made him and a sandwich.

"One day I'll repay you." Cameron reached for his black coffee before handing Tessa her cappuccino.

"Not for a *very* long time, my friend." Caring for his siblings had taught JC the qualities needed in a good father. His mother had said he'd be a perfect dad someday, but he didn't want to rush it. Actually helping his mother raise his brothers and sisters had acted as its own form of birth control. He was almost afraid to touch a woman for fear he'd end up with nine children he couldn't afford. Twins ran in his family for generations, and in his family there were three sets of twins, leaving only JC and the youngest two as single births.

"We'll see," Tessa mumbled before settling onto the chair next to him.

* * *

With Express-Ohh's lunch rush dying down, Rebecca's peace returned as well as the memory of the hunk of man that stood before her only a short time ago. Picturing his solid body in her mind, she wondered what injury cut his career short. He seemed in perfect physical and mental health. Maybe he had an underlying mental issue that left him unfit for duty. Regardless of his injury, he was one hunk of man she'd like to dig her nails into.

Her cell phone's vibration on the counter pulled her from her fantasy. She leaned forward and read the screen. *Dad.* Hitting the Talk button, she brought the phone to her ear. "Hi, Dad."

"Becca, how are you, sweetie?" His raspy tone came through the line, reminding her of a strong espresso. Maybe it was the strong, rich, flavor of the coffee that made her compare her father's strength, to her love of espresso. Her father was still full of life, as long as he was away from her mother.

"I'm good, Dad. What's going on? You never call in the middle of a work day." Her suspicion rose.

"Can't a father call his only child because he misses her?"

"Dad…" Rebecca frowned. Something was up.

"I miss you, and I have a few days off. Why don't I come for a visit?" There was a hint of hesitation in his voice.

Her father never took time off work. He only travelled to get away from his wife. It was his escape and Rebecca couldn't fault him for it. After he retired from the Navy he tried to settle down, to be the man her mother wanted, but all the years of him being away had left a wedge between them. Rebecca's mother was unwilling, or unable, to give up the bottle for her husband, and he couldn't stand to be around her in a drunken state. Dad had said divorce wasn't an option because he loved her.

"Are you visiting alone or with Mom? Because you know how I feel about that."

"Alone. I need to see you Becca. What do you say?"

She nodded as if he could see her. "Okay. When?"

"I'll be there tomorrow."

"Tomorrow?" She abruptly stood from the chair, nearly knocking it over.

"Yeah, if that's okay. I'm in Denver for a job so I'll drive up and get a room at Winterbloom Bed and Breakfast. Are you working tomorrow?"

Her mind raced with everything she'd need to do before her father's arrival. "No…no, I'm not working. I'm off the next two days. There's no reason to stay at Winterbloom, I've got a guest room. You'll stay with me. You have my address. What time should I expect you?" She tried to hide the panic from her voice, but her gut was telling her something was amiss. Her father didn't just drop by for a casual visit, especially not in the middle of a work week, no matter how close he was to Clearwater.

"I'll leave first thing in the morning and I should be there around two. We can have a late lunch in Jackson Hole and catch up. It's been too long since I've seen you."

She caught the edge of sadness in his voice. She was accustomed to hearing him miss her. He had been away most of her life with deployments and training. He had been a good father, better than her mother was a mother, even if he had been absent a lot. "Sure, Dad. I look forward to seeing you…but are you sure everything is okay?"

Rebecca heard commotion in the background and her father speaking to someone else. "Okay, I'll be right there." There was a long pause of silence before he returned to their conversation. "I just want to see you, but Becca I have to go now. I'll see you tomorrow. I love you."

"Love you too, Dad." She ended the call and snatched the pen out of her hair to make a list. First, was a spring clean of her apartment, especially the guest bedroom. She tapped the pen on the counter, her mind more on her father than the list. There was something in her father's words, but she couldn't put her finger on it. He wasn't just missing her, he was hiding something.

Chapter Four

Rebecca glanced around the apartment again, checking to make sure everything was in order. It had been nearly eight month since she saw her father, and even longer since she saw her mother. Clearwater allowed Rebecca to keep her distance from the problems her mother created, but she hated the distance it caused in her relationship with her father.

The clock struck two and a knock sounded against the thick wood door of her two-bedroom apartment. She timidly stepped to the door, her heart beating frantically in her ears. Taking a deep breath, she turned the handle.

Even nearing fifty, her father was toned. His years in the Navy had instilled good values. To this day he worked out at the gym three times a week, and every morning, rain or shine, he went for a two mile run. Rebecca envied his dedication.

His hair had grown out a little from the crew cut he normally sported. The only sign that showed his age was the hit of grey showing around his temples. The deep brown tan, from hours in the sun, reminded her proudly of the job he took after leaving the military. Instead of deployments and training, he was now an architect, designing and building homes for military men and women who were injured as a result of their service.

He dropped his small, black duffle bag. It hit her floor with a thump.

"Dad." She smiled as he extended his arms wide. He wrapped his arms around her, filling her lonesome heart with love. Clearwater had become her home and she had made many friends, but without any family around, she was lost and alone. Her father's hug drained away the loneliness and doubts.

"Becca, I've missed you."

She wanted to remain in the comfort of her father's arms, but finally stepped aside to allow him inside her apartment. "Come in. You've had a long journey. Do you want to rest for a bit before we go for lunch?" Once the words were spoken she realized how stupid they sounded. Her father had never taken a nap in all the years she'd known him, no matter how long he had been awaken. He just couldn't sleep in the afternoon.

He shoved his bag with his foot before stepping into her apartment, and shutting the door. "I'm fine. The drive was good. I left Denver before rush hour traffic. I'm hungry. How about we have lunch in Jackson Hole? I heard there's a delicious Italian restaurant there, and I know how much you love Italian."

"Sure. Let me grab my purse. If you want to put your bag in the guest room, it's the first door on the right." She nodded toward the hall leading from the great room.

"Thanks," he said.

Collecting her purse from the kitchen, she slipped it over her shoulder and tucked her cell phone into the pocket of her jeans. She wanted to ask why her father chose now to visit. Was he terminally ill? Had her mother drank her liver to failure?

As her father returned from the bedroom, she stuffed away her questions. He'd tell her in his own time. Pressuring him wouldn't make him spill whatever secret he was hiding any sooner.

* * *

JC added the last student's information into the first self-defense class database that was set to start in two weeks. He then pushed away from the desk. It had been a long day and he still had two hours to go. Coffee, that's what he needed. He considered going to Express-Ohh's, not just because their coffee was better than the crap sitting in the pot in his office, but also to see Rebecca again. She weighed in his thoughts since their first encounter.

"JC, got a minute?" Jordan leaned against the doorframe. Jordan, a former Marine, was now retired and settled into a quiet life with his wife Chloe, running Winterbloom Bed and Breakfast.

"Sure, come on in. I was just pouring myself a cup of coffee, would you like some?"

"No, thanks." Jordan sank into the chair in front of JC's desk. "Cameron asked me to teach a self-defense and weapons training class specifically for business owners in Clearwater. One evening a week, an hour long each, over the course of three weeks. I'd prefer Thursdays, but any day except Fridays works for me. Can you set this up?"

"Sure. With so many of the business owners being female, it would be good for them to learn basic self-defense. Clearwater is pretty safe, from what I hear, but being so close to Jackson Hole you could have tourists passing through who cause trouble." JC glanced at the computer screen, checking the scheduled class rooms. "How about Thursday evenings from seven to eight, starting the second week of September? The course will be complete before tourist season."

"Works for me. I'm flexible on the number of attendees, but ten would give me more hand–on-hand training. If there's more interested, maybe we can split into two classes, one at seven and the next at eight. Whatever works in the schedule, just send me a list of the participants so I can tailor some of the training to their needs." Jordan rose from the chair and nodded toward JC's coffee mug. "You need the good stuff from Express-Ohh's."

JC laughed and walked Jordan out. He went back to his office and took another drink of the muddy coffee. His stomach rumbled in protest. He ignored it and sat at his desk. Instead of making a run to town to catch a glimpse of Rebecca, he had more work to get done. It was for the best. He didn't need to be anywhere near her, even if he craved to see her again. *Friendship only.* He vowed.

He grabbed his notepad and jotted down the names of some local businesses that might be interested in the new class. He'd create a flyer and head into town tomorrow to get people to sign up.

* * *

The Italian restaurant overlooked one of the ski hills, but without snow the scenery didn't have the same attraction it boasted in the winter. Rebecca arched her back against the booth, trying to ease the tension that had settled there. An awkward silence settled between Rebecca and her father, which was very unusual for her normally talkative father.

"Dad, what's going on? This isn't like you." She leaned forward, placing her folded hands on the table.

"I was hoping to tell you after lunch, but I can see it's unavoidable." He placed his hand over hers. "Your mother and I are getting a divorce."

The surprise of his blunt comment stole her words. "What?"

"I know this is a shock, but our marriage just doesn't work any longer. It's time to accept that."

Doesn't work any longer? Where had he been all these years? Her parents' marriage hadn't been good since she was a child. "I'm astonished that it's taken you this long to realize it." She shook her head, swallowing all the nasty words she wanted to say about her mother, and about their suffering marriage. "You said you could never leave her, that she needed you. What changed?"

"Becca, I've always loved your mother, that hasn't changed. But your mother…she's found someone new. She filed for divorce last week." Sadness thickened his voice.

"I'm sorry." She held his hand, giving it a little squeeze. "Nothing I say will lessen what you're going through, but you deserve better."

"Oh Rebecca, if you could have known the woman I fell in love with." Her father glanced at their entwined hands before continuing. "Your mother was so full of life. My career stole that from her, and stole the mother you should have had. For that I'm truly sorry."

"This isn't your fault. She made the choice. She didn't have to stay in a marriage she wasn't happy in. She chose the bottle over us." Rebecca wanted to say something else to remove the pain from her father's eyes, but nothing she said would bring him any comfort. He had stayed with her mother because he loved her, even if she was a mess. Whereas, Rebecca could barely stand to be in the same room with her mother for five minutes without wanting to scream. "What now?"

"I'll get an apartment in Denver, it's central to the airport, and with my job that's important. Plus it's close to you. I'm hoping you'll allow me to visit from time to time."

"I never wanted to separate from you. I just couldn't live like that. Mom was driving me insane. I needed to get out of there, to make a life of my own. Moving to Clearwater has been the best decision for me, made me stand on my own feet."

He nodded, his thumb trailing over her knuckles. "I'm proud of you. You're twenty, supporting yourself, and nearly finished your degree. You've become your own woman."

"Thank you." All her life she strived to please her father. Her throat tightened and tears slid down her cheeks. "I hope you'll visit often."

Chapter Five

JC had been looking forward to Saturday and the town picnic since meeting Rebecca, but now that the day was upon him, here he sat working. Nothing needed his attention that couldn't wait until Monday, but he was using work to stall going to the picnic. Part of him craved to see Rebecca again, while the other half thought she deserved better than him. She was young and had her whole life ahead of her. While he might be young in years, he grew up too fast. Being the man responsible for his family's home and a stand-in father for his siblings, his childhood and rebellion years were cut short.

Before his injury, he longed for a steady relationship—for a woman to settle down with. His fear of ending up like his mother, with children he couldn't afford, prevented him from taking that step. JC's family dream was unreachable. He already had a family to provide for...and now he wasn't a complete man, capable enough to be a husband or a father.

"JC."

He glanced up from the paperwork to find Tessa standing in the doorway.

"Aren't you coming to the picnic?"

"I should stay here. There's a lot of paperwork that needs to be dealt with and phone calls to return." He pointed to the paper scattered on the desk.

"Come on, that stuff can wait."

"Not only is my wife beautiful, but she's always right." Cameron stepped beside his wife, with Rosie nestled against his chest. Tessa slid her arm around his waist. "Phone calls, seriously? You won't get any response because everyone will be at the picnic. So come with us. It will be good for you to meet some of the residents. Many of them you've spoken to, and now you can put a face to the name."

Nodding, JC slid the papers back into the folder and rose from the desk. He followed Cameron and Tessa to their truck, reminding himself his interest in Rebecca was as a friend, nothing more. Who was he trying to kid? Just the thought of her sent his nerves on edge.

A refreshing breeze brushed his shoulders, cooling his heated thoughts of Rebecca. Waiting for Cameron to strap Rosie into the car seat, JC glanced back at the shop. In two weeks the place had transformed. The boys had finished adding landscaping around the building. The mature trees around the area brought shade and also gave an appearance they had been there for years instead of only a few weeks.

On Monday the manager's flat would be completed. The furniture he had chosen from Country Home Fixing's would be delivered and he could finally move it. Cameron and Tessa were great, giving him space, but he wanted his own place, where he could relax and not have to worry about being in the way.

Cameron pulled the truck to a stop not far from where everyone had already gathered. The sun glistened off the lake, gleaming like a diamond in the rough. People gathered on blankets and around picnic tables, while children ran to and fro. A few were even playing in the lake water with their watchful parents nearby.

JC felt like an outsider, watching everyone having a good time with their families.

"This is your home now too." Tessa met his gaze as she slipped the car seat out careful not to disturb the sleeping Rosie from her car seat. "We are one big family here. You'll enjoy the picnic if you let yourself."

It was crazy to run now. He couldn't sit in the hot truck and wait for them. He was here and would make the best of it. Opening the door, he stepped out and his gaze immediately found Rebecca. She was wearing a pair of jean shorts, a pale pink tank top, and her long, brown hair was pulled into a ponytail. An older man sat across her.

A twinge of jealousy passed through him, but he had no reason to be jealous. There was nothing between him and Rebecca, even if he wanted to heat up the night with her next to him.

"Hey, Cameron, JC, over here." Jordan waved from a picnic table with Chloe and Jennifer.

JC followed Cameron's lead toward the table. He knew Jordan and Chloe, and he had met Jennifer once when she dropped something off at the house for Tessa. Being surrounded by new people always put JC on edge, making the hairs on the back of his neck stand on edge, but he quickly grew comfortable with the people of Clearwater.

"Want a beer?" Jordan asked JC as he handed one to Cameron.

"Sure." He lowered onto the corner of the bench, obtaining a clear view of most of the crowd, and Rebecca. Taking the bottle from Jordan, he twisted the cap off, and took a long swig.

"Let me hold my sugarplum." Chloe bent, unhooking Rosie from her car seat. "I've missed her."

"Now that Jordan's finished your log home and Holly's running most of the day-to-day operations for Winterbloom, you need to visit more," Tessa said, taking a seat next to Chloe. "Cam's always busy, and I only get goo's and gah's with Rosie. I need some adult interaction."

"I've cut back now that JC's here." Cameron added defensively.

"Before you newlyweds bicker too much, Tessa, why don't you ask my workaholic wife how she's doing with giving up the reins to Winterbloom." Jordan held his hands up in surrender as Chloe whipped around to face him.

"Chloe?" Tessa raised an eyebrow.

"Winterbloom has been my life since I was a child, running it with Gram until she passed. It's my heart and soul, and hard to give it up."

"But there's life outside of the Bed and Breakfast." Jordan slid his hand down Chloe's arm.

"He's right," JC added. The minute the words escaped his lips he wished he could take them back. Everyone turned to him. He gave them a halfhearted smile. "I didn't expect to make it after...I left the Marines, but now that I'm here, I do my best to live every day to the fullest. Chloe, you just need to find a balance. All you need is a competent manager for Winterbloom. Let that person handle the daily operations while you sit back and enjoy your family. My mother has worked two jobs most of her life, never having the time to spend with her children. Now they are growing fast, and she regrets the lost time. Don't miss out because of work."

"Wow." Tessa broke the silence that followed JC's comments. "So young and knowledgeable. Cam needs to take your advice. Thankfully with you running the shop he finally gets to spend more time with Rosie and me." She smiled at her husband.

"I am, and JC is learning the ropes quickly, but it's a new business, which I still need to keep my hands in. Once the classes start I'll have even more time to spend with you." Cameron leaned to kiss his wife.

JC sat there for a moment realizing he had told everyone at the table that they needed to live their life, yet he wasn't following his own words. "If you'll excuse me, there's someone I'd like to say hello to." He rose from the table and headed toward Rebecca before the courage escaped him.

Her gaze found his as he neared, and his heart skipped a beat when she smiled. Her grin was like a lighthouse in the middle of the darkest night, guiding him like a beacon. Speeding up his pace, his lips curl upward, returning her smile with one of his own.

"JC, I'm glad you could make it." She waved a hand to her father. "This is my father, Robert James. Dad, this is JC."

JC accepted the man's extended hand, giving it a firm shake. "Juan Carlos Marquez, sir, but please call me JC."

"None of that sir stuff. Robert is fine. What branch are you in, son?" Robert tapped the bench, offering JC a seat.

JC sat across from Rebecca. He was surprised that her father knew he was in the military. "I was a Marine, but an injury cut my career short. How did you know?"

"It's the way you carry yourself. A fellow service member recognizes another. I was in the Navy for over twenty years. What brings you to Clearwater? Or are you originally from here?" Robert's brows furrowed over his eyes, almost as if sizing up JC. To determine if he was good enough for Rebecca?

"Cameron White was my commanding officer. He needed help with his shop, Clearwater Combat and Guns, so here I am. Do you live here or are you in town visiting?" One thing JC didn't miss about dating was impressing the parents, not that he dated often before his injury.

"Visiting. I'm returning to Denver in the morning." Robert turned to Rebecca and nodded. "I'll leave you two for a bit. I need to make a couple of phone calls."

"Okay, Dad." She watched her father leave the park before glancing back at JC. "I didn't know he was coming into town until yesterday." She shook her head. "I'm really glad you came."

"I'm glad I came too." He smiled, suddenly feeling like a schoolboy again. "I don't want to interrupt your visit with your dad, but I'd like to talk to you for a few minutes. Could you take a short walk with me?"

She glanced over her shoulder at her father, who was in the parking lot talking on his cell phone. "Okay."

JC walked away from the noisy picnic area, hoping to gain a little privacy for what he wanted to tell Rebecca. She stepped in beside him. Once they neared the far edge of the lake, he nodded toward the bench. "Let's sit."

She sat on the bench, staring at him intently. "You seem tense, is everything all right, JC?"

"Sitting over there with Cameron, Jordan, and their wives, I realized something." He paused and inhaled a deep breath. What he was about to tell her might change how everyone in Clearwater saw him. He'd no longer be the new guy in town. He could become the new handicapped guy in town. How he hated that label. Even without his leg, he was still the same man he was before. It took coming to Clearwater to help JC understand that there wasn't anything he could do before his injury that he couldn't still do.

"What is it?" A hint of concern filled her voice.

"I gave up living life to the fullest after I was discharged from the Marines, but that's about to change. I told you I was injured on my last mission. The truth is, I lost my leg in an IED explosion. I don't know if I'd have made it through without Cameron. I owe my life to him. He's the reason I moved here. I'm telling you this because I want to be honest with you and it's only right that you know up front. If you're okay with my disability, I'd like to take you out sometime." He let the words fly off his tongue, desperate to get them said.

A glimpse of sadness shadowed her hazel eyes. "I appreciate you telling me this, but I'm wondering if I should be offended that you thought I'd have an issue with your injury."

"Rebecca, that's not what I meant." He ran his hand down the length of his jeans. "Damn it. This isn't coming out how I wanted it to."

She laid her hand over his. "JC, you're still alive, that's what should matter. You lost your leg, but you're alive and healthy. Many of our military members are denied a second chance at life. When my father retired from the Navy, he took a job as an architect, designing homes for injured military members once they've been discharged. I've met some of the people he has helped. They've suffered loss from this war, but they are alive and that's what counts. Their families are grateful to have them. I've also seen the families of those who never made it home. In honor of the soldiers who will never make it home, you need to live the life you were meant to. You've been given a second chance. Don't let it pass you by." She didn't bother to wipe away the tears that slid down her cheeks.

"When I first woke up in the hospital and realized what happened, I prayed for death. My mother is a single mother of nine children, and I've always been the man of the family. I helped her make ends meet, with the younger children, and whatever else she needed done. It was the reason I joined the Marines. Without my career I didn't know how I was going to continue taking care of them." He sighed. "My mother was beside my bed and cried, not for the loss of my leg, but because I made it home. My heart broke at the sight of my mother crying." If he would have died it would have been worse for her and his whole family.

"It sounds as though you're close to your mother and your siblings. If not for yourself, you need to be strong for them." She frowned. "Why are you here, instead of being with your family?"

That was the one question he didn't want to answer. Why he ran as quickly as his legs would carry him from North Carolina. "I'm close to my family, they mean everything to me, but I had to leave."

"Why?"

She wasn't going to let the subject drop, leaving him with two options, be rude and ask her to drop the inquisition or to tell her the truth. If he expected her to go out on a date with him then rudeness was out of the question. "Everyone back home knew what happened. I didn't want their pity. When I went anywhere, I saw the sympathy in people's faces. I got tired of their sadness and their questions. If I was ever to move on with my life, it had to be somewhere else. Home only reminds me of what I lost. The whole town is Marines. Military is a way of life there."

"For some people it's the only way they know how to deal with tragedy. I'm sorry you had to leave your home because of it. What about your family? Will they remain there?"

He noticed sadness in her eyes, but thankfully no pity. Rebecca treated him like a person and not a former shell of who he once was. "I don't know. I've been thinking about options. Mom and the kids need to get out of where they're living. The apartment is too small, and Mom needs more help. Lee and Laya, the next oldest, can only do so much. Laya is like a second mother to the younger siblings and Lee has stepped into my shoes since I left. He has a chance to make something of himself, to go to college on a full football scholarship if he can keep his grades up. He only has a year left." JC glanced over the lake. "I want them to come here. Clearwater would be good for my family, but I'm not sure I can convince my mother. I've been putting together a plan, to convince her."

She squeezed his hand. "I'm sure your mother misses you. If anyone can find a way to bring them here, I know you can. Finding a place big enough might be a challenge, but I can help."

"Thank you. I have money put aside to do this and it doesn't have to be a huge place. They live in a small four bedroom apartment now. I hope I can find something better." The loneliness of not having his family close by stung. "I just want them here. They deserve better than what they have now."

She ran her thumb over his knuckles. "I'm off tomorrow, why don't you come by my place and we'll put together a plan to convince your family to move here."

"Only if you promise you'll let me take you out to dinner afterward?" He hoped she'd say yes because he was growing short on alone time with her. It wouldn't be long before her father returned, or Cameron and Jordan wondered where he had taken off.

"Okay. How about one o'clock?"

"Give me your address, and I'll be there. It looks like your father is done with his calls." He nodded toward Robert approaching.

"I rent the apartment above Express-Ohh's, park around back and you'll see the door." She smiled and turned to her father. "Hey, Dad."

Robert stood behind them. "I hope I'm not interrupting."

"Of course not. I should be going. Cameron and Tessa will be wondering where I disappeared. Enjoy your visit, Robert." JC rose from the bench, careful to not raise his leg too high so his pant leg didn't show his prosthesis. Cameron, Jordan, and their wives knew, and now Rebecca, but he didn't want everyone in town to know. He couldn't face a repeat of pity on people's faces here too.

"I will, and I hope to see you again when I visit." Robert stuck out his hand, smiling, and nodding as if giving JC permission to date his daughter.

JC returned the handshake and smiled. He then grazed his fingers along Rebecca's arm. "Thank you for listening and understanding."

"I'll see you tomorrow." She grinned.

For the first time since JC woke up in the hospital bed, he truly felt alive. Life was no longer passing him by.

Chapter Six

Rebecca stretched her legs on the sofa, a bowl of ice cream in her hand. She was still adjusting to the information that her parents were divorcing. "Dad, I know Clearwater doesn't have an airport like Denver, but have you thought about staying here? Between jobs?"

He sat catty-corner across from her in the black recliner. He laughed. "You don't want me around cramping your style with a new gentleman friend."

She shoved a spoon full of chocolate ice cream into her mouth. "Seriously? You were gone a lot when I was growing up, but now we can make up for lost time. There's no reason for us to be miles apart. Would you at least give it some thought?"

"You didn't deny my *gentleman friend* comment." His eyebrow rose. "I'm not your only family. You still have your mother. Maybe with this new guy she's dating, she'll get her life turned around."

Years ago, Rebecca gave up hope that her mother would pull her life together and give up the bottle, so she chose to ignore her father's comment about her mother. However, his comment on JC couldn't be avoided. Her father wouldn't give up until he knew what was going on between her and JC. She'd always be daddy's little girl, no matter how old she was. "I just met JC. He's a super nice guy and we're going to dinner tomorrow night. I don't know if it will turn into a relationship."

"Why not? You're an attractive, smart girl."

"Thanks, Dad. JC's got his own issues he needs to work out."

He sat his glass of sweet tea on the coffee table. "Issues?"

Without going into many details, she explained what JC had told her at the lake. "His family means a lot to him. I don't know if he'll stay in Clearwater if his mother and family refuse to move here too."

"So make it so they can't refuse?"

"What do you mean?" She placed her bowl of ice cream on the end table and tucked her legs under her.

"Let's build them a house, give them a true home they can't say no to. JC served his country, it's time his country gave back to him."

He pulled his phone from his pocket, and then glanced at her. "The project in Denver is done in three weeks and I don't have anything lined up after that. Do you have Cameron's number?"

"You know Cameron?" She slid her phone from the pocket of her sweats and tossed it to him. "It's under Tessa."

"Yes, we met several years ago. If anyone can help, it's him. Let me call him before it's too late. Maybe I can get the ball rolling, and you can tell JC the plan tomorrow." He rose from the chair and headed down the hallway to the spare room.

* * *

With her father on his way back to Denver, and his promise to consider settling down in Clearwater part time, Rebecca was hopeful. If JC gave the go-ahead to build his family a home here, she'd be seeing a lot of her father in the near future.

Glancing over the quick plans her father was able to draw up over breakfast, a sliver of nervousness passed through her. If only her dad could have stayed to go over things with JC. Housing plans and land space was not her thing. She was a business major and knew next to nothing about building houses.

A knock on the door made heart flutter. With a quick glance at the clock, seeing he was a few minutes early, her nervousness quickly changed to excitement as she went to open the door. She hoped he would be as excited about the building plan as she was. When he spoke of his family the longing was clear in his eyes. He could never truly be happy without them nearby.

Opening the door, her breath caught in her throat. The faded blue jeans and grey T-shirt he wore did little to hide his toned body. She took a step back. Why would he think a woman wouldn't be interested in him because of his injury? He was one fine specimen of pure hunk. Regaining her breath, she invited him in. "Come in."

"There's this girl that works at Express-Ohh's that got me hooked on their coffee." He laughed and handed her one of the to-go coffee cups in his hand. "Jennifer fixed your regular."

"Thank you." She brought the cup to her lips and sipped. She loved French vanilla cappuccino. "This girl at the coffee shop, is she pretty? Should I be concerned she'll steal away your attention?" she teased.

"She's beautiful and had the focus of my attention since I walked into the shop." She shut the door behind him and waved a hand toward the dining room. "I grabbed today's edition of the Clearwater News, to check the rental ads."

"Actually, I have an idea about that. Please, sit down." Butterflies danced in her stomach as she strolled toward the dining room table. Setting her coffee cup down on the table, she waited for him to sit across from her. She then took a deep breath and told him about the new plan. "I was talking to my dad about your family's situation and he mentioned another option."

"What option?"

She pushed her cup aside, leaning forward to wrap her hands around his. "Let's build a home for your family."

He sat straight, but didn't pull his hands away. "I have some money saved, but not enough. I don't know if I could get a loan to buy land and build, especially since I just started working for Cameron."

"I wish my father was here to explain this to you because I knew I wouldn't do it right." She bit her lip, taking a moment to consider her words so he'd understand. "I meant building with my father. You're an injured vet, trying to put your life back together." She smiled. "Dad did some research last night. There's a strip of land just outside of town, big enough for building." She reluctantly let go of his hand and grabbed a green folder. Pulling out the sketches her father worked on that morning, she handed them to JC. "It's a rough design of what he could build and you can change anything you want. The idea of a duplex allows you a place of your own and your family next door. Normally with a duplex you have equal sides, but with eight children still living at home, Dad changed the design a little. Your mother's house would have six bedrooms, as well as a nice size playroom while the kids are younger and can be turned into a family room as they grow up, while your house would have four bedrooms." She gave him some time to review the floor plan.

"It's a great idea, but I wouldn't qualify for your father's organization. It's for injured vets and their families—spouse and children, not mother and siblings." He slid the paper across the table as if he couldn't stand to think about something so far out of reach.

"It's not through the organization. We're going to do it. Dad called Cameron last night and got things moving. Cameron, Jordan, and some of the other residents are going to do the work. Dad will oversee the operation, and the materials are being provided by Kelly's

Hardware." She pulled her laptop closer, opened the top, and turned it toward JC. "Here's the land information. It's a foreclosure and a good price. Before he left, Dad and I drove by the area this morning to make sure it would fit your needs." She sat back, giving him time to adjust the information.

"I don't know, I can't allow people to do this for me. I don't deserve it."

"But you do. You served your country for three years before your medical discharge. The Clearwater residents want to give back. These are times when small towns like Clearwater pull together to help someone that's done so much for them. You can set roots here, and your family can finally have a real home. Your mother can stop working two jobs and actually watch her children grow." She closed the computer screen. "Why don't we go look at the property and you can think about it? If you're interested in putting an offer in we'll meet with the realtor, Allison. Then you can make a decision with the rest of the paperwork. What do you say?" She rose from the table, holding out her hand. "Come on, looking won't hurt."

He stood and raised his hand to cup her cheek. He lowered his head to hover his lips just above hers. His breath was warm against her skin. "Thank you," he whispered, and then without hesitation he pressed his lips to hers.

The kiss was sweet and timid, and completely caught her off guard. With her slight hesitation, he started to move away, but she placed her hand on the back of his head, drawing him in for a deeper kiss. Adrenaline flooded her veins, as she opened her lips, allowing him entry to her mouth. His tongue slipped between her lips, and she explored the spicy taste of coffee, devouring it until it slid away. He placed one final kiss on her lips before stepping aside, leaving her longing for his touch.

* * *

Returning to her apartment after their tour of the land, JC sat on the sofa with the plans for the house spread on the coffee table. The town's help with construction as well as the supplies, had him thinking he could swing the costs as well as have enough savings to cover any bills that would occur, at least until his mother found a job.

Rebecca plopped down next to him. "Allison is drawing up the paperwork for your offer, and she'll meet us downstairs in an hour. Do you want to call your mother before you sign the paperwork?"

He leaned back, turning to her. "While you were on the phone, I made a call to Cameron. I need to do this in person. The classes haven't started yet, so I'm going to take a few days off and fly back to North Carolina." He met her gaze and took her hand in his. "What are your plans for the next few days? Do you have to work? If not, I'd like you to come with me."

She shuddered, blinking uncontrollably. Maybe she didn't hear him? Or was she trying to find the words to let him down easy. "Why?"

"This was your idea, and I want you with me when I tell my family. What do you say?" His thumb glided over her knuckles. She shuddered again. "What better time to meet my family?" He teased.

She laughed. "I can think of at least a dozen better times."

"I've met your father and I'll be seeing him a lot in the coming months. It's only fair that you meet my family. How long did your father say the project would take?"

"Eight to ten weeks, for the design in your hand. Minor changes wouldn't change the date, but bigger adjustments could extend another two to four weeks. You'd have to talk to my dad if you want to change anything. He'd be able to give you a better length of timing."

"I'll leave any changes up to my mom." JC glanced back to the plans on the table. He still couldn't get over the fact this might happen. He didn't deserve it, but he couldn't turn the offer down. He'd have to find a way to repay the residents of Clearwater for their kindness. "So are you coming with me? It will probably take the two of us to convince her and the family to move."

"How about we have that dinner you promised before we go rushing off to meet your family?"

He smiled, satisfied that at least her answer wasn't *no*. "Okay, we'll go see Allison and then have dinner." He rose from the sofa, snatched her hand and drew her to him. "You're beautiful, and amazing to boot." He wrapped his arms around her, pulling her closer to his body, before pressing his lips to hers.

Chapter Seven

The following afternoon, Rebecca sat sandwiched between JC and the small window of a plane. Her palms were sweaty, and nerves turned her stomach upside down. Closed spaces did little to help the tension coursing through her body. The worst thing about living in Clearwater was flying in and out of the airport on the small planes. The airport didn't have big enough landing strips for large planes, and there were never enough passengers unless it was winter.

"I didn't realize you were scared to fly." JC tucked a strand of loose hair behind her ear. "You should have told me."

"Sorry." She smiled, halfhearted. "I agreed to come. I've never let my fears hold me back from anything I want to do, and I'm not about to start now."

"You're an amazing woman. Thank you." He lifted the armrest between them, sliding his arm around her to pull her closer.

"Hello, sir. It's nice to see you've chosen our airline again. I hope you enjoyed your visit to Clearwater." The flight attendant stood next to the aisle, a hint of hostility colored her eyes as she stared down at Rebecca.

"Actually, I live in Clearwater now. We're going to visit my family." JC's fingers tickled over Rebecca's shoulder.

"Oh. Please fasten your seatbelts, we will be departing shortly." She shot a glare at Rebecca before moving down the aisle.

"Did you know her?" Rebecca glanced at JC.

"I met her when I flew in."

"To give me a threatening stare as she did, I would have thought you had history."

"Do I detect a hint of jealousy?" The plane began to move, picking up speed as it made its way down the runway. A shiver of fear coursed through her again. He ran his arm down her arm, his touch trying to make her forget they were hurling down the runway about to be airborne. If people were meant to fly they'd have wings.

"Do I have anything to be envious about?"

"Not at all." He kissed the top of her head. "You're the one I want."

* * *

Night had fallen over the area when JC parked the rental car in front of the apartment building where his family lived. He didn't call to let them know he was coming, he wanted to surprise them. If his mother knew he was coming home after only a few weeks in Clearwater, she'd be suspicious. Shoving the gearshift into Park, he took a deep breath. "Are you ready?"

"As ready as I'll ever be. It's nerve-racking to meet someone's family for the first time. I hope they like me."

"They will." He opened his door, slid out, and walked around the car to open her door. He took her hand and led her up the walkway.

"JC?" Laya opened the door, surprise evident in her eyes.

"Laya." He released Rebecca's hand and rushed toward his sister. She was so mature, standing there with Kelly clinging to her hand. "It's so good to see you, I've missed you both." He wrapped his arms around Laya before bending to pick up Kelly.

"What are you doing here? I thought you were in Clearwater for that job." Laya glanced between JC and Rebecca.

"I needed to speak with mom, and the whole family." Settling Kelly in one arm, her hands locked tightly around his neck, he wrapped his other arm around Rebecca's shoulders. "Laya, this is Rebecca. Rebecca, this is my oldest sister, Laya, the one who keeps her twin, Lee, and the rest of our siblings, in line."

Rebecca and Laya exchanged greetings while he enjoyed the youngest of the Marquez siblings in his arms. Kelly was four, and he had been the only father figure she had known. She yawned and nestled her head into his shoulder. "I think Kelly is ready for bed. Is Mom upstairs?"

"Yeah, she just got home. Kelly was sick today, so Ms. Betty watched her while Lee and I took the rest to the park. Since she was sleeping, Ms. Betty kept her while I fixed dinner and got the other kids settled for the night. Come inside." Laya stepped aside, letting them enter the house.

They followed Laya, and by the time he entered the living room, Kelly was asleep in his arms.

"Mom, guess whose home?"

"Shhh, Laya, the younger kids are in bed." JC's mother walked out of the kitchen. "JC!" Tears fell over her cheeks as she ran to him.

Rebecca moved to the side, giving his mom full access to him. He wrapped his arm around his mother as she came in for a hug. She clung to him, like she hadn't seen him in years instead of only a few weeks.

She pushed back from him, tears flowing freely down her face. She glanced between him and Rebecca. "Why didn't you let me know you were coming?"

"I wanted it to be a surprise." He handed his sleeping sister to Laya. "Would you mind putting Kelly to bed? I need to talk to Mom."

Laya reached for Kelly.

"Mom, could we sit out on the porch, I'd like to talk to you before the rest of the family."

"Of course, honey." She turned to Laya. "When you get Kelly settled can you make sure everyone else is still in bed. I gave a few of them permission to read for a little while, but lights out in ten minutes." Laya nodded and walked down the hallway toward a bedroom. His mother smiled at Rebecca. "Since my son has lost his manners, I'll have to introduce myself. I'm Jackie and you are?"

"I'm sorry, Mom. This is Rebecca." He held out his hand to Rebecca and drew her next to him.

"Let's go outside then." She pointed toward the sliding glass doors off the kitchen.

On the small patio, JC let his mom and Rebecca sit on the only two chairs, while he leaned on the iron railing. With the cool night air dancing around him, he glanced out to the city. He missed the lights, but the noise he could do without. Hopefully he'd be able to put North Carolina behind him, and his family could join him in Wyoming.

* * *

Rebecca hoped she didn't appear uncomfortable as she listened to JC explain the benefits of moving to Wyoming. He told his mother what he had planned. She felt like an outsider, eavesdropping on a personal family moment. JC needed time with his family, to convince them to move closer to him. He didn't need to have his girlfriend hanging around.

Girlfriend? When did she start considering herself his girlfriend? Maybe it happened when they booked one hotel room, instead of two. At that moment, she realized she wanted more than a friendship with JC.

"How do you play into this?" Jackie's question dragged Rebecca from her thoughts.

She fidgeted unnervingly on her chair, glancing briefly to JC for support. His smile gave her the encouragement she needed. "It was my father's idea."

Jackie glared at her son, anger lighting her eyes. "You told her father about our situation?"

Rebecca refused to let JC take the blame. "Ms. Marquez, that was actually my doing. I'm sorry. I was only trying to help."

"Mom, Rebecca and I were going to look at apartments, to find somewhere for you to live closer to me. Robert's solution is better for everyone. I've put an offer on the land and we can begin building in three weeks." He leaned forward, handing his mother the folder. "Will you at least look over the plans and think about it?"

"I've made up my mind already." She didn't take the folder, just pushed it aside.

Lee slid the door open, walked out on the patio, and hugged his brother. "JC, Laya said you wanted to talk to Mom privately, but Kelly's throwing a fit. She wants you to tuck her in bed. Could you come in for a moment?"

JC glanced toward Rebecca. She nodded and he turned back to his mother. "Mom, stay here until I get back, please."

Rebecca could see the disappointment in JC's eyes. He wanted Clearwater to be a place for his family to start over, but he would have a difficult uphill battle to convince his mom.

Once JC and Lee left, Rebecca turned to face Jackie. It was time for a woman-to-woman chat. Hearing about the plan to move from an outsider was going to go one of two ways, either Jackie would realize it was best for her and the family to move to Clearwater to be with JC, or Jackie would take offense to Rebecca for butting into family business. "I apologize if I might be out of place to speak about this, especially since I haven't known JC for very long, but I do know his family means the world to him. He enjoys living in Clearwater, and it's been very healing for him, yet being so far away from you and his siblings is difficult."

When Jackie opened her mouth to respond, Rebecca raised her hand. "Please, just hear me out. JC told me a little about you. That you're working two jobs to support your family. JC joined the Marines to help the family, but…his injury prevents him from doing that now. He's starting over in Clearwater and wants to continue providing for his family. You're going to turn him down without hearing him out? I realize your pride is at stake, but isn't keeping your family together more important?"

"Do you have children?"

Rebecca shook her head. "I don't, however if I did, I'd want to be close. I know it's not possible for all families, but it is for you. You don't know how much longer you will have that opportunity. Lee and Laya are finishing their last year of high school, and then maybe they'll be off to college. JC tells me Lee's an amazing football player and is up for a scholarship."

Jackie glanced down at the folder before returning her stare to Rebecca. "Your kids aren't supposed to help you financially, or raise their siblings. That's been JC's whole life. He doesn't deserve that responsibility any longer."

"He can't turn off something he's been doing for years. Being away from you is tearing him apart. Clearwater is giving him a chance to rebuild a new life without the daily reminders of the military. Unfortunately, he won't stay with such a distance between him and his family."

"You seem to know my son rather well." Jackie's eyebrow rose.

Not knowing how to respond, Rebecca went with the truth. "We've become very good friends and have talked a lot about you and the kids." She left out the part about sharing a few kisses. Their relationship was moving slow and she was okay with that. She wouldn't rush JC. He needed time to adjust to the new developments in his life without her pushing him for more.

"It seems like there's more between you and my son then just a few chats about family." Jackie's eyes were filled with curiosity.

Thankfully JC chose that moment to return. He slid the patio door open and stepped outside. "Kelly's asleep. I checked on everyone else and they are either sleeping or reading in their rooms. Lee went for a run and Laya is studying for an upcoming exam." He placed a hand on Rebecca's shoulder, giving it a gentle squeeze.

She hoped he wouldn't pick up on the tension that had settled over Rebecca and his mother.

"Mom, it's been a long trip for us. We'll go settle into the hotel and get some rest. Maybe tomorrow we can take you and the kids out for lunch?" JC pulled out Rebecca's chair for her and took her hand in his as she stood.

"Hotel?" Jackie's voice rose.

"Staying in a hotel is only practical. Lee is in my room now and there's no room for us here. I didn't want to put anyone out. We are just down the street. We'll be back in the morning." He slid his hand around Rebecca's waist.

"If you would have called, we'd have made room for you. It's crazy to waste money on hotel rooms when you could have stayed here." His mom rose, meeting JC gaze.

"Mom, we've already checked in and we are only here a few days. There's no reason to cram the kids any more than they already are."

Prior to their arrival, Rebecca warned JC that his mother probably wouldn't be happy about their hotel accommodations. Even with Jackie's clear irritation, Rebecca was relieved that she wouldn't be surrounded by his family. His mother seemed nice, but the tension created over the conversation to move was unsettling. Rebecca didn't know where her relationship with JC was going. She secretly longed for something permanent and hoped his family issues wouldn't hinder their progress.

Chapter Eight

The cool night air didn't soothe JC's thoughts as he stood on the balcony. He was stupid to put the move in motion before his mother could consider it. He never thought it possible that she'd turn down the chance to get away from North Carolina, and away from the constant reminder of the military. Or maybe it was just him that was affected by the reminders. Would his siblings feel shorted by having to leave their schools and friends behind? Laya and Lee were seniors this fall and might not want to be uprooted. Maybe JC should have considered his whole family's position further before signing his name on the dotted line for the property.

"Can't sleep?" He turned to find Rebecca leaning on the glass door, a blanket wrapped around her, and her long brown hair slightly tousled from sleep. "It's late. You need to get some rest."

She came to stand next to him. "How long have you been awake?"

He glanced down at her, his hands itching to touch her. Awake? Heck, he never got to sleep. When they checked into the hotel, all the double queen bedrooms were taken, leaving one availability—a king room. It was almost as if the cosmos were aligning, bringing him and Rebecca together. Because the bed was so large, they agreed to stick to their own side. His thoughts jumbled as he lay awake next to her. The smell of sweet vanilla from her shampoo, and the round curves of her body hardened his shaft as soon as he had settled down next to her. He had to get fresh air or take her right then and there. "A bit." He lied.

"What's on your mind? Are you worried Jackie won't agree?" She slid her arm across his back, the blanket now wrapped around them both.

You've been on my mind since I stepped into Express-Ohh's. He turned to gaze into her eyes. "If Mom doesn't want to come to Clearwater, I can't force her. I just feel bad we have everyone lined up for the building."

"It will work out."

Her hand caressing his back broke the final straw of his control. He wrapped his arms around her, pulling her to his body, and lowered his head. Their lips met with desire. Her lips slid open, letting his tongue explore her mouth. His hand slipped under the blanket, grabbing her ass to lift her off her feet. She wrapped her legs around his waist, her arms locked around his neck drawing them closer.

Passion pulsated in his groin. He wanted nothing more than to take her to bed and have her scream his name. He broke the kiss, enjoying her warm breath over his face. "We shouldn't."

"Why? I want this. Don't you?" Her breath came in gasps.

"I've wanted you since I first laid eyes on you. I don't think I've ever wanted to be with someone as much as I want you." Adrenaline flooded through his veins.

"Don't stop. I want your hands on my body, your lips on mine. Please…" She begged.

Without further invitation, he walked the two quick strides to the bed. He lowered her on the bed, the blanket discarded on the floor. Whisking her nightshirt over her head, he took in the sight of her naked body. He tossed her nightshirt aside, slid his hand over her waist, and knelt before her. He wedged his body between her legs. Trailing kisses along her neck, hunger coursed through him. He wanted to take his time, to get acquainted with every inch of her body. He claimed her nipple with his mouth, sucking it, and flicking his tongue over them.

"Oh, JC," she moaned, and tugged at his shorts.

Reluctantly, he released her nipple to travel kisses over her shoulder and up her neck, until he could gaze into her hazel eyes. "You're beautiful." Her cheeks reddened as he pushed her back on the bed and crawled next to her. "I want you on top, to see your body riding mine. I want to see your beauty highlighted by the moonlight." He rolled onto his back, pulling her with him until she lay on top, and caressed the curves of her body.

"What about your leg? Do you need to…?"

"I'm fine." He slid his hand between their bodies, his fingers teasing her pleasure and entering her core, tantalizing her with yearning. She arched her back, giving his fingers deeper access. As the moonlight accentuated her body, she rode his fingers to an orgasm.

"JC, please, I need you." Her voice was full of desire and need.

He moved his hands to her hips and lifted her. "Up." When she hovered above him, he adjusted so his shaft stood just below her entry. She slowly lowered down. Filling her inch by inch, he pushed up on her hips making her rise again before entering her completely with his manhood. His steady strokes fed her fire like tinder set to dynamite. His hands on her hips guided their pace.

He leaned forward, locking his mouth on her nipple and sucked until she moaned in pleasure. Her hips increased pace, driving the force of each pump. His thrusts became deeper and faster into a perfect rhythm. They moved together with such precision, as if in a well-choreographed dance.

Her body tightened around his shaft and her nails dug into his chest. "Oh, JC!" she cried out as his own release followed.

Breathless, he brushed her hair from her face. He wanted to see her. Rebecca's eyes were glossy and dreamy—the aftermath of amazing sex. She slid off him, lying next to him. Snuggling next to his body, she sighed. He pulled the sheet over them. His breath returned to normal as contentment filled him. He cradled her, caressing her spine with long, lazy strokes.

"I know you're worried," Rebecca whispered, her fingers rubbing small circles down his chest. "But I have a feeling everything will work out."

He kissed the top of her head. "It doesn't matter."

She glanced up at him. "Don't lie to me. It does matter to you."

She was right. Would he stay in Clearwater if his family chose to remain in North Carolina? He knew he would…now, with Rebecca by his side. Clearwater gave him a fresh start and possibly a new life that included Rebecca.

* * *

Dawn peaked through the sheer curtains hanging from the patio door. Sleep barely touched JC through the night, and when it did, it left him with nightmares. Being back in his hometown, seeing the service men and women at every turn had brought back the memories of his final mission. He had worked with a therapist months before and the dreams disappeared, for the most part. Since settling in Clearwater, the terror had left him. He needed to return to his new home soon.

When he took off his prosthesis so he could attempt sleeping, he was concerned Rebecca would cringe. But she surprised him. Instead of turning away, she clung to him tighter. She was truly an amazing woman.

She yawned. "The time change is playing with your sleep schedule. You barely slept. Maybe we should make arrangements for dinner instead of lunch." She curled in his arms, her left leg and arm draped over him, cuddling close.

"We leave tomorrow night. If I'm going to convince Mom to move, it has to be today. Then we can relax and enjoy family time." He draped his arm over her. "You didn't sleep much either. If you want to stay behind, I'll understand." She had been his rock through this and he wanted her with him, not only to convince his mother, but to be next to his side.

"No, I'll go. Unless you want to spend time alone with your family?" Her gaze met his.

"I want you there with me. I just didn't want to pressure you."

She laughed, sliding her hand up his chest. "I don't want to walk on eggshells around your family."

"I don't want that either." He placed his index finger under her chin, lifting her lips to his for a soft meaningful kiss. "My family can be a bit overwhelming. I don't want you to feel uncomfortable."

"Your family is an extension of you. I'm looking forward to all the embarrassing stories they can tell me about." She kissed him again. "I need to shower."

"Maybe I should join you." He winked.

"We'll never make it to your family's house if we end up fooling around in the shower. I'll take a rain-check for when we're back in Clearwater."

Watching Rebecca pad naked to the bathroom caused his shaft to harden with desire. He wanted to follow her, to see the soapy water cascading down her silky body, but there would be another day for that. Right now he had to get dressed and prepare what he'd say to convince his mother to move.

Chapter Nine

JC opened Rebecca's door just as Lee jogged up to them.

Lee approached them, his arms crossed over his chest. Anger sparked in his eyes. "I didn't think you were coming back? Mom said you were, but I figured you had to get back to your new life and job?"

"Boy, I hope you haven't lost your manners while I was gone." JC frowned.

"Sorry." Lee held out his hand. "I'm Lee. It's nice to meet you, Rebecca."

She accepted his hand. "Same to you. I'm sorry we left before JC had time to talk with you last night. That was my fault. I was tired after the plane ride."

Lee poked his finger at JC's chest. "It's your fault. You left us. You left Laya and me to handle everything. Poor Laya's got so much to handle, and I have football practice starting in two weeks. Why'd you bother to come back?"

"Lee, I'm sorry you had to pick up some of the slack with me gone. I had to go. Today, I'm here to take everyone out to lunch, to enjoy some family time. I've missed you all." JC had always sheltered the kids, doing his best to allow them each to have a childhood, but when he left, Laya and Lee had no choice but to take over. Lee resented it, and while that tore at JC's heart, he had no real choice. He was useless to his family before.

"We don't need you here." The muscles in Lee's neck bulged.

"Damn it, Lee, stop acting like a spoiled brat. I know you had to give up partying with the team and cruising the streets, but damn it we're talking about our family. Your siblings needed you too." JC's anger peaked. He was tired of Lee acting like he was the only one that gave things up to help. "What the hell did you want me to do? I was a mess when I returned from duty. I wasn't any good to anyone. Leaving was one of the hardest decisions I made, but it was right for the family."

"You're wrong. Mom was worse when you left, she cried all the time. When you were on a deployment she worried, but when she sat by your bedside she realized she could have lost you. Then you just picked up and moved across the country. It broke her. Kelly cried for you, night after night. Nothing any of us did would comfort her. She's finally getting over missing you. She asks for you, but there's no fighting at bedtime. Do you realize what coming back will do to Kelly? She woke up this morning searching for you and when she couldn't find you she went back to bed crying. You're the only father she's known. Hell, you abandoned us all." Lee uncrossed his arms, and for a moment, JC thought his younger brother was going to hit him. Instead he took off running down the street.

JC leaned against the car. His heart sank. Was coming back a mistake?

"JC." Rebecca laid her hand on his arm.

"Oh, Rebecca, I'm sorry you had to witness that. Let's go inside. I'll deal with Lee when he comes home." He glanced down the sidewalk to see Lee rounding the corner. He pushed away from the car.

"JC, wait." She pulled his arm. "Lee is upset. I think some of his anger stems from missing you. It wasn't just your mother that nearly lost you, it was your whole family. You're their hero. They look up to you and you've been a standup father to them, especially the younger ones."

"I did my living through Lee. He has my dreams of playing football and going to college. To see him so angry, breaks my heart. I don't know how to fix it." He shook his head.

"I think he wants your freedom. With you here, being the man of the family, he had it. Maybe the possibility of going to college in a year and leaving his family behind, he feels guilty. You said you did when you joined the Marines and when you moved to Clearwater. Go find him and tell him the reason you're here."

"What about you?"

He had to go after Lee, but he couldn't just leave Rebecca standing on the sidewalk. Who knows how long he'd need with Lee.

"I'll go inside. I have a feeling your mother has some questions she's dying to ask me about what's going on between us."

He shook his head, sliding his arm around her waist. "I won't put you through mom's interrogation."

"It won't be that bad, and maybe I can soften her decision on the move. Now go on."

"Are you sure?" He looked for a hint she didn't want him to leave.

"I'm sure. I'll see you inside."

He leaned and kissed her. "You're amazing." He went after Lee, knowing Rebecca could handle his mother. He was more worried about the knowledge that he was falling in love with Rebecca.

* * *

Rebecca took a deep breath and knocked on the apartment door. She needed a swift kick on the behind for offering to go in alone, but JC needed to work through his issues with Lee without her. She either waited in the car or went inside.

Jackie opened the door. Her slightly greying hair was pulled back in a clip. "Rebecca? Where's JC?"

"He went after Lee. They need to talk. I thought I'd wait for him here. I hope you don't mind."

Jackie stepped aside. "No, come on in. Did Lee run-off at the mouth again? He never knows when to keep his damn trap shut. If he goes making JC feel guilty about coming home there will be hell to pay."

Rebecca shut the door and glanced around the room. The small apartment was fairly quiet. Laya sat on the sofa with a school book on her lap.

"Did you bring JC back?" Kelly peeked over the back of the sofa. She was in her princess pajamas and had tears streaming down her face.

The little girl pulled Rebecca's heartstrings. She walked closer to the sofa, hoping to offer what little comfort she could. When she bent, almost eye level with Kelly, the little girl climbed over the back of the sofa. "Aww sweetie, JC will be here soon. He's just downstairs talking to Lee."

"You swear?"

"I promise." Rebecca made a cross over her heart. "You should go get dressed so you'll be ready when he arrives."

Kelly swung her arms around Rebecca's neck. Rebecca lifted her.

"Kelly, I'm sure Rebecca doesn't want to carry you around. Now get down." Laya scolded her younger sister.

"She's fine." Rebecca moved Kelly to rest on her hip, her arm tight around the girl's back. "You're just excited to see JC, aren't you?"

"I've missed him." Kelly whined, snuggling her head against Rebecca's shoulder.

"I know, sweetie." She wanted to do something to ease the little girl's pain. If Jackie declined the move it would be hard on Kelly when JC left again.

"Laya, why don't you take Kelly to get dressed and make sure everyone else is ready too. I want to talk to Rebecca alone." Jackie nodded.

Laya had to pull Kelly off Rebecca before she was able to do as her mother asked. She left Rebecca and Jackie alone in a heavy silence that seemed to fill the small apartment. Rebecca wondered how nine people lived in such cramped quarters. The living room was barely big enough to allow six people to sit. It had to have been worse when JC lived at home.

"Don't judge me." Jackie sat down on the recliner.

"I wasn't. I was actually admiring how spotless the apartment is. Parents with fewer children have a hard time keeping up with all the toys and clothes lying around. Your home is so tidy." Rebecca sat on the sofa across from Jackie.

"I can't take credit for that. Laya does most of the cleaning." Jackie smiled, glancing around her home before her attention fell back to Rebecca. "I've thought about JC's offer."

Rebecca fought the urge to ask what she had decided. Pushing Jackie might put her further from a positive decision. She wouldn't do anything to hurt JC's chance at having his family closer.

"Aren't you going to ask what I've decided?"

Rebecca shook her head, pushing a strand of hair behind her ear. "I figured you'd prefer to wait for JC. I'm only here to support JC, not to force you into anything you don't want to do."

"So if I said we were staying here, you wouldn't pull that guilt shit you did last night?" Jackie's tone made Rebecca cringe.

"I apologize if I came across harsh. I only told you the truth and hoped you would consider moving a good opportunity—for you and the kids."

"I can see in my son's eyes that you mean a lot to him. He seems to like living in Clearwater." Jackie turned to study the picture of her son in his dress blues. His face so young and innocent, it had to be shortly after he enlisted.

"JC might stay in Clearwater, but not because of me. He's gained peace there. I've seen a change in him after being home one day. This visit has brought back his anxiety and stress. I don't think he could live here again. He'd lose all the progress he's gained. You have to realize that."

"Are his nightmares back?" When Rebecca remained silent Jackie added. "He tried to hide them, but the walls are thin here."

"Yes, last night."

"But not in Clearwater?"

Rebecca didn't have any first-hand knowledge, only that he had told her he hadn't had any since he moved to Clearwater. "None that I know of."

"I saw the tension in him last night when he was here. I don't want to be the one to cause him any further grief in his life. He's a good boy and deserves to be happy, that's why I've decided to go to Clearwater, as long as the kids agree."

The door creaked. JC and Lee entered the apartment. Both were smiling and JC had his hand on Lee's shoulder. "Did I hear you right?" JC approached his mother.

"It's not up to me. The kids have to have a say in this, especially the older ones."

"JC!" Kelly ran to him and wrapped her arms around his neck, crawling onto his lap. "I've missed you."

"Are you really certain you want to move?" Lee questioned his mother.

"Everyone sit. I'll gather the kids for a family meeting." Jackie rose from the chair and walked down the hall.

"What did you say to her?" JC sat next to Rebecca, Kelly still clinging to his side. He wrapped his other arm around Rebecca's shoulders.

"Nothing," She whispered and leaned against him. "She sees what being back here is doing to you." She tickled Kelly's stomach. The little girl giggled. Rebecca was happy that JC would have everything he wanted, which she hoped included her.

Chapter Ten

With a positive consensus reached, JC's family would move to Clearwater on the condition he found them a rental home before the school year started. It meant his family would have to move twice, but at least they would all be together.

Instead of going out for lunch, they ordered pizza and spent time together as a family. JC and Rebecca cuddled on the sofa, Kelly dozing in his arms, while his mother sat across from them.

"Why don't you ship what you don't need over the next few weeks to the new house? We can buy new furniture in Clearwater and you won't need a moving truck?" JC made a mental list of everything to be done.

"What about the cars? Lee's got your old one, and there's mine. I'm not sure they'll make it, but we can't be without a vehicle."

"Clearwater is a small town. The house will only be a few blocks from the high school so Lee doesn't need a car right away. I can get you one before you arrive." JC smiled. "I don't want you and the kids doing that long drive, especially in two separate cars. Flying would be easier."

"Flying is expensive." Jackie didn't seem convinced.

"Driving is too. Hotel rooms, food, and gas, it all adds up."

"Okay. I'm still worried about a job."

"Don't be," Rebecca replied. "A friend of mine is a secretary for Dr. Bowmen, an OBGYN in Clearwater. She's retiring and needs someone to replace her. JC said you do that type of work. I scheduled a phone interview for Monday, if you are interested in applying. The only catch is, Dr. Bowmen needs someone to start in three weeks."

"Wow, you're amazing." JC leaned toward her, careful not to disturb Kelly, and kissed Rebecca. "That's tight, but we'll make it work. Once we get back to Clearwater tomorrow, Rebecca and I will start searching for a rental."

Kelly's eyes shot open. "You're leaving? You can't! Please don't leave me!" Tears fell down her little cheeks, breaking JC's heart.

"Oh, Kelly, we're going to be together soon. All of us. We'll just be apart for a short while." He picked her up, cuddling her against him, and rubbing small circles on her back.

His mother rose, arms stretched to take Kelly. "I think she needs a nap. She didn't sleep well last night."

"It's okay, I'll put her down." JC stood, contentment filling his heart.

* * *

Rebecca leaned in the doorway of Kelly's bedroom, watching JC interact with his sister. She was more of a daughter than a sister to him. Maybe it was because Kelly was the youngest at only four, with nearly a five year age gap to the next sibling.

"Did Mom scare you off?"

"No. I just wanted to talk to you alone." She entered the room and shut the door behind her.

"Did Mom say something that upset you?" He frowned.

"No. I was thinking about Kelly. She's really attached to you." She moved closer to him.

"I know. Leaving tomorrow is going to be hard on her."

"And hard on Laya and Lee for the next while until Kelly sees you again." Rebecca glanced down at the sleeping child. "I was thinking...why don't we take her home with us?"

"What?" His voice rose, shock clear in his tone.

"Hear me out." She rested her hand on his arm. "The rest of the family will be joining you in a week or two, three max. Why not bring her with us now. She needs you."

"I'm still at Cameron's. I can't spring a kid on them. Even if I could, there's no room."

She took a deep breath, wondering how he would feel about her next statement. "You could stay at my place. I have a guest room. Kelly can sleep there."

"I have to work. The shop isn't the best place for a child."

"I'm part time at Express-Ohh's. I'll watch her while you're at work, and when we both have to work we'll make arrangements. It's only temporary. We can make it happen." She rubbed his arm. "I know seeing Kelly so upset breaks your heart. If your mom is okay with Kelly coming with us, then why not? It will give Lee and Laya a break as well."

"You're sure you want to do this?"

"I wouldn't have offered if I didn't. We'll find your mom a great rental, and everyone will be together in a few weeks."

He wrapped his arms around her, squeezing her tight. "Thank you."

* * *

By the time they arrived at Rebecca's apartment, Kelly was so exhausted she could barely keep her eyes open. JC turned to Rebecca, catching a glimpse of Kelly from the corner of his eye. She was stretched out across the backseat, asleep. "I'll take her up, tuck her into bed, and then I'll come back for our bags."

"The bags are light, I can grab them."

He glanced back at Kelly, the muscles in his shoulders tightening. "Are you sure about this? I could get a room for us at Winterbloom."

"Stop worrying. I want you both here." Rebecca laid her hand on his thigh, giving it a gentle squeeze. "Now come on, she needs to be in bed."

He nodded, opened the truck door, and stepped around to the passenger's side. She stumbled as she stepped out of the truck. His shaft hardened as her chest brushed against his. His body itched to hold her in his arms, to touch her. There was no doubt that he had fallen head-over-heels in love with her. It just wasn't the time to make his feelings known.

He reached in the backseat, pulling Kelly into his arms. She didn't stir or even bat an eye. He turned to see Rebecca with the bags in her hand. "I told you I'd get those."

"It's fine. Let's go inside. I want a hot bath and a glass of wine before bed." She stepped away from the truck and toward the door that led to her apartment.

JC bit his tongue, refusing to force the issue. It wasn't that he thought she couldn't handle the bags, his mother had taught him to respect women. Carry their bags, open doors, and be a true gentleman every time. Tonight he'd let Rebecca have her way. It had been a long day of travel, and morning would arrive before long. All he wanted to do was relax, hopefully with Rebecca in his arms. Tomorrow he had to get back to work and find a rental house.

Opening her apartment door, Rebecca stepped aside for him to enter. "The guest room is the first door on your right as you go down the hall. I'll bring the bags and a nightlight for the room."

Kelly woke as he headed down the hall. "Shh, sweetie." He rubbed her back.

"Where are we?" Her voice was a soft whisper and her eyes were still shut.

"We're at Rebecca's. I'm going to put you to bed, so you can get some sleep." He kept his voice low. Stepping into the guest room, he realize it would be the first time Kelly ever slept by herself. The only bedroom she ever had was shared with two other sisters. If she awoke before morning it was going to be a rude awakening in a strange room all alone. He wondered if he should sleep in here with her and decided the sofa would be better, in case his nightmares plagued him.

The creamy white walls and ebony queen bed showcased the room. A turquoise comforter and small blue and white throw pillows decorated the bed. A large picture of waves crashing on a pristine beach hung over the bed. It seemed a better fit for North Carolina than landlocked Clearwater, Wyoming.

"It reminds me of home." Rebecca explained, coming to stand behind him. "With Dad in the Navy, I grew up by the water. It inspired the decor for this room."

"Do you miss home?"

She pulled back the bed sheets. "Moving around so much I learned home was where you make it. But if you're asking do I miss the ocean, sometimes. But Clearwater is my home now. It's where I want to be and I don't plan on leaving."

JC didn't want to wake Kelly to change her clothes, so he put her into bed as she was. Her leggings and T-shirt would have to do as sleepwear for tonight. He tucked the blankets around her and stared down at her. Rebecca and Lee were right, while he played no part in her conception, Kelly was like a daughter to him.

Rebecca cupped the side of his face with her hand. "You worry too much. She'll be fine. She has her teddy, and we're just down the hall. If she calls out, we'll hear her."

He nodded. "I know. You go prepare your bath. I'll bring you a glass of wine."

She rose up on her tippy toes, bringing her lips inches from his. "I've got a better idea."

"Oh, do you?" He closed the distance between them, pressing his lips to hers.

When the kiss ended, she tugged his hand. "Come on."

He followed her down the hall, his shaft already hardening. It had been a long day, but his energy was suddenly renewed. Being led down the hall, he didn't take anything else in but the sway of her hips. When she opened her bedroom door he was amazed with the space. This larger room was decorated completely different than the guest room. The walls were a warm topaz with the accent wall behind the bed a few shades darker. The large canopy king bed, outfitted in a brown comforter with gold swirls, dominated the room. Gold, brown, and black pillows were piled neatly on top of each other. Sheer, white curtains accentuated the sides of the bed, pulled back with gold ties.

"It's different than the rest of the house, but it's cozy." She pulled her sweater over her head, letting it fall to the floor, before strolling to the bed. "Shut the door in case Kelly gets up."

He watched her ass saunter in the black yoga pants. He wanted to pull those pants off with his teeth, before tasting her sweet spot. He shut the door and when he stood in front of her, her hands immediately pulled the belt of his jeans. Unhooking it, her fingers flicked the button. "In a hurry, Sugar?"

"I want you naked and inside of me." The sound of his zipper echoed in the room.

His mouth claimed hers, while his fingers unhooked her bra, with skills he didn't know he still had, and slid it off her shoulders. His fingers found her nipples, teasing them gently into harden tips, his mouth eager to lay claim to one at a time.

She leaned back.

Lifting his head, he kissed the base of her neck, working upward until he found her sensitive spot just below her ear. "I want you on the bed, naked."

His jeans hung loosely on his hips. Her hand traveled between the rough material and his skin until she found his hardened shaft, standing at attention. "On one condition…"

"Name it."

"Don't pretend." Pushing his jeans out of her way, she wrapped her hand around his shaft, gliding her fingers along the length of it. "There's no need for the prosthesis. I know the other night you were worried about my reaction. It changes nothing between us. Take it off and let tonight be about us."

"I don't know."

"JC, I didn't turn away when you took it off in the hotel. I cuddled against you. That should prove to you it doesn't bother me. You are still the man I want to be with, and the prosthesis doesn't make me think any less of you whether it's on or off. I want tonight to be about us. Please."

He could barely think a coherent thought as her hand continued to run the length of him. "Fine, but I want you naked and on your back." He lowered to the bed, while she stripped before him, shaking her hips to drive him wild. He regretted the decision to take his leg off, but if their relationship was going to progress then he had to get comfortable with it eventually. He rolled up his jeans, until he reached the lever that would release the pin, allowing his prosthesis to come off with ease.

With the pin released he was able to lift out. The only thing left to do was to remove the sleeve that fit just below the knee, where his leg was gone to half way up his thigh. The long pin stuck out the end, which connected to the inside of the leg. He pulled it off before tugging his jeans down and letting them fall on the floor.

"Oh, don't stop there." Rebecca winked.

"What?"

"Lose the boxers and shirt, and get your ass in bed." She sat on the bed, her fingers tugging the hem of his shirt.

"Woman, you're so demanding." He laughed and let her pull the shirt over his head before sliding down his boxers. He pushed her against the pillows. "You're supposed to be on your back."

She nudged some of the throw pillows off the side of the bed and rested on the king size pillows, her arms above her head. "As you wish. Now what?"

"Anything I want." He positioned his body between her legs, his fingers going for her special core, while his thumb teased along the outside of her lips until it reached the center spot that would drive her crazy. As he teased, he watched her. Her eyes were closed and a moan escaped her lips.

"I won't last long if you keep doing that."

Ignoring her words, he didn't stop. He leaned over her body, kissing along her thigh and working his way to her hip. He placed kisses over her stomach and up to her breast. His mouth claiming one, his tongue traveled around the edge of the nipple, hardening it again, before sucking it into his mouth and nibbling.

"JC, please, I want to feel you in me," she begged. Her fingers tangled in his hair, pulling him to her body.

"Someone is impatient tonight." He rose up on his elbows and angled between her thighs. He eased inside, the slow friction a delicious torture for him. With his shaft firmly inside her, he eased back out before sliding home again. As he quickly found the perfect rhythm, she writhed against him, encouraging him with sweet little gasps and tight muscles. Every stroke added to the tension coiling at the base of his spine.

Her body clenched around him and she clawed his back, marking him as she exploded around him. The heat lacing up his spine turned molten and his climax followed seconds later. He leaned his head back and cried from the pleasure coursing through him.

JC rolled to his side, pulling her to lie next to him, her arm across his chest. He could only see the faintest outline of her features in the now darkened room. "I'm falling in love with you, Rebecca."

She glanced up, meeting his eyes. Her hand continued to run the length of his chest. "I'm falling for you too. I've never felt this way before. It's happening so fast, but I don't care."

As sleep claimed Rebecca, and JC's eyelids grew heavy, his heart was more content than ever before. He had found a special woman who accepted all his faults. His life had purpose once again.

Chapter Eleven

Rebecca sat on the sofa with her law book on her lap, trying to study while Kelly played with her dolls. The last week of being stand-in parent for Kelly had enlightened her. After her own unfortunate childhood, Rebecca wasn't sure she wanted children. She didn't know if she could even be a good parent, but Kelly had proven she could. This parenting test had been a reminder of how much she loved children and wanted some of her own.

"When will JC be home?" Kelly glanced up from her dolls.

"Soon, sweetie." She was thankful that in the last week JC had been able to work from home part of the day, giving him time with Kelly, as well as finding a rental home. Today he had to meet with the principal of the local school about doing a self-defense class, once school resumed.

As if summoned from the little girl's inquiry, JC opened the door. His dress pants and shirt were such a dramatic change from his normal T-shirt and jeans Rebecca wouldn't have recognized him if she hadn't seen him leave this morning. Damn he looked good.

"JC!" Kelly ran to him.

He bent down and picked her up before winking at Rebecca. "Is Kelly the only one that missed me?"

She rose from the sofa and kissed him. "You know I missed you. How did your meeting go at the school?"

He put Kelly down, who returned to her toys on the floor, and slid his arm around Rebecca's waist. "Better than expected. I got a lead on a rental house."

"Really? From who?"

"Ms. Marcie Lewis, she's the principal. Her mother decided to stay in Florida after her recent vacation. Ms. Lewis hasn't had time to put her mother's house on the market yet. She offered it to me until the construction is complete. We can see it this evening after dinner."

"Wonderful. I have dinner in the oven now, but it's not ready yet." She was hopeful this rental would be the one, because right now they were at a loss as to where his family would stay when they arrived the following week. There were very few rental properties in Clearwater, and most of them were apartments above shops, or seasonal rentals for winter. The one place they did find, the landlord refused to rent to such a large family, which put their search back to square one.

"Good, then I have time to shower and change." He leaned close to her ear. "Care to join me? You did promise once we got back home." He kissed the nape of her neck.

She nudged his arm. "Not with Kelly right there," she whispered.

He glanced at Kelly playing on the carpet. "I love her as if she was my own child, but I can't wait until we are alone. I have plans to make you scream my name in every room of this apartment, especially the shower." He tapped her butt and strolled down the hall, leaving her with the urge to follow him.

Rebecca looked forward to Jackie's arrival, but also dreaded it because it meant Kelly would be leaving. JC might also leave too. He wouldn't have to stay here once Kelly was gone. He could return to the apartment over Clearwater Combat and Guns.

A chill of loneliness ran down her spine. She tossed her law book on the sofa and joined Kelly on the floor.

* * *

"It's a beautiful home, and even better since it's furnished. I did mention there will be eight children, as well as my mother. Are you sure you're okay with that?" JC wanted to make sure Ms. Lewis was aware of all the children before he signed a lease and committed to payments for the next six months or longer if the construction became delayed.

Marcie Lewis laughed. Her skirt and white blouse were unwrinkled from the long day, and her red hair was still neatly pulled back in a stylish twist. She appeared no older than thirty-five—if that, yet she gazed at Kelly with such longing, as if she wanted children of her own. "This house has been full of children for years. I'm the youngest of seven siblings myself. We're all grown up now, and my mother is in Florida. The house is so quiet. Your family will bring laughter and joy back."

"JC, I love it. Is this going to be my new home?" Kelly tugged his hand, wanting to be picked up. "I don't want to go back. I want to stay with you!"

"Kelly, remember your manners. This is Ms. Lewis. She is the principal at the school you will be attending in the fall."

"She's fine. She's just excited." Ms. Lewis squatted in front of Kelly. "Why don't we let your brother and Rebecca talk for a few minutes, and I'll show you the room I had as a child. There's a secret passage way between two of the bedrooms. It has a small room that my sister and I played in."

"Can I?" Kelly stared at JC, excitement glistening in her eyes.

"Go ahead, but mind your manners." When Ms. Lewis and Kelly left, JC glanced around the living room again. It was furnished with a large sectional that would easily seat his whole family. A fireplace dominated the back wall with windows on each side. The dining room off to the right had a long table for family dinners. It was perfect for his family, and even had five bedrooms. Most of the children would have to double up, but there was still enough room to spread out. The downstairs family room would provide a great place for the children to play, giving his mother, Laya, and Lee a little peace upstairs.

"What do you think?" Rebecca was taking a few pictures to email his mother.

"It's perfect. I know Mom will love it, and Lee can walk to the high school without needing a car. I just have to find mom a car and pick them up at the airport next week." He wrapped his arms around Rebecca. "It's all coming together because of you. Thank you."

"You've done most of the work. I just sparked the idea. I'm glad it's working out. You seem so happy with the idea of your family moving here." She slid her arm around his back.

"Are you okay with them being so close? I know they can be a bit much." He loved the way her body fit in his arms, and the way her sweet vanilla shampoo excited his senses. "Will my family being here make you miss your family more?"

"No. This move brings my dad here too. So it works out for both of us."

He leaned to hover his lips over her forehead before pressing them against her cool skin. "What about your mother? You never talk about her."

"She's a drunk and the reason I left home."

JC frowned. Rebecca's statement was firm and blunt.

"She filed for divorce, which is why my dad is moving to Denver. His job requires a lot of travel, so he needs a good airport and Jackson Hole has limited service. I've tried to talk him into staying here. Maybe spending time here while your house is being built will convince him to stay, at least part time."

"I'm sorry. My father drank himself to death before Kelly was born." JC understood what it was like to live with a drunk and didn't wish it on anyone. It was hell watching his father throw his life away for the bottle.

Kelly ran into the living room at full speed, a big smile on her face. "JC, there's a secret passage that leads to a pink room. There are dolls and a coloring desk. Can it be my room? Please."

"Sounds like she's sold. What about you JC?" Ms. Lewis entered the room a few steps behind Kelly.

"If Kelly is happy then so am I. Did you bring the contract?"

"Sure did." She pointed to the dining room table where her bag was sitting.

"Come on, Kelly, why don't we go check out the back yard while JC goes over the boring paperwork." Rebecca took Kelly's hand and led her out the back door.

"Now that we're alone, I wanted to mention something that might be helpful to you." Ms. Lewis dug the contract from her bag before turning back to JC who sat at the table. "As I mentioned before, I wanted to sell the house, but haven't had time to get everything straightened out. Your family will be starting over, leaving everything behind, but if your mother is interested in the furnishings here, she can take them when they move into their new house. Your family won't have to spend all that time shopping to fill the house, and I won't have to figure out what to do with it."

He glanced around again. Some of the items had to be antiques. "What would you want for everything?"

"Nothing. I want you to have them, as long as they fit your tastes. Or more importantly your mother's, since she's the one who will have to live with them."

"I couldn't...there are antiques here. Belongings you've grown up with. You and your siblings must want some of them."

"We have what we want. Our memories are more important than any possessions." She pointed to the furniture. "They'll get used to the furniture while they are here, which will make the move to their new home easier. Your family can start over again, comfortably. I heard Jackie will be working in Dr. Bowmen's office, and the kids will be starting school in the fall. Your family will be part of the community. This is what we do for our fellow residences when someone is in need. Look at it as a gift, not charity, for you gave so much to your country."

"Thank you." He was in awe by the generosity of the Clearwater residents. It was more kindness than he had ever known. He owed so much to the town and somehow he'd find a way to pay them back.

* * *

The day was growing late, but Rebecca didn't want the night to end. She snuggled against JC, her head against his chest as a movie played on the television. She couldn't focus on the movie while waiting for her time with JC to end. His family was arriving in two days, and she hated the thought of him leaving. The apartment would be empty without him. She'd miss their quiet cuddle sessions after Kelly went to bed. He couldn't continue to stay here…or could he?

"Sugar, you seem a million miles away. What's wrong?" JC's fingers trailed up her arm.

"I was thinking how quiet it will be when Jackie and the kids arrive, and Kelly leaves. You'll be going back to the manager's flat above the shop." Saying the words made her sound like a child who didn't want to be left alone. She didn't want him to think she was pouting.

"I don't have to."

"What?" Her heart skipped a beat.

"I could stay, if you want me to? Or you could stay with me. Wherever you want to be is fine with me, as long as I have your body curled around mine each night, I'm happy."

Excitement coursed through her like a wave of cool water. The tension from the thought of being alone disappeared. "Then stay here. My apartment is bigger. Or I can move in with you so you can be close to work. I don't care either, as long as we're together."

Chapter Twelve

Five Months Later...

With the house finished, JC conned Chloe and Tessa into keeping his family occupied while the men moved the stuff from the rental into the new house. He wanted the house to be perfect when his family saw it for the first time.

"They're coming up the drive, is everything in place?" Rebecca asked JC from her post next to the front door.

"Cameron and Jordan are putting the dresser in Mom's room and that's it." JC walked toward Rebecca. "Everything's perfect. I wish your father could have been here, after all he's the one that made this possible."

She slipped her hand into his. "He promised he'd be over later. This is a family occasion and he didn't want to intrude."

With her hand in his, he opened the door, allowing his mother and siblings to enter. "Welcome home."

Kelly shot past everyone, running to the room he had promised would be hers.

"It's beautiful!" Tears welled in his mother's eyes as she glanced around the room. The house had an open floor plan, providing the family with as much space as possible. The hardwood floors added a touch of class, while keeping the floors simple for upkeep. "Thank you."

"You're welcome. I hope you're happy with everything." His mother had a say in most of what was done, but there were a few added features JC had worked on with Robert to be a surprise to his mother. One of them included a small reading nook in the master bedroom for her to unwind at the end of a long day.

Bringing up the rear, Laya and Lee stepped inside. JC pointed down the hallway. "You two, go down there until you see your names. There's something special waiting for you." Their eyebrows rose before doing what he said.

"What did you do?" His mother walked around the living room, her arms stretched open.

"Robert and I made a few changes to allow them to have their own rooms." When his mother opened her mouth to speak, he held up his hand. "I know Lee's only has one year of high school and then he will be going off to college. Believe me, he'll be thankful for the privacy, and so will you." He laughed. "Laya said she wanted to stay at home and attend the online college she's currently enrolled with, so she'll need her own space. That will leave the twins, Ann and Marie, sharing a room, with Kelly right next door. The boys, Brian, Keith, and Jason, will share the other bedroom, and the twins can move into Lee's room when he leaves for college. They are all used to sharing so it won't be a problem. Laya and Lee deserve some privacy, especially with their studies."

"Laya's going to love that. She thought she was going to share with Kelly again."

"I know." Letting go of Rebecca's hand, JC took his mother's hand in his. "We have a year before Lee leaves, to make this a true home. A home all the kids will want to come back to. Our apartment was never truly home, but you can create one here. You'll have more time now that you only have to work the one job at Dr. Bowman's office."

"All because of you. I couldn't have asked for a better son." She hugged him tight, and then stepped back to reach Rebecca's hand. "Thank you, Rebecca. You opened my eyes to what I tried to stay blinded from. You not only brought my family happiness, you returned the son I had before his injury. I can never repay you for that. You are a true blessing to my son, to me, and my family."

"I'm honored to help. JC means everything to me." Rebecca put her arms around JC's waist.

"Don't let her go, she's truly a catch." His mother winked.

"I don't intend to ever let her get away. I love her." JC smiled at Rebecca. "I have to go to Express-Ohh's to pick up the lunch I ordered. Want to go with me?" His stomach churned, worried she'd say no, which would throw his next plan off track.

"Sure." She grabbed her purse and met him at the door.

"Mom, we'll be right back." He followed Rebecca down the front steps, and for the first time since leaving the military, he was nervous.

* * *

Entering Express-Ohh's Rebecca frowned, as if surprised to find the place empty. JC had actually arranged it to be that way. He wanted to propose in the same spot he met the woman of his dreams.

She glanced around the room and checked the back office. When she returned to the front counter, JC was bent to one knee.

"Rebecca James, since the day I walked in here you haven't left my mind. You're an inspiration to me. You brought my family together, and most important, you made me feel like a whole man again. You made me a better man. You're everything I've ever wanted and more. I love you, Rebecca, and I ask you in the same spot we first met, will you marry me?"

Tears glistened in her eyes. "I love you, JC. Yes, I'll marry you!"

He slid the ring on her finger and stood. She wrapped her arms around his neck, clinging to him. "You've made me the happiest man."

She kissed him hard on the lips.

Everything in his life had come together. He found a place to call home in Clearwater. His family was here, and he had a future wife and hopefully children of his own in the coming years. He may have lost his leg, but he gained so much more.

Christmas Countdown

Jasmine Pierce has been burned by her family and by love. Leaving her past behind, she longs for a quiet place to start over and raise her daughter. Upon learning about a grandmother she didn't know she had, she inherits not only a house, but a chance at a new future.

Snowbound in a cottage, twelve days before Christmas, Jasmine meets Logan Clarke. His kind personality and loving nature has her considering the possibilities, but she's already played the game of love and lost.

Could this have been her grandmother's plan all along? For Jasmine to return home and find the missing pieces, bringing her dream of a real family and her heart's longing for love finally within reach?

Chapter One

December 10

Jasmine Pierce rocked her six-month old daughter in her arms while she waited in the hotel lobby for the attorney. Her mind raced, trying to understand why Dave Johnson, an attorney from Wyoming, had traveled to Virginia to meet with her. It probably had something to do with her ex, who went missing months ago, but that situation was over. She wasn't going to bail him out—never again.

The lobby was near empty at this time of day, which she was glad of. Everyone had finished breakfast and gone on with their day. The owners' two kids were waiting for the school bus outside, leaving no one close enough to overhear whatever shame her ex had gotten himself into this time and expected her to bail him out of.

"You must be Mrs. Pierce." A man approached her and held out his hand. She accepted his hand, giving him a halfhearted handshake. "I'm Dave Johnson, we spoke on the phone. I appreciate you taking the time to see me. Let's have a seat." He led the way into a little nook the hotel offered, with a small sofa, two chairs, and a fireplace, giving it a homey feel.

Jasmine sank onto the comfiest chair the room had to offer, which wasn't saying much. It was stiff and had a straight back. She turned her attention to the man before her, wanting to get this meeting over with before Alyssa stirred. "Please, call me Jasmine." She hadn't been Mrs. Pierce since the divorce, but she didn't want to get into that conversation with a man she just met. "I don't understand why you requested to see me. What do you want?" She prayed it had nothing to do with her ex. She wanted to move on with her life and to provide a loving home for her daughter.

"I've come from Wyoming searching for you. I've been your grandmother's attorney for years. She passed away in September, but asked me to find you a few months prior. I had a difficult time locating you since your mother changed your last name and then you married."

She leaned against the hard back of the chair, taking a deep breath to steady her nerves. *Grandmother?* Her mother had always said she had no family left and that her own mother had died years before Jasmine was born. "I'm sorry, but you have the wrong person."

He scooted to the edge of the stiff brown couch. "Let me explain." When she nodded he continued. "Your mother ran off with you when you were very young. She sent pictures to your grandmother, but wouldn't allow her to see you. They, your grandmother and mother, had a difference of opinion that led to an estrangement." Mr. Johnson leaned down to pull a stack of envelopes, tied with a red ribbon, from his briefcase. "These are letters she wrote to your mother. They were returned unopened. Your grandmother said they explained the distance between her and your mother. She tried for years to make things right, but your mother refused her letters and calls. But that's not why I'm here. I came to give you the deed to her house. When she passed, your grandmother left everything to you."

Chapter Two

December 13

Two long days later, Jasmine parked her SUV in front of her grandmother's—now her—home, in Clearwater, Wyoming. She sat there a moment, taking in the large, two-story log house with a huge wrap around deck. Enough snow blanketed the ground to make the cabin stand out against a wooded background. She was exhausted and aching from sitting in the car so long. Driving from Richmond, Virginia to Clearwater with Alyssa, and her sweet, but cantankerous little Cocker Spaniel, Floppie, was not an ideal trip, but it was what she had to do. After all, she had nothing else, so what did she have to lose?

Having a grandmother, she didn't know she had, leave her everything was a mixed blessing. It allowed Jasmine to start over and give her daughter a true home instead of an apartment. However, it also scared her to death to start over in a new place. Not knowing anyone in Clearwater set her nerves on edge, especially since winter had settled in.

The late afternoon sun dipped low in the sky, leaving her with little hope she'd be able to unload much from the car before night was upon her. She'd grab the few essential things she couldn't do without for the night, and get Alyssa settled. Then a hot shower and a good night's sleep is what her body needed.

Pushing open the door, one leg out of the SUV, she realized there was something familiar about the house. A distant memory, just barely there, but somehow she remembered being here. Maybe once she was inside it would jar the complete memory to the surface. A detailed look around inside would have to wait until she had Alyssa in bed.

She glanced over her shoulder at her daughter. "Let's get inside and turn the lights on before it gets too dark." She stepped out of the vehicle, digging the key Mr. Johnson had given her out of the pocket of her jeans.

Opening the back door, she let Floppie jump out and then unbuckled the car seat. "Come on, Sweetie, let's see if we have heat in that house." Alyssa had been fussy through the whole trip here and now that they had arrived, she was sleeping through the excitement. "Typical. When I need her to sleep she won't, but when arriving at her new home, she's out like a light." Jasmine shook her head, slipped the diaper bag over her shoulder, and lifted the car seat. She ran her hand through her dark brown hair, tugging it away from her face, before slipping it behind her ear.

Trudging through the snow to the deck, the winter breeze chilled her bones. She would need to buy warmer clothes and a winter jacket for both her and Alyssa. Jeans and sneakers just didn't cut it in all this snow. Struggling to unlock the door with already frozen fingertips, she attempted to turn the key in the unforgiving lock. "Damn it!" She bent to concentrate on the lock when Floppie started barking. "Shh, boy. I know you don't like the cold either. We'll be inside in a minute." She patted his head, but that didn't quiet him.

"You must be Jasmine." A deep, husky voice called from behind, startling her.

She whipped around to face the stranger, her senses immediately on high alert. "Who are you?" She raised her voice a notch louder so he could hear her over Floppie's continuous barks.

"Here, let me help you with that." He moved in between her and the door and, taking the key from her hand, he expertly unlocked the door. He moved aside and shrugged. "Years of practice. You have to know how to slide and click the old thing."

She stood rooted to the deck, blinking like a complete fool. With fear coursing through her, she didn't know if she should run for the car or slug this man while she had a free hand.

He extended his hand. "I'm Logan, I rent the cottage by the lake." He nodded to his right. "I've been expecting you. I saw you pull in. I thought I would offer to help unload your car and check on the old furnace. It's been acting up lately."

She couldn't tear her gaze from his eyes. He had the face of an angel, high cheek bones and incredible, emerald green eyes. His wavy, chestnut brown hair held tight to his forehead. She continued her inspection. The front of his heavy, winter coat hung open, giving her a glimpse of the tight thermal shirt that clung to his chest. He obviously worked hard to achieve such a sculpted body.

Her apprehension dissipated as she peered back into his eyes. She wasn't sure she could trust him, but if he was willing to check on the furnace while she got Alyssa settled, Jasmine was willing to take a chance. Mr. Johnson had warned her that a tenant rented the small cottage beside her, which also belonged to Jasmine now, but she expected some crotchety old man. "Thanks. I need to get my baby inside. If you could check on the heat that would be great."

He nodded, pushing the door open for her to enter. The chilly air that met her as she stepped inside caused her to frown.

"Shit," he mumbled, as he headed to check the furnace.

Kicking the door shut, she hoped the lack of heat wasn't a foretelling that something was wrong with the furnace.

Jasmine left Alyssa in her car seat until she could get the crib from the car and set it up. Grabbing another blanket from the diaper bag, she wrapped it around her daughter before glancing around the large living room. People said you could learn a lot from the belongings a person owned, but she couldn't tell much about the woman that was supposed to be her grandmother because the furniture was covered with white sheets to keep the dust off them while no one lived here. She had a lot of work to do over the next few days to get this place livable.

A faint memory of many afternoons playing in this room scattered past her thoughts. A rocking horse sat next to the fireplace where she would rock for hours on end while her grandmother crocheted. It seemed so long ago, and up until that moment, Jasmine wasn't even sure she had lived here. She was so young when they left.

Her thin sweater was nothing against the cold air in the house. Rubbing her hands down her arms for warmth, she thought about how much her life had change in just a few short days. She went from living in a small studio apartment, barely making ends meet, to moving across country to a large, two-story home. Jasmine needed a change, one that would make a better life for her and her daughter. Moving to Clearwater provided her with everything she needed—a home, money her grandmother left, and an income from Logan who rented the cottage.

She caught a glimpse of her reflection in the window. The dark circles under her eyes showed her exhaustion from the long drive, and Alyssa's constant fussing. Her hair was a mess and her makeup faded long ago. What a way to meet the tenant next door.

A picture hanging above the fireplace caught her attention. Stepping closer to see it better, she saw her mother with a baby in her arms. It had to have been taken shortly after Jasmine was born. *What happened between her mother and grandmother all those years ago?* She would need to go through her grandmother's letters to learn more about their relationship.

"Bad news."

Pushing aside the mysteries that lay in her past, she turned to find Logan standing in the doorway. "Oh?"

"Deader than a doornail. Jasmine, the furnace isn't working. You can't stay here, not with a baby and all."

If it's not one thing it's another. Would this roller coaster ride ever end? She sighed. "Don't worry. I'll call someone in the morning. I'll make a fire. Alyssa and I can camp here in the living room. We'll tough it out tonight."

He shook his head. "This house is way too cold, and I'm afraid you won't get anyone out here for a few days, at the least. There's a major snowstorm arriving tonight. It's expected to drop three to four feet of snow over the next two days."

"I'll drive back into town then. I think I saw a motel." The thought of driving again exhausted her already tired body, but what choice did she have?

"I wouldn't."

She frowned. "Well, it's obvious I can't stay here, not with a baby and a dog. The furnace isn't working, and I'm not sleeping in the car. I have to head back into town."

"You won't make it. Look outside." He pointed to the large front window. "The snow is coming down pretty hard now. Besides, Winterbloom Bed and Breakfast is the only place in town, and it's full. With the ski resort in full swing, there's not a room available for at least fifty miles."

She crossed her arms over her chest, trying to retain as much warmth as she could, as well as control her anger. It wasn't Logan she was angry with, it was life in general. It was always an uphill battle, nothing could ever be simple. "Well, I don't see any other alternative."

"I do. My place."

"Oh, no. I don't know you." *I'm not risking my baby and dog to a stranger.*

He stepped closer. "Look, Jasmine. I've known your grandmother all my life. I'm harmless, I promise. If I let you and your little family head out in a storm at this time of night, I'm pretty sure your grandmother would return long enough to tan my hide. I insist, and I have the room."

What was she supposed to say? He was right. She couldn't stay here with no heat. The storm was getting worse, and her SUV didn't have winter tires. It made sense to stay with Logan. Her grandmother obvious trusted him, to allow him to rent the cottage beside her, and he seemed to know his way around this place. "Okay, if you're sure we're not putting you out."

* * *

Jasmine sat in the living room of Logan's cottage, playing with Alyssa. She tried to keep her daughter awake while Logan set up the crib. Hopefully Alyssa would then sleep through most of the night, allowing Jasmine to sleep too.

Logan stepped out of the guest bedroom Jasmine and Alyssa were taking over. "Alyssa's crib is ready. While I make dinner, why don't you get settled?"

Too tired to argue, she did just that. She changed Alyssa and finally put her in her comfortable, warm bed. With Alyssa's sleepy eyes closing, Jasmine brushed her hand along her sweet girl's face. "Sweet dreams, Sweetie."

Once Alyssa was asleep, Jasmine unpacked a few of their things. As she placed a stack of diapers on a dresser, she glanced out the window. The dock and lake triggered a memory of her as a child, maybe four years old. She had learned to ice-skate on that lake. This area was definitely part of her past, and for the first time in a long time, she finally felt like she was home.

Chapter Three

December 14

Jasmine woke late the next morning to a dark and snowy day. The cottage was quiet. Logan had obviously gone out to do whatever he needed to do. The snow was falling hard and fast so there was no way he could have gone far. Alyssa slept peacefully while Jasmine dressed and went in search of coffee.

In the kitchen, she found a pot of coffee already brewed. Pouring herself a cup, she wondered about the condition of the furnace. Floppie padded beside her and cocked his head. "I'll call someone today, so they can get out here to fix the heating as soon as the weather calms."

"Want to go out?" she asked, as if her dog would answer. She took a sip of coffee before letting him out. From the open door, she watched the snow continue to fall while Floppie ran out to do his business and then rushed back inside. "I don't blame you. I don't want to be out there either."

Shutting the door, she thought she'd be able to sit and enjoy her coffee, but Alyssa chose that moment to wake up. Her cries echoed though the small cottage. Rolling her shoulders, she headed to her daughter. Thankfully Alyssa had slept through the night. The last thing Jasmine wanted was for Alyssa to keep Logan awake after he opened his home to them.

Her daughter was truly the light of her life. She wanted to give her baby girl everything she didn't have and more—a life surrounded by family and love. Sadly the family part hadn't work out so well since Alyssa's father walked out, but Jasmine had plenty of love to give.

She found her daughter lying on her back, tugging on her toes. "Morning, Sweetie." Jasmine lifted her from the crib and hugged Alyssa close. "Did you sleep well?"

Her daughter cooed. One of her former co-workers teased Jasmine by saying she should enjoy the quiet now because before long the word *no* would be a key part of her child's vocabulary.

The front door creaked open and snowy boots crunched on the hardwood floor. "Jasmine?"

Stepping out of the bedroom, she balanced Alyssa on her hip. "Oh my! What is that?"

He flashed her a sideways grin. "Silly, it's a Christmas tree. I thought we could decorate it."

Not able to prevent it, a smile creased her cheeks. She barely knew Logan, but there was something about him that put her at ease, removing her original apprehension of him. "I know what it is. Where did it come from?"

"There's a stand of pines in the woods on the other side of your house. When I was younger, your grandmother let us cut one down every year. I know it's a little large, but Alyssa is pretty small, so I'm assuming this is her first Christmas. She deserves a real tree. I found your grandmother's old ornaments in the house. They're out on the porch. Come on, it'll be fun."

He leaned the Christmas tree against the wall. Was he trying to impress her? She wasn't sure, but if he was, it worked. She wanted to decorate the tree with him, even if she'd be doing it again in her own home after the storm. Alyssa did deserve a real Christmas. She might be too young to remember, but it would be a memory that would stick with Jasmine.

Dealing with a heartless mother, who cared more about getting high than giving her daughter a good life, Jasmine had a very isolated childhood. She had been deprived of many things—things she vowed her daughter would never crave. This year marked a special Christmas for them. It wouldn't just be Alyssa's first Christmas, but it would also be Jasmine's first one, starting a new future.

"You hear that Alyssa? We're going to have an old-fashioned, family Christmas." She tickled her daughter's belly. "I know you have no idea what is going on, but this is going to be your first of many happy Christmases." She glanced from her daughter to Logan "Thank you. Let me get Alyssa settled and I'll help."

* * *

Later that evening, they sat in front of the crackling fire, the Christmas tree lit, and the snow falling outside the bay windows—a perfect scene to share with family. She had just met Logan, yet it was if they'd known each other for years. While they had decorated the tree, conversation flowed smoothly and easily.

"Alyssa looks just like you when you were a baby, so adorable and innocent. Your grandmother loved to show off your pictures to anyone who visited. Through all the stories and pictures she shared, you became a part of my life." He paused when she frowned. "I know this sounds strange, but I've been waiting for you to return. It's why I've stayed here. I've been waiting for you my whole life." Logan smiled at Alyssa, her eyes closed as she lay nestled in his arms.

Waiting for me? Jasmine wasn't sure how to take his statement. It explained the instant ease he had around her and maybe her comfort as well. She glanced down at her daughter. Sadness filled her that Alyssa would never know her great-grandmother, the woman who helped provide the life she'd now be able to have. Logan gently rested Alyssa in the crook of his arm and slipped his other arm around Jasmine, pulling her close. She let him, wanting the comfort he was willing to give, even if for only one night.

Thoughts of her own childhood plagued her, wondering what life would have been like if she had been able to grow up in Clearwater. She smiled at Logan, sensing his gaze as she stared at the twinkling lights of the Christmas tree.

"You seem lost in thought. What are you thinking about?" Logan's finger trailed along the edge of her shoulder.

She glanced at her daughter, who lay peacefully sleeping, wondering what this move would mean for Alyssa. It seemed her young daughter had already accepted Logan, which was a shock. Since she spent most of her time with Jasmine, Alyssa didn't usually take to other people. "I was just thinking about how astonishing it is that she took to you so quickly."

He let out a hearty laugh. "See, I told you I'm harmless. Children are great judges of character. Alyssa likes me, and Floppie likes me too. Now what can I do to convince you?"

She decided to tell him the truth. "Trust is not an issue. The problem is, maybe I like you too much, too soon."

The more she got to know Logan, the more her emotions sparked with possibilities.

Chapter Four

December 17

The deep snow left her stranded at Logan's. Being snowbound with him the past few days was like being on the best winter vacation. Alyssa cooed and played contentedly, while Logan and Jasmine sat for hours talking and playing games. Adult time was rare. Since the divorce, her life had revolved around the pregnancy and then her daughter. Friends fell to the way-side, because they were either still happily married or single and wanted to go out, leaving Jasmine lost in the mix.

She did what she could around the house, including cooking the meals, while Logan chopped wood and kept the fire going. There was a comfort to their routine, as if they had been doing it for years, instead of just days. "You seem to know a lot about my grandmother, why is that?"

Logan chuckled, pouring more coffee in his cup. "Growing up in Clearwater, there isn't a lot to do. My dad was the Sheriff before Ryan took over. Dad worked long hours, and my mom worked as a teacher during the day and took online college classes at night to get her Master's degree. With my parents so busy, your grandmother became more of a surrogate grandmother to my sister, Lexy, and me. She was always yelling at me for something, keeping me in line, and Lexy became one of the best cooks in Clearwater because of her. She was a great lady."

Listening to Logan speak so fondly of her grandmother, Jasmine couldn't prevent the twinge of jealousy. The woman he described seemed wonderful, leaving her to wonder what happened between her mother and grandmother that forced a distance. To deprive a daughter of her grandmother, who could have been there when she needed her, wasn't right.

Growing up, Jasmine craved a real family, envious of those around her who had what she longed for. She wanted a large family with grandparents, aunts and uncles, and siblings. Instead her life had been one uphill battle, moving from one place to another when her mother got fired from yet another job. Jasmine vowed, when Alyssa was born, her daughter would not be an only child.

Coming out of the bedroom from putting Alyssa down for the night, she returned to her spot on the sofa next to Logan. The cracking fire and the lights of the Christmas tree brought a romantic edge to the room. Pulling her legs up under her, she turned to face him.

"Instead of playing cards tonight, I thought you could help me read a few of the letters my Grandmother sent to my mom. Her lawyer gave them to me, and I've been meaning to go through them, but the time slipped away with packing and then the trip." She held up a pile of letters, bound together by a fraying red ribbon.

"Sure." He patted the spot next to him on the sofa. "I've always wondered what happened to cause such a rift between them because it was obvious to me that your grandmother missed you and your mother."

Jasmine sank down next to him, her body tense and on edge, nervous about what the letters held. She untied the ribbon carefully, wondering what her grandmother must have been thinking as she tied it, knowing her only daughter had rejected her.

Taking a blanket from the back of the sofa, she wrapped it around her legs and settled down to read the first letter while Logan read the second one.

My Dearest Daughter,

It has been over six months and still no word from you. When you stormed out of here I never realized it would be for good. You've take my only grandbaby away, refusing me any contact. The words spoken were the truth, yet they were also said in anger. I stand by those words.

You chose to have a child with Robert Melvin, so it's only proper that you tell him. He has the right to know his child, even if it means a scandal in our small town.

Oh, Daughter, what were you thinking when you laid down with a married man? Did you not think your actions would have consequences? Were your actions because of something I did? Your father and I did everything we could for you, and still you chose to go against everything we taught you.

You should have known better than to fornicate with someone you didn't love, and there was no love between you and Robert, only lust. You were young and naïve to believe that he'd leave his wife.

I'm a strong woman and never give in, but for Jasmine's sake, I'm asking for your forgiveness and for you to come home.

Your mother.

Jasmine sat there in shock, her mouth hanging open. She wished she hadn't opened the letter, hadn't learned the reason for her mother's quarrel with her grandmother.

After all these years, Jasmine finally knew who her father was, a married man. Did Robert Melvin still live in town? Did he ever find out he had a daughter?

* * *

The hour grew late, and the fire was nearly out by the time they finished the letters. She learned nothing more, only that her grandmother had wanted to put their differences aside, and for Jasmine's mother to come home. Parts of the letters were filled with town gossip and events as if her grandmother hoped to entice her daughter back with what she was missing.

"Are you okay?" Logan asked, his arm comforting around her shoulders.

"I guess. I just can't believe it. Does Robert still live here?"

"No." He turned away from her, obviously hiding something.

"What is it?"

"I hate to be the one to tell you this." He slid his hand over hers, giving it a squeeze. "Your mother wasn't the only woman Robert had extramarital relations with. A few years after your mother left, Robert's wife found him with another woman and left him. She moved out of Clearwater, to the other side of Jackson Hole. Not long after that, Robert left as well. The town all but shunned him, and with his garage no longer doing any business, he had no choice."

What a mess! "Did anyone know my mother was sleeping with him? Or that I'm his child?"

"Not that I'm aware of, and trust me if people had known then it would have recirculated when the town residents heard you inherited your grandmother's land. No one but you and I know, and we can keep it that way. This can still be the new start you hoped for."

That sat there for a while longer, letting the fire die out. She stayed locked in his embrace until her eyes grew heavy. "We should get some sleep, Alyssa will be awake soon."

He placed his hand over hers, drawing her attention. "Years ago, through the stories your grandmother told, I believe I started to fall in love with you. It seemed like a childish crush to love someone I had never met, but now I know it's real. Jasmine, I'm falling in love with you. I know it's fast and I don't want to scare you away. I just thought you should know."

Her heart skipped a beat, and her mind raced. She loved the comfort they shared. Why did he have to make a statement of love, which had the possibility of ruining their friendship? *Love?* She already played the game of love and got burnt. She wasn't sure she wanted to play with that particular fire again.

Chapter Five

December 18

For most of the night, Jasmine lay in bed thinking about Logan's confession of falling in love with her, and by the early morning she wondered if her own feelings matched his. There was a deep connection between them, one she wanted to explore, but the fear of getting hurt again held her back. Or worse yet, having her daughter hurt.

She couldn't rush this relationship, especially with having Alyssa to think about. She was just a baby, and Jasmine didn't want her daughter getting attached to a man who might eventually leave. The pain of her ex-husband running out on her when she was pregnant with Alyssa hid beneath the surface. The slightest hint of betrayal could open the healing wound. She wasn't willing to risk her heart again.

This move was supposed to be her change, to make something of her life that didn't involve a man. A second chance provided by her grandmother. Maybe Logan was part of the package. Maybe her grandmother wanted him to be the final piece to Jasmine's happiness. Could she really walk away from Logan just because she was afraid to get hurt?

When she slipped out of bed, she was convinced she wasn't ready for another relationship, no matter how much she enjoyed Logan's company. Easing the bedroom door open, careful not to wake Alyssa, she saw Logan in the living room with another woman, his hand resting on her arm. Pangs of regret instantly shot through her heart. The turmoil of emotions she went through with her ex-husband returned.

Logan glanced over the woman's shoulder, smiling at Jasmine. How dare he act so innocent!

"Jasmine, this is my sister, Lexy. Lexy and her husband live in the next house over. John is the best handyman I know. I called him this morning after the snow stopped to see if he had the part for your furnace."

Thankful Jasmine had misread the situation. She released a deep breath and returned Lexy's smile. She dragged her hand through her sleep tousled hair, hoping to look presentable. Disappointment coursed through her at the thought of her furnace being fixed. She enjoyed the time spent snowbound with Logan and wasn't ready for it to end. "Hi, Lexy. Thanks for coming over in this weather. Hopefully John can fix my furnace so my daughter and I can get out of Logan's hair. He's been great, but I'm sure he's looking forward to having his house back and not having toys all over the place."

Lexy stood and wrapped her arms around Jasmine. Being in a stranger's embrace was new and awkward. Jasmine's arms froze at her sides, unable to return the woman's hug. Her discomfort must have shown because when Lexy stepped back, she frowned. "Sorry, it just feels like I know you. Your grandmother talked about you all the time and would show us the pictures your mom sent. Every few months an envelope with pictures of you would arrive, those times filled your grandmother with such happiness. She was like an adopted grandmother to Logan and me. Seeing you makes me miss her more."

She wished she had known her grandmother. The way Logan and Lexy talked about her, she must have walked on water. Jasmine wanted to know more. Did she look like her grandmother? Did she have any of her traits? Growing up, her mother hadn't shown her any pictures from before she was born, and rarely took any as Jasmine grew up. She was shocked that her grandmother even had pictures of her as she didn't know any were being taken. There would be plenty of pictures to mark every stage of Alyssa's youth.

Whenever the furnace was fixed, she'd have to find a picture of her grandmother, to finally see the woman everyone spoke so highly of. Jasmine prayed she was more like the grandmother she never knew than the mother that had let her down in so many ways.

She joined Lexy at the kitchen table and listened to Lexy tell her stories about her grandmother while Logan cooked a huge breakfast. The sizzling bacon made the small cottage smell like home. Logan dished out four plates, placing one in the oven for John when he returned from Jasmine's house.

When Alyssa's cries signaled she was awake, Logan set a plate in front of Jasmine, and then laid a hand on her shoulder. "Start eating, I'll get her."

Before she could respond, he strolled toward the bedroom. Jasmine's eyes filled with tears. Never before had someone offered to help with Alyssa. Everything her daughter needed, she was the only one around to provide it.

"He's just like that, you know." Lexy chewed on a piece of bacon.

"What?"

"Logan is a nice guy. He would give anyone the shirt off his back if they needed it. He's just that way. Always has been."

Jasmine picked at her eggs with her fork, trying to put the thoughts in her head into words. "He's been great, and Alyssa has really taken to him. I'm just not used to all the help."

"You've been doing everything on your own?" Lexy's chewing paused in mid-motion.

Jasmine nodded. "I had to. There's no one else."

Tossing the half piece of bacon on her plate, Lexy placed her hand over Jasmine's. "Maybe that will change."

Jasmine couldn't place hope that her life would change so quickly. For her, dreams never came true, leaving her with little confidence that the dream of having someone to share her life with Alyssa would either. "I should check on Alyssa. I'm sure she needs to be changed, and she'll be hungry."

Before Jasmine stood from the breakfast bar, Logan stepped out of the bedroom, carrying a still sleepy and somewhat weepy Alyssa. Her sweet daughter took more after her and was not a morning person. Logan passed her to Jasmine. She cuddled her daughter against her chest.

"Logan, why don't you take Jasmine to town today? I'm sure you need some stuff, especially since I hear there's another storm coming. I can watch Alyssa." Lexy put her hand up as if she knew Jasmine was going to protest. "Logan can vouch for me, I love children. You have nothing to worry about. I'm sure you need more diapers and stuff for Alyssa. Around here you never know how long you'll be snowbound, so you should always stock up."

The timing seemed a little suspicious, like Lexy was trying to push them together, but Jasmine did need to a few items for Alyssa, especially if more snow was expected. "I'm game. I need to get more diapers. I also planned on picking up a few more gifts. If there is a children's store in town, I would love to stop there."

Logan stood by the fireplace, drinking his coffee, a sly grin stretched over his face. "Sure, but I have to run up to Old Man Miller's and check on him on the way home, if you don't mind."

Jasmine nodded, already excited to get out of the house.

Logan grabbed his jacket from the closet. "Lexy, if you're sure you'll be okay here, we'll go in a few hours. I want to cut more wood, and then I'll check in with John to see if he needs any help. While I'm doing that, you ladies can get to know each other better."

* * *

While in town, Jasmine picked up the essentials for Alyssa, while Logan bought enough supplies to be snowed in for the next month, and still be okay. She was surprised how quaint the small town was with the core businesses lining the Main Street. She had always pictured living in a place like this. How blessed her daughter would be to be raised here.

The Tiny Treasures Baby Store on Queen Street had so many cute things for Alyssa. Now that Jasmine didn't have to worry about money, she couldn't stop from picking up a few new outfits, as well as a few toys to replace the ones they left behind. She even picked up a Christmas present for Logan to show her appreciation to him for opening his home to her and Alyssa.

Heading out of town, toward Old Man Miller's house on the mountain, she took in the picturesque views of Clearwater. Even with all the Christmas spirit in town, with the shops and houses decorated for Christmas, her eyes widened as they stopped in front of a small home resembling a gingerbread house. The Christmas lights twinkling in the semi-darkness, highlighted by the setting sun, were breathtaking.

"Here we are. Come in and meet Old Man Miller, he's expecting us." Logan parked his truck and pulled his keys from the ignition.

Inside Old Man Miller's house was even more surprising. A large white couch sat in front of a crackling fireplace, a small bistro table hugged close to the huge bay windows, and candles were lit all around.

"Old Man Miller is a chef," Logan explained, shutting the door behind them. "He mostly does catering for town events with his apprentice, but he also rents this house out for special events. It's a popular place for proposals. The rental provides a catered dinner for two, made by Old Man Miller himself." He turned to her, his gaze deep and piercing. "Jasmine, during the short time since you and Alyssa walked into my life, I've never had such strong emotions. You put a spring in my step and a smile on my face. I wanted to do something special for you. Taking you out to dinner in town wouldn't be anything like what Chef Miller can provide. He's the best chef, but retired a while ago to spend more time with his wife. Besides the wonderful food, there is a magnificent view of the town. Come enjoy dinner with me."

She couldn't decline. Logan had been amazing to her and Alyssa, and she should have been doing something special for him, not the other way around.

An hour later, their stomachs full, they admired the incredible view while enjoying a cup of freshly brewed coffee. Soon they would have to head back into the cold night, but Jasmine never wanted this moment to end. "Thank you, Logan. No one has ever done something so special for me. I will always remember this night."

Logan reached across the small table and cradled her hand in his. "I'm glad. I hoped tonight showed you that you're special to me. Clearwater is a wonderful place to raise a family, and there are so many fun things to do here. It's truly a winter wonderland."

She pushed her chair back and walked to the front window to get a better view of the town. "Clearwater is just like the town I always wanted to settle down in, somewhere small where everyone knows your name." Gazing out at the town all lit up, she could see the houses decorated for Christmas. "The town is beautiful from up here."

Logan stood behind her, wrapping his arm around her waist. "You're the beautiful one." He turned her to face him, and before she had a chance to think, he lowered his lips to hers. His kiss was long and sweet, and likely the best kiss she ever had in her entire life.

Was he trying to seduce her, to win her over? She wanted to take a chance with Logan, to risk her heart again. She only hoped he didn't leave her shattered.

Chapter Six

December 20

Jasmine was loading the lunch dishes into the dishwasher when the front door opened, letting in a gush of cold winter air along with a few snowflakes. Lexy nudged the door with the tip of her boot, her arms full of toys. "I figured Alyssa needed more toys to keep her busy, and I wanted an excuse to visit," she said, smiling. She possessed the kind of face that could light up a room, and her smile only made it more effervescent. "Why don't Alyssa and I play while you and Logan go for a walk or something? I'm sure you're feeling restless."

That was the understatement of the year. Living on the East Coast most of her life, Jasmine wasn't used to being snowbound. Sure she dealt with snow, but not like this.

Lexy laid the toys on sofa and returned to the kitchen. "Oh, I have some bad news. John said the wrong part came in for the furnace. Kelly's Hardware is ordering the correct one in this week."

"Thanks for letting me know." She honestly didn't care about the furnace, being secretly content with staying at Logan's. "It would be nice to get out of the house for a short time. I haven't been stuck indoors this long before. I'm going crazy. Would you like to go for a walk?" She glanced at Logan who was playing on the living room carpet with Alyssa.

He jumped up. "I know the perfect spot."

Jasmine closed the dishwasher door and grabbed the heavy winter jacket she'd bought in town. She waved to her daughter as she slipped her feet into her boots. Lexy settled down by Alyssa, making Alyssa giggle as Lexy tickled her cheek. Jasmine was amazed by the changes in her daughter since arriving in Clearwater. Alyssa went from always being stuck on Jasmine's hip, to accepting Logan, Lexy, and even John. It was almost like being part of a real family.

Logan led her down to the pond and up a small hill, where a winter wonderland appeared below. Some kids were sledding, while others built snowmen or had snowball fights. On top of the hill sat wooden benches where parents could rest and watch their children.

Logan swept the snow from a bench with a gloved hand, clearing a section for them to sit. Jasmine smiled and watched the children playing. Logan wrapped his arm around her shoulders. "Before long, Alyssa will be playing outside like this."

She sat, silent for a moment, realizing how quickly her daughter was growing up. "I can't believe it. Some days it seems like she's growing right before my eyes, and other days I wonder if I will ever get through the baby years."

"Don't worry, we will." He gave her shoulder a gentle squeeze.

We? Something about his declaration of being part of Alyssa's growth made her stomach jump nervously. Her heart raced with excitement.

Logan turned to face her. "If you could go anywhere in the world, where would you go?"

She didn't have to think about it, because there was only one place she had always wanted to visit. "Paris. I would like to go to Paris. Back in Virginia, one of the girls I knew attended high school there as an exchange student. She loved it. She told me all about her travels and showed me pictures." Jasmine wanted to experience the same thrill and excitement. Unfortunately, once she had Alyssa, she had spent all her savings for her trip. She didn't get to Paris, but her baby girl was worth every last cent. Maybe someday, once her daughter was grown, she'd be able to take the trip of a lifetime to Paris. For now, her dreams would have to suffice.

Paris was a fantasy. If she had to pick any other place to be in the world, it would be right here, right now.

Chapter Seven

December 24

Jasmine had been in Clearwater for eleven days now, and every day was like a new adventure. She felt like a teenager in love. Lexy came by daily to spend time with Alyssa, which allowed Logan and Jasmine time to get to know each other better. There was something special about the Clarke family, because not only did Jasmine's heart cling to them, but Alyssa's as well. Lexy's eyes lit up whenever she saw Alyssa. She had a longing for children, and it wasn't until a few days before that Jasmine found out Lexy and John had been trying to have a child of their own for the last few years, with no luck.

The day the furnace part arrived, John made the repairs, allowing Jasmine and her daughter to return home, but Logan had asked her to stay until after Christmas so Alyssa could enjoy the tree and the decorations they had put up. Jasmine wouldn't have time to redecorate with Christmas right around the corner. It made sense, even if it was just an excuse for them to be together.

With Christmas Eve now upon them, the second snowstorm had finally let up, enough for a trip into town to attend the church service that Logan's family went to every year. Since this was the first year Jasmine had anything to be thankful for, she agreed.

She was blessed with so much—her beautiful daughter and the Clarke family. Since her mother walked away from her family, Jasmine's grandmother probably adopted the Clarkes as her own. Jasmine was gradually doing the same, just in a different way. Even if a relationship didn't continue between her and Logan, the Clarkes were her neighbors. Lexy was becoming a fast friend and great with Alyssa.

Butterflies danced in Jasmine's stomach while Logan drove into town. It had been years since she attended church, and the thought of being surrounded by Logan's whole family had her on edge. What were they going to think when she walked in with Logan? Would they think she was only trying to find a father for her daughter, instead of someone searching for love and to fill the loneliness of her life?

Since the roads were slick from the earlier snowfall and made the drive slower, they arrived after the church services had started. Parking, Logan walked around the truck to help her out, before reaching back in to lift Alyssa from her car seat. "Put your arm through mine so you don't slip." He tucked an extra blanket around Alyssa.

They took their time across the slippery parking lot, and as they entered the church, a few heads turned in their direction. As if sensing her nervousness, Logan placed his hand on her arm and directed her to one of the back rows.

During the service, her gaze wandered until she spotted Lexy and John a few rows ahead. The older the woman sitting beside them had to be Logan's mother because she kept glancing at Logan. While waiting for the service to end, Jasmine couldn't quite settle her rattled nerves. If Logan's family disliked her, or resented the fact she had a child already, they could end whatever was growing between them.

When the service ended, everyone rose. In a strange and hurried rush, Logan escorted her out the side door before anyone made their way down the aisle. "I have a surprise this way. Come on or we'll be late."

"Where are we going?"

He opened the door and there in the parking lot stood two beautiful chestnut-brown Clydesdale horses in front of a white carriage. "I thought we'd take a ride around town to see the Christmas lights. Then we can stop at the lighting of the large Christmas tree on Main Street. What better way to see all the lights than in a horse drawn carriage? Climb aboard, Mi'lady and we shall ride." Holding Alyssa in one arm, he offered Jasmine his other hand. Once she was settled on the seat, he handed her Alyssa, and then climbed in.

"Clearwater has a number of smaller Christmas tress located around town, but the Main Street tree has always been lit on Christmas Eve. The whole town gathers around after Christmas Eve service. It's something you don't want to miss." Logan thanked the driver for the heavy blanket, and then tucked it over her legs and around Alyssa. He nodded for the driver to go and then leaned back, wrapping his arm around her.

Alyssa sat on Jasmine's lap, giggling and smiling as the horses trotted through town. Her daughter was having a blast.

"How do you like Clearwater so far? Is it all you hoped for?" Logan flashed a saucy grin.

"Clearwater is a unique town, and I have a very friendly neighbor."

He leaned in and kissed her, ever so softly. "I hope you're planning to stay."

Caught up in the moment, she laid her head on his shoulder. "Oh, yes," she whispered. "Thank you for everything. You have made this the best Christmas ever."

He chuckled. "Remember that tomorrow when you're stuck having Christmas dinner with my insane family. You might regret agreeing to go with me."

Chapter Eight

December 25

At four o'clock, Christmas morning, Alyssa woke crying. "Hush, sweetie, it's too early to be up." Jasmine carried her daughter to her bed. She had just pulled the warm covers over them when a soft knock hit her door.

"Jasmine, I heard Alyssa cry. May I come in?"

"Sure." Logan poked his head around the door. "I hope this isn't an omen of what she will be like on future Christmases, waking up before dawn to see what Santa brought. Sorry she woke you."

Floppie laid curled in a ball on the edge of the bed. His head perked up to see what the commotion was at such an early hour. Obviously deeming they weren't important enough to be awake, he laid his head back down.

Logan stepped into her room and sat down next to them on her bed, wearing only his blue and grey, plaid pajama bottoms. His chest was bare and insanely sculpted. The light from the moon shone through the curtains enough to highlight his body. "Don't worry about it. I've been awake for hours."

His fingers fiddled with the corner of the blanket at the foot of the bed. She had never seen him unsure of himself. He seemed almost nervous. "Is everything all right?"

He took a deep breath. "Jasmine, I love having you and Alyssa here." He took another breath. "I love you, and I can't picture my life without you."

A lump formed in her throat. "Logan..."

"Please, let me finish."

She wasn't sure what he was going to say, but all thoughts were lost when he grasped her hand and then dropped down on one knee beside the bed.

He pulled a ring from his pocket and held it between two fingers. "Marry me, Jasmine. I love you. Take me as your husband, and allow me to be the father Alyssa needs."

Tears filled her eyes. Her life had changed so much in the last two weeks—all for the better. She loved Logan, and Alyssa would have a complete family. *Was this all too soon? Are we caught up in being snowbound in the cottage? Would everything change once normal life set in?*

Even with doubts running through her head, she did what her heart wanted. "Yes."

He jumped from the floor and back onto the bed, sliding the ring onto her finger. "Oh, darling, I was worried you would think we were moving too fast. *Now*, this is the best Christmas. I can't wait to tell Lexy, she's going to be so happy. She's been bugging me to ask you since I showed her the ring."

"It's beautiful."

"It was your grandmother's wedding ring. She gave it to me many years ago. I had it cleaned and have been saving it for the perfect girl. It seems only right for you to have it. Almost like your grandmother knew this would happen."

Thank you, Grandmother.

During the excitement of Logan's proposal, Alyssa had fallen asleep in Jasmine's arms. Logan nudged Jasmine's hip so he could lie beside her on the bed. He slipped his arm around her and cuddled close, talking about their future and wedding.

After the holidays, they would move into her grandmother's old house and make it their home, and then after New Year's, they would have an intimate wedding. But before any of that could happen, they had to tell his family, and have Christmas dinner at Lexy's.

* * *

Remember when you're stuck having Christmas dinner with my insane family, you might regret agreeing to go with me. Logan's words ran through her mind as she added a pair of silver and red dangly earrings to complete her outfit. She took a step back, taking in her full appearance. Her long brown hair was curled and flowed around her shoulders. She wanted to fuss with it, since it was normally pulled back in a clip, but didn't have time. She hoped meeting his family wouldn't be as bad as he made it sound, because in a few short weeks they would be her family too.

"Jasmine? You ready? Everyone is going to be sitting down to eat if we don't get a move on."

She had spent the last hour going through her clothes, being a typical woman and not finding anything to wear. Was her procrastination intentional or just one of those things? She wasn't sure. Dressing Alyssa was easy. During their trip to town, she had bought a red, with black trim, velvet Christmas dress. Her outfit was complete with a small red bow for her hair. Her daughter looked adorable.

Jasmine, on the other hand, was unsure and insecure about her outfit *and* meeting her potential in-laws. Alyssa, would generally start off shy and coy around strangers, but eventually opened up and showed off. She was a happy baby. When it came to Jasmine, she was shy and didn't easily open up. She worried that people wouldn't like her and found it hard to break out of her shell. What would his parents think? She hadn't even been in town twenty-four hours and she'd been living with their son. Not in *that* way, of course, but still…

"Jasmine!"

"Okay, I'm coming." She picked Alyssa up from her crib. "Come on, sweetie. Time to go see Aunt Lexy." She entered the living room and put Alyssa in her car seat. Logan stared at her, smiling. He then stepped closer and took her in his arms. "Honey, you are a breath of fresh air. You look incredible."

Her cheeks heated with embarrassment. She never had anyone compliment her so much. "Thank you. You're pretty amazing yourself." She hesitated, feeling suddenly uneasy again. "But are you sure, this dress is all right? That I'm—"

He stopped her with a finger over her lips. Logan didn't see her imperfections and past baggage. He didn't mind that she was a single mother and had no family. His loving gaze said he only saw her, and to him that seemed to be worth everything. "Darling, you are perfect. You're just a little nervous, but there's nothing to worry about. Lexy and John already love you, and they're the hardest to win over. Lexy hasn't liked a single girl I have ever dated. Everyone is going to love you and Alyssa. Now come on, we're going to have a wonderful time, and the best part will be coming home with you tonight."

* * *

With the roads still a mess of snow, the drive was slow to Lexy's. If they didn't have Alyssa, Christmas gifts, and food, it might have been quicker to walk through the field that separated the houses. Fifteen minutes later, Logan stopped in front of Lexy and John's house. It had so many lights covering the trees and front porch, Jasmine was sure the house could be seen from space. A large Christmas tree, decorated with red and white ornaments and lights, sat in the front window. Every spot of the house had Christmas lights, and in the yard by the porch stood a large sleigh and reindeer with Santa waving.

"I forgot to tell you, Lexy and John go all out for Christmas, which is why we always have Christmas dinner here. It's the most festive."

He reached into the back seat to unbuckle Alyssa. The front door flew open and Lexy waved at them. "Hurry up, slow pokes! I want to introduce Jasmine and Alyssa to everyone. Don't worry about the car seat. I have a feeling everyone is going to want to hold that bundle of joy. It's been so long since we've had a baby here at Christmas!"

Jasmine took a deep, steady breath. This was sure to be an eventful evening. Through the window, she could see a house full of people. Everyone seemed to be having a good time, but all she could think about was if it was too late to turn and run.

"I'll get Alyssa, you grab the other stuff."

Logan rubbed her back, pulling her out of her thoughts and back to the reality she was about to face. No time to escape now. She reached in the truck for the diaper bag and the gifts. Logan touched her cheek.

"On second thought, all that can wait until after you've met everyone, and feel more at ease." He kissed her cheek and wrapped his arm around her waist. She walked beside him to the house, his arm at her waist lessening the stress, but in reality she was scared as an abused dog, ready to run.

At the door, she resisted the urge to turn back to the truck. The crowd was larger than she had thought from outside, and crowds weren't her thing, especially when they were people she didn't know. Logan's family was even larger than she expected. There had to be at least thirty adults and eight or ten children milling about.

He must have sensed her panic because he squeezed her a little tighter to him. "You said you always wanted to be a part of a big family." He whispered, and then winked, giving her the encouragement to continue.

Alyssa held out her arms for Jasmine. She held her daughter, taking comfort from her small body against hers. Alyssa buried her head in the nook of Jasmine's shoulder.

Most of the men crowded around the large television, while the women sat around the dining room table, or huddled in the kitchen. The children were spread out in each room.

Lexy put her fingers between her lips and whistled. "Hey everyone! Meet Jasmine and her daughter, Alyssa! Jasmine is Grandma Vivian's granddaughter. They moved into her house."

A chorus of *hello* and *nice to meet you* followed.

Jasmine leaned onto Logan's chest for support. "Hello, everyone. Thank you for inviting us." Even to her own ears she could hear her voice shaking. If anyone noticed, they didn't let on.

"See, darling, I told you it wouldn't be too bad. Come on, I want to introduce you to my mother before she has a nervous breakdown. I'm sure Lexy has told her all about you. Didn't you, Lexy?" He frowned at his sister as he guided Jasmine across the room and into the kitchen, where a group of women mingled and cooked.

She spotted Logan's mom, recognizing her as the lady next to Lexy in church. She was a short woman, with brunette hair perfectly curled in a bun. Logan's mother leaned against the counter, staring at Jasmine. Even with the woman's size, Jasmine still found her intimating. Her deep, brown eyes seemed to search into Jasmine's soul. Logan led her forward, forcing her feet to move.

"Mom, I'm sure Lexy has already told you all about Jasmine. Jasmine, this is my mother, Patsy."

Jasmine held her breath, waiting for the woman to say something first.

A smile broke across his mother's face. "You are a pretty little thing. My goodness, Lexy, she does resemble Vivian. And oh, Alyssa is adorable! May I hold her?"

Jasmine nodded and released a breath while Logan's mother took Alyssa from her arms. Alyssa hid her face behind her hands— her usual reaction when she was nervous.

"I hear you stole my son's heart," Patsy said, playing with Alyssa's fingers.

Heat raced over Jasmine's entire body, bringing all her fears to the surface again. She feared Pasty thought she wasn't good enough for her son. Her heart pounded so loud, she assumed everyone could hear it. She glanced at Logan for support.

He smiled. "Oh, yeah, my mom is a little forward, but she's like that with everyone. It's just worse when you're about to be part of the family."

Jasmine admired Patsy's strength and hoped she could learn a few lessons from Logan's mother.

With her pulse galloping, she took another deep breath. "Don't worry, Mrs. Clarke, I might have stolen your son's heart, but he has mine in return. I love him."

Bouncing Alyssa on her hip, she studied Jasmine's face. "That's good to hear."

"On that note, Mom, I have something to tell you. I asked Jasmine to marry me and she said yes. We are planning a small wedding after the new year."

Jasmine's fingers gripped Logan's shirt.

"Well, I'll be." Patsy stepped around the island in the kitchen, taking Alyssa with her, and waltzed into the living room. "Logan's getting married! I can't believe it. My son is finally getting married. Hopefully he will be adding more children like this precious darling to our family!"

Jasmine sighed, a smile creasing her cheeks. *Maybe dreams do come true. Alyssa and I will be part of a loving family.*

Everyone called out their congratulations. Lexy pulled on Jasmine's arm, bringing her back to the kitchen. "I am so happy for you. Welcome to the family."

Lexy embraced her in a long hug, tears flowing freely down her face. When Jasmine asked Lexy to be her matron-of-honor, Lexy squeezed her tight again.

"I would love to! Anything I can do to help, let me know. We're going to be like sisters, and I have always wanted a sister."

The rest of the day flew by. It was Jasmine's first Christmas with a family and a traditional dinner all wrapped up in one. Hopefully, it was the first holiday of many more to come. This was the life she craved—to be surrounded by family and friends. Now Alyssa would have that and so much more, and if Logan's mother had her wish, Alyssa would have plenty of brothers and sisters to play with in the near future.

Thanks to the Clarkes, Jasmine grew closer to her grandmother every day, and she was sure Logan and his family would continue to share their wonderful stories about her.

When they returned home, and Jasmine tucked Alyssa in bed, Logan took Jasmine's hand and guided her to the living room. He pulled her close beside him as they sat by the warmth of the fireplace. As she stared at the fire glistening in the diamond on her finger, Logan held her other hand. "I have a present for you. Remember when I asked you about the one place in the world you wanted to go? You said Paris." He handed her a long narrow box. "Open it."

She untied the box and lifted the lid. Inside the box was a photograph of Paris. "Oh, my!"

"I thought we could go to Paris for our honeymoon."

"Oh, Logan, thank you. This is amazing, but we can't. I…"

He frowned. "What's wrong?"

"I love the thought, Logan. I can't wait to be Mrs. Logan Clarke, and honeymoon in Paris. I never thought I would ever get to go there, but of all the places in the world I want to be right now, this is where I want to be the most." She paused as tears filled her eyes. "I love you, Logan Clarke."

"And I love you, my sweet, Jasmine. I promise to make you the happiest woman. Whether in Paris, or in your grandmother's old log home." He pulled her closer and sealed his promise with a kiss.

The Surrogate

Surrogate pregnancy…

Eight months ago Jessi Macis was artificially inseminated as surrogate mother, never imaging it would land her with more than she bargained for. Giving her word and her eggs to help the man she pined for have the child he longed for would have been more than some could handle but Jessi did it because of their friendship.

Divorce…

Doctor Michael Johnson's divorce came as a huge surprise to him, but not nearly as big as the one when he realized he never truly loved his ex-wife. That he had always longed for the woman that stole his heart when he was just an intern. Now with a successful practice and twins on the way can he convince her he wants to be more than just the father to the twins?

Christmas and babies…

Add in the holiday season to the mess he created, will it be enough to soften her heart and bring the two together at last?

Chapter One

Jessi Macis white-knuckled her car into the driveway of the Johnson's household thankful she made it there. During parts of the trip she thought the snow would get the best of her little car. Just shy of eight months pregnant, she had no desire to get stranded by the weather. She wouldn't let the blizzard stand in the way of the commitment she made to spend the holidays and last few weeks of the pregnancy with the child's parents.

She pushed open the car door surprised no one had come outside. They should have been expecting her, especially since she was two hours late. There had been times she didn't think she'd make it at all. The cold air whipped in swirling eddies sending shivers through her as she slogged through the snow to the house.

The large three-story house had huge white pillars lining the front, with large windows to take advantage of the beautiful setting surrounding the house. White Christmas lights trimmed the house giving it a warm feel without being over the top with the holiday decorations. To look at the house and realize the twins she would give birth two in just a few short weeks would grow in up that house was amazing. She never thought she'd do such a thing, but Jessi had agreed to be the surrogate for Doctor Michael Johnson and his wife Peg.

The feeling of giving children to a couple who could give them so much more than just love was a mixed blessing. She felt honored to help them have a family, but sad that in a few weeks she'd have to leave the children she had grown attached to as they grew in her womb.

Jessi stomped the snow from her boots, then rang the doorbell. Seconds passed and the entryway light didn't come on. She pushed the bell again, before wrapping her arms around her body. Gosh, it was cold. Even if something had happened, the housekeeper should have been there.

When she was about to go back to the car, to the warmth of the heater, and call Michael, the door opened. He stood before her, his hair shaggy and tussled from dragging his hand through it. He gazed at her as if he didn't recognize her, there was something haunting in his eyes. His clothes were wrinkled, the tie he normally wore was loose and just draped over his shoulders, while the first two buttons of his dress shirt lay undone. She had never seen him so disheveled, not even when he was an intern and worked the long hours at the hospital in Denver.

In that moment she forgot about the chill. "Michael, it's me Jessi. Is everything okay?"

"Jessi?" He dragged his hand through his hair, pushing it out of his eyes. He shook his head, as if trying to focus and it seemed to push away the cobwebs. "Jessi, what are you doing here? You shouldn't be out in this."

"What? I'm here as we agreed upon. Michael what's going on? Where's Peg?" She looked past him, trying to see into the house.

"Come in. You're going to catch your death out there." Still in a daze, he moved away, allowing her to step into the warmth of the house.

Jessi pushed the door shut and shrugged out of her coat, before she unlaced her boots. Something was wrong with him and she was eager to get to the bottom of it. She touched her hand on his arm, to draw his attention. "Let's sit down and you can tell me what's happening."

"I need a drink." He moved from her touch and into the family room.

Somewhat taken aback, she followed. Even when Michael and her brother James were in medical school together he rarely drank. In all the time she had known him, she only saw him drink once, and that was at the graduation celebration she put together for them. He had a half of a glass of champagne for the toast, and not another sip through the rest of the party. Stepping into the living room was even more of a shock to her already overloaded system.

The normally spotless house looked—the only word she had for it was lived in. It wasn't dirty, or even a mess, it was just lived-in. His suit jacket was flung over the back of one of the chairs, an open pizza box that was barely touched on the coffee table, with a large bottle of whiskey and glass next to it. A stereo played soft jazz in the background. Old memories pushed to the surface, Michael was the one that took her to her first jazz club, one night after his intern shift at the hospital. It was a night she'd always remember, it was also the night they shared their first and only kiss, provided by a few drinks.

She refused to let the memory of his lips on hers cling to her. Right now there were other issues that needed to be attended to. "Where's Peg? Is Betty here?"

Michael poured himself a large whiskey. From the way his eyes seemed to gloss over, she was sure it wasn't his first. "She's gone." He sank onto the couch, his shoulders slouched in defeat as he took a long drink from the glass he just poured.

"Gone? As to the store? To work?" It was highly doubtful that Peg, a lawyer, was called to work at this time of night. She mostly dealt with divorces and some family law. Why would she go out in a storm like this, especially when she knew Jessi was due to arrive? Even if Peg was out, it didn't explain the absence of Betty.

"No, she's gone for good. Divorce papers were served a month ago."

"Divorce?" Her voice was so low she wasn't even sure he heard. Running her hand along the curve of her stomach she couldn't believe it herself. A month ago—that was right around the time of her last doctor's appointment. He'd come to it alone. Had the papers been served then? If so, why didn't he mention it? What would happen to the twins now? He was in no shape to provide for them, especially not alone. She became a surrogate mother because the child, or in this case children, that she delivered would have a family home. She wouldn't have agreed to do this for a single parent.

He finished the glass of whiskey in record time, his head rested against the back of the couch and his eyes shut.

He'd be no use to her tonight, she'd have to head back out into the snow to get her luggage and find a guest bedroom, because the snow was now fully upon the sleepy town of Clearwater. Jessi got up from her perch and went to him. "Michael, wake up." She shook his shoulder until his eyes opened just a crack. "Where's Betty?"

"With Peg." His eyes closed again and this time there was no waking him.

With her host passed out she was left to find her own guest room. "Guess we're on our own." She looked down at her protruding stomach and wondered what would happen now. She had no means to provide for twins, but she was damn sure that unless Michael got his act together she wouldn't let him have them. She had to have some rights to stand on. After all it was her egg that helped create the twins. Besides, there was never any paperwork signed between them, it was all a verbal agreement. Before then it never struck her as odd, but now she wondered why Peg being a lawyer never forced the issue. She'd have to think about that later.

* * *

Michael woke to the chimes of the grandfather clock in the hall. It was after three in the morning. "Shit, Jessi!" He looked around the room. Had she arrived last night? He couldn't remember anything after the pizza came. Flipping open the lid of the box he saw only the piece he started to eat last night was gone. If she had been there, she didn't eat any of it, nor was there another glass to be seen. Not that she would have joined him in drowning his sorrows in whiskey. Jessi would have been left alone with his bottle of whiskey to mark the end of his marriage. Those damn divorce papers peeked out from under the pizza box as a faithful reminder.

The instant he stood from the couch his head spun. Too much alcohol on an empty stomach, he would feel worse in the morning. Now he had to see if his pregnant guest had arrived. He made it to the window before his stomach revolted. Through the thin curtains he saw her little red car parked in the driveway. Thankful she made it safely Michael stood there a moment giving his stomach time to settle before he tried the stairs.

He still needed to find out where she had settled for the night, and if by chance she was awake he owed her an apology. How could he be so stupid as to try to drink away his problems on the night she arrived? This was the woman who carried his children. He had to show her he was still fit to raise the twins even if he was alone.

Each step was pure hell, a clear reminder why he never drank. He couldn't handle a beer without feeling its effects in the morning. What made him think half a bottle of whiskey would be better for him, he'd never know.

At the top of the stairs he skipped the first door, knowing it was just an empty room now that Peg had taken her things from her home office. That left three other guest rooms between him and the master suite at the end of the hall. He moved up next to the first door, it took his eyes a moment to focus in the dark room. The bed was undisturbed. Two more to go.

He made his way down the hall, his eyes unfocused because of the alcohol and the semi-darkness. The door was only slightly ajar, unlike the others that were open. It had to be the room she had chosen. It was the room he would have selected for her. It fit her completely, the large queen bed sat on an ebony frame, with a high headboard, the comforter was a rich shade of gold, and lighter gold and white pillows decorated the bed. It was also the larger guest room, with a private seating area and in-suite bathroom.

"Michael, is that you?" a sleepy voice called through the darkness.

"Jes, I'm sorry." He stepped into the doorway so she could see him.

She scooted up so her back was pressed against the headboard. Even in the moonlight, he could see her long blonde hair cascaded around her shoulders.

"Come in." When he did she patted the side of the bed for him to sit. "How do you feel?"

"I was so drunk I don't even remember you arriving and you sit there asking me how I'm feeling." He slammed his hand onto the bed, thankfully missing her legs. Pain coursed through his head from the sudden action. "Dammit, it was irresponsible of me. You could have been stranded, or worse yet, injured."

She laid her hand over his. "But I arrived safely. Now tell me what happened."

"There's nothing to tell. Peg left." He really didn't want to talk about it, but she had a right to know the full story. This late at night wasn't the time to get into it, if he could avoid it.

"Why did she leave?"

"Could we do this later?" Maybe never, he added silently.

"I think I deserve some answers, but since it's late and I'm sure you have to work in a few hours I'll let it slide for *now*."

The way she stretched the word now, he knew she wouldn't wait long. "I took tomorrow off. Unless there's an emergency I don't have to go in until Monday." He sat there a moment before he decided to just tell her everything now. It might be selfish but he had no desire to go to bed to only lay there wondering how she would take the news.

"I want you to know I never deceived you. Peg and I didn't have problems until recently." He frowned, not able to help himself.

Would things have been different with their relationship if he never wanted children? He wasn't sure, but he couldn't give up his dream of parenthood because she couldn't have them, not when there were other alternatives. When they explored the surrogate mother option, she seemed completely on board, it wasn't until months later he realized she wasn't.

"Recently, as in when? You said the divorce papers where served a month ago, why didn't you tell me before?"

"I didn't know, I guess I should say I wouldn't admit it until you were about five, maybe six months along. Looking back, Peg was distant from the time the pregnancy was confirmed, but I wouldn't admit it to myself." He hated that he didn't recognize it sooner, if they had been patients of his he'd have seen it, maybe he could have prevented it. "She came back from a doctor's appointment with you when you found out it was twins. That's when it came out."

"What did?" She leaned forward, at least as much as her stomach would let her, her hand in his.

"That she only agreed to the surrogacy because I wanted it. She tried, but she didn't want a child that wasn't hers. She couldn't get past the fact the doctor wasn't able to use her eggs, and in the end she couldn't accept the babies." He rose and walked to the window. He needed to look away from the very pregnant and beautiful woman lying in the bed wearing only a thin blue nightgown. "It's better that I found out now, before the twins are born. This way I can provide a life for them, without the tension. The divorce changes nothing when it comes to the children."

"Actually, I think it changes a lot." She adjusted in bed to look toward him.

"What?" His head whipped around so fast, he felt the muscles pop and his stomach heaved. "What are you saying, Jes?"

"I agreed to this when I thought the children would be raised in a home filled with love and two parents. Michael, you work long hours. How are you, alone, going to provide the care to two infants?"

She had him there. He hadn't actually worked that out. He got as far as a nanny, but that was it. A nanny wouldn't replace an actual family but what choice did he have? "I'll hire a nanny and I'll cut back on my hours. Whatever I have to do."

"Your practice is almost as important to you as children. Not to mention you're the only pediatrician in Clearwater. What will your patients do without you?"

"A better question would be, what would my children do without me?" Anger rose but he fought it. His anger shouldn't be pointed at Jessi. After all, things could have been so different if he would have expressed his feelings for Jessi long ago. She might have been his wife now.

"Not without you. Hell, I couldn't raise these children on my own either. I'm saying you will need help and, to be honest, yes, this put doubt that I made the right decision, but as you can see it's a little late now." She pushed the covers away, exposing her stomach. "We got ourselves into it and we'll have to figure out a way to provide for the children."

He stalked to the bed, glaring down at her. "I will provide for them just like I said I would."

"Michael, don't start. You know damn well that I could fight you for the twins. I might not win in the end, because I don't have the means to support myself and two children as you do, but I could make things hell for you. So let's act like adults here and figure out what's in the best interest of the babies."

He took a deep breath, calming himself. He swore that he'd find a way to work things out with Jessi. What he didn't need was to fight her in court, he had seen enough of lawyers and the legal system to last a lifetime.

Chapter Two

Jessi was cleaning the family room when Michael shuffled down the steps. The late morning sun reflected off the marble entryway making him growl and shield his eyes.

"Morning. You must feel like hell to just be getting up. There's fresh coffee in the kitchen."

"You shouldn't be doing that. Leave it, I'll get it," he told her as she cleared the coffee table.

"I'm pregnant, not handicapped. I can take care of the few things you left about."

Her words made the guilt of last night rise in him. He meant to hire another housekeeper when Betty went with Peg, but he never got around to it. In that moment he wished he would have. He didn't need Jessi cleaning up after him. "After some coffee, I'll call the agency in Jackson Hole that helped me find Betty. Maybe I can get a housekeeper to start today."

"I don't mind. I think we have bigger things to worry about." She moved past him holding the leftover pizza out before her as if it assaulted her sense of smell.

"What about now?" Between the hangover and no caffeine in his system, he was grumpy. He needed coffee before she dove into what problem she had discovered.

"I'm due in less than four weeks." She ran her hand along her swollen stomach, as if saying, remember these babies.

He laid his hand on the cool granite countertop trying to suppress the drums that beat against his temples, and poured himself a mug of the coffee she so graciously had ready. He breathed in the deep aroma, filling his senses with the strong vanilla roast he preferred and took a sip before he faced her. "I know when you're due. What I don't understand is the problem you think we should be worried about."

"Have you seen the nursery?" She placed a glass into the dishwasher and looked up at him.

The nursery was another reason he should have realized something was wrong before Peg dropped the divorce on him. It was completely empty. They'd sold the furniture from the room after Jessi's positive pregnancy test in order to make room for what they thought would be one child. He was glad now they chose one of the larger guest rooms as the nursery since it was also the closest to the master suite, but with twins they'd need the room. "Yeah, I know." He took another sip of coffee, his brain struggling from its slumber. "Tiny Treasures Baby Store is right in town. How about you help me pick out what's needed and I'll get it set up this weekend?"

"I don't know why you need me." She opened the fridge and her eyes became wide. "It's empty."

"Guess we should get groceries while we're out." He felt embarrassed, the refrigerator should have been stocked. "I'm sorry."

Her lips curved down into a frown as she leaned against the counter looking at him. "Michael, we've been friends for years. I've never seen you like this. How do you expect to care for the twins if you can't even remember to buy food?"

"It wasn't I forgot. Without Betty here I've grabbed food at the hospital. I'm a disaster in the kitchen. Even if I wasn't, it's pointless to cook for one." He finished his mug of coffee and poured another. It was at least a two-cup minimum morning, but he suspected that if she wasn't staring him down he'd have drunk the pot himself. Something about her gaze made him uneasy. Or maybe it was the suddenly claustrophobic kitchen.

There he stood next to the one woman that always appeared just out of his grasp. It wasn't just her brother would break his hand if he touched her, it was more the fact he always believed he was never good enough for her. When they were the closest he was a medical intern, which meant two things long hours and very little sleep. It wasn't a time to get involved even if she wasn't the younger sister of his best friend.

"I cook all the time for myself." She shook her head, a strand of her long blonde hair fell from the barrette she had it tied back with. His fingers itched to reach out and tuck it behind her ear. "I'll go. If you went to the store alone who knows what I'd end up with when I tried to make dinner."

"I told you, I'll get a housekeeper. In the meantime we can eat while we're in town." He wanted to deny the fact he couldn't shop but it had been years since he bought any groceries.

"I'm pregnant, I have cravings at weird hours, so there needs to be stuff here. You don't need to rush to find a housekeeper, I can do what needs to be done around here and I don't mind cooking. Actually I enjoy it."

"I'll call and see about someone anyways. Give me twenty minutes and we can be on our way." He placed the coffee mug in the dishwasher.

"Will we make it out? It was pretty nasty last night, and more snow is supposed to come in this afternoon."

"Don't worry, my truck is used to the weather. This is nothing compared what we normally have at this time of year." Tiny Treasures Baby Store was right next to Fast Check Groceries, so they'd be able to knock both things out quickly and head home before the storm hit again.

* * *

Tiny Treasures was adorable inside. So many cute outfits, toys, and beautiful furniture. Exploring the store sent a twinge of regret through Jessi—regret that when the twins were born she'd no longer be a part of their lives. Instead of keeping distance between herself and the children, she stood inside Tiny Treasures picking out the items for their nursery. *Why did I get myself involved in this?*

"Michael," a woman called as she came toward them. Another woman with a baby in her arms followed.

"Chloe." He leaned close and gave her a quick hug and kiss on the cheek. "How unexpected to see you and Tessa. This is Jessi. Jessi, Chloe, Tessa, and one of my favorite patients, Rosalie. How is she doing, her allergies better with the medication?"

The women shared a nod, and Jessi was acutely away he didn't explain who she was. Did the residents of Clearwater know she was his surrogate?

"Rosie is good, growing like a weed. No more problems with the allergies. We came to pick out her Christmas dress and to give Chloe and idea of furniture for the nursery." Tessa rocked the little girl gently in her arms.

"I wanted to wait until after the holidays to let anyone know. You know how news spreads like wildfire here in Clearwater. Let everyone talk of who's getting what, not about my soon to grow stomach," Chloe teased her friend.

Feeling slightly awkward, Jessi stepped away from the group, her attention turned back to the cribs on display. There was a slight twinge of jealousy with the way he interacted with the women. It was the way things had been between them at one time, an easy, friendly relationship that she missed. Things never seemed more strained than today.

He was trying, she'd give him that, but with so much left up in the air concerning the twins she wasn't sure how they'd move past the tension that seemed to surround them. Maybe some of that tension was from the fact she couldn't wrap her head around the divorce. He was the man that every woman wanted. He was a successful doctor with a heart of gold. Why hadn't she noticed Peg's tension the last time they were together?

Minutes later Michael returned to her side. "I'm sorry."

She stared into his green eyes. They reminded her of dew-covered grass first thing in the morning, dark and deep like they went on forever. "For what?"

"Letting myself get caught up with Chloe and Tessa. When I took the position at Clearwater Hospital I stayed at Winterbloom Bed and Breakfast. I was there for weeks before I could find a suitable place, and we got to know each other. Over a year ago Chloe and Jordan married, he built them a beautiful log home behind Winterbloom. They have wanted to start a family since." Michael moved to the next crib before continuing. "Tessa is new to Clearwater but the women have become close so I've gotten to know her at the town picnics, and Chloe's dinner parties and bar-be-ques. She loves to entertain."

"There's no need to apologize. This is your home, you can't change things just because I'm here." She ran her hand along a beautiful walnut crib. "What do you think about this one?"

"What exceptional taste you have. Chloe's husband, Jordan, does woodworking in his spare time. His specialty is nurseries. The owner Zoe Noble sells them here. He made a beautiful set for Tessa, I wanted to order a custom one from him, but things got away from me." He looked toward the counter, for the owner. "I'll see if Zoe has two in stock. Why don't you take a look at bedding?"

"Okay. We'll need the changing table and dresser to match. Might want to get two dressers. They are adorable and the kids can use them as they grow up." She watched him walk to the counter, before turning her attention to the bedding.

Scanning the shelves, Jessi wasn't completely surprised to find that most of what she saw was for one sex or the other. Nothing seemed to be unisex and since Peg didn't want to know the sex of the children, they'd never found out.

He came to stand next to her. His shoulder brushed hers, neither of them moved. "Zoe has two of the cribs in stock as well as the changing table, but only one dresser. We can order another one. It should be done at the end of January. How's the bedding coming?"

"Not very well actually, since most are for either a boy or a girl. It's one thing to get blue and it be a girl, but I doubt you want pink with the possibility they might be boys. What do you want to do about it? We'll run into the same problems with clothes and toys." How had Peg planned to decorate the nursery without knowing? Or maybe she didn't want to know the sex because it was another way to keep her distance.

"Then let's solve that." He unclipped a cell phone from his belt and held it up to his ear. "Richard, it's Michael. I need a favor."

Jessi stared at him for a moment, wondering what he was up to now. He walked away from her, as if he wanted to keep whatever he had planned a secret. What did he have up his sleeve? Her appointment with the doctor who would take over and deliver the twins wasn't for another week.

Chapter Three

They were ushered into an exam room at Doctor Bowmen's office without a wait. Jessi only felt slightly bad that she was pushed in front of the others who had appointments. Michael gave a quick wave to someone he must have recognized as they made their way through, but his attention was completely focused on her. He seemed to share in the excitement that was coursing through her. Finally she would know the sex of the twins she carried.

A man no older than thirty-five, in grey slacks and purple dress shirt stepped around the corner. She wasn't sure why but had expected someone older. "Michael, good to see you."

"You too. Richard, this is Jessi. Jessi, Doctor Bowmen." Michael nodded.

"Doctor Bowmen, it's nice to meet you. I appreciate you willing to deliver the babies here." Her hand glazed over her stomach again, it had become a habit since she found out she was pregnant.

"Please call me Richard. We're very informal around here. Most of us know each other, see each other around town." He opened a door and stepped aside. "Come in. Since you're here I'll do your exam now and find out the sex of your children."

She stepped into the room with Michael on her heels and Richard bringing up the rear. Sitting on the exam table she didn't feel anything but excitement.

"So Jessi, tell me about your pregnancy. Any problems I need to be aware of? Since your appointment wasn't until next week I haven't had time to look over the file your OBGYN sent from your last visit." Richard stepped to the sink to wash his hands.

"It's been a smooth pregnancy, no issues at all. I'm aware that with twins most people don't make their due date, but as of my last appointment everything was fine. The doctor believed I'd at least make it close to the date." Knowing the routine, she leaned back on the table.

"Excellent." He stepped up beside her waist, forcing Michael to move closer to her head. "Were you not able to find out the sex of the twins before, or did you just change your mind?"

Michael laid a hand on her shoulder. "Changed our minds, it will be easier to decorate the nursery and purchase items for them if we know what to expect. I really appreciate that you fit us in."

"Anytime. Now if you'll pull up your shirt we'll see how the little ones are." Richard drew the sonogram machine a little closer, before angling the second screen to allow Michael and Jessi an easy view of the twins.

She tugged up her shirt, baring her stomach, and tried to find a comfortable position on the table. Lying on her back wasn't easy or comfortable. Her back ached from the position but it wouldn't last long and, more importantly, it was worth it.

He squirted a warm gel on her skin before taking the wand and moving it over her stomach. Instantly the sound of two strong heartbeats filled the room, her eyes filled with tears. It wasn't the first time she'd heard the heartbeats, but this time the sound of those two little drums tore at her heart. Up until now she was able to distance herself from the twins. How could she ever look at the holiday season the same again when it would always remind her of the loss of her twins?

"Everything looks good. They've developed well. Their lungs look good. There's no need for additional worry, I believe your babies will be healthy even if you delivered today," Richard explained, his gaze on the screen before him.

He moved the wand and one of the twins' faces came onto the screen. Jessi's hand reached out as if to touch her child through the screen. "Can you tell their sex?" Her heart was cracked and tears now flowed freely down her cheeks. The additional information would no longer allow her to think of them as just babies but as her sons or daughters, yet she had to know.

"Let's see." He moved the wand down the length of the first child slowly, almost teasingly so.

She wanted to cry out for him to hurry, that she couldn't wait a second longer when Michael took hold her hand, interlocking their fingers. Their gazes met and she saw tears glistening in his eyes.

"Not that it will change anything but I always ask my patients, what would you like?"

Jessi look to Michael with the hope he'd answer. "Hopefully they have their mother's good looks, so girls." He smiled down at her.

Good looks? She was completely knocked off guard by his statement. All the times they had known each other, nothing like that had ever come to light. Did he really think she was attractive, or was he just being kind?

"Well, it's too early to say who they look like, but baby number one is a girl." Richard moved the wand over her stomach, to find the perfect spot for the second baby. "Baby number two is also a girl. Looks like you two need to go back to Tiny Treasures and buy pink." He lifted the wand and set it to the side before he grabbed a towel and wiped off her stomach.

"Daughters." Michael stood, still gripping Jessi's hand. His eyes were glazed over.

"The look that crossed through your eyes…I can tell you're worried about their teenage years. You're going to be one of those dad's with a shotgun anytime they have a date, aren't you?" Richard teased Michael with an ease that let her know they were close friends.

"Just wait until you have kids and see what a paranoid father you will be." Michael was able to gain control of his face, hiding the fear that was there only moments ago, which only made Richard laugh harder. Michael held out a hand to her. "Come on, we'll leave him to his hysteria. Your time will come, Richard."

She pulled her shirt over her stomach, then placed her hand in his before gliding off the table. "If there's nothing else?"

Her question seemed to sober him, forcing him back to business. "No Jessi, you and the babies are in good health. If you have any concerns or questions, Michael knows how to reach me, otherwise I'll see you when you go into labor."

Michael's arm was snug against her waist as they made their way from the office building at the back of the Clearwater Hospital where a number of doctors had their offices. It was also the location of Michael's office, allowing him quick and easy access to the hospital when needed.

Snow was falling when they finally got back to his large pickup truck. He walked Jessi to the passenger side and helped her in. She was finally able to take in the extended cab, checking to see if there'd be room for two car seats. Thankfully there would be, because she wasn't sure her little car would be adequate in the snow when they brought the babies home.

Michael hopped into the truck and started it. He shoved the shifter into Drive and looked over at her. "Can you believe girls? Me, a father to two little girls. What the hell do I know about raising girls?"

She laid a hand on his thigh. It felt somewhat intimate but it was the only spot she could touch to give him comfort that wouldn't interfere as he drove along the snow-covered roads. "Don't doubt yourself now, you will be a great father."

"I hope so." His words didn't sound very convincing, but only time would show him that he'd be a good parent. He leaned forward, looked up at the sky. "I don't think the snow will get too bad for another hour or so. We'll stop by Tiny Treasures and get some groceries then go home."

The drove back to the store in silence, each of them lost in thought. Jessi's emotions were running havoc, her stomach churned. She was happy, yet she felt like crying for her broken heart. It was all becoming too much for her to bear. The nine months of pregnancy was enough to form a strong bond between her and the children before they were even born. It would only get worse once she gave birth. She wondered, not for the first time, why she got into the surrogacy parenthood. Why did she think she could walk away from the babies without being torn in two?

* * *

Michael carried the last bag in from the truck. The food had been put away before he lugged in the bags from Tiny Treasures. Jessi sat on the couch with her feet on the coffee table. As anxious as he was to get the nursery set up he still refused to allow her to carry anything in or upstairs. She had done her part by helping him pick out the stuff, and now with the cribs delivered he could prepare the room for his daughters.

He balanced the bedding sets in one hand and locked the door before he stepped into the family room. "I'm going upstairs to get things in order for the nursery. You coming up?"

She shook her head. "Leave the bedding down here, I'll get it washed."

"Laundry is upstairs. The previous owner had the place plumbed for it. Guess it makes sense with the family bedrooms upstairs, but it took time to get used to." He set the stuff down. "What's wrong? You seem distant, upset."

"It's nothing. Go ahead, do what you need to."

It only served to raise his suspicions something was off when she refused to meet his gaze. "Jes, over the years we might have drifted apart, but I can still tell when something's eating at you." When she continued to remain silent he racked his brain to figure out what was wrong. "Did you want boys? Is that what this is about?"

"It doesn't matter what I want, they're *your* children."

Suddenly he felt even more confused. "What?"

"Dammit, Michael! I know I'm supposed to just be some damn incubator but things have changed. This is all messed up now. Peg's gone, taking with her the happy, home filled with love that I thought the children would be raised in. Helping with the nursery, finding out they're girls—it all just brings home that in a few weeks you will have your family and I'm supposed to just go back to my life in Denver. I can't cope with it." Tears ran down her face, breaking his heart.

"What does this all mean?" Fears of her running off with the twins played through his mind. He knew he had rights to the girls even without paperwork. It was his sperm that helped create the twins, but it didn't mean she couldn't make things difficult for him. After all, she was the biological mother.

"It means nothing. I've never been one to go back on my commitments. This will be no different." She pushed off the couch, stormed past him, and up the stairs. Michael stood there dumfounded.

He wanted to follow, to say something that would make her feel better, but he wasn't sure what would make the situation better. How was he supposed to help when he wasn't sure about raising twin girls himself?

Chapter Four

For the next two days they moved around each other like strangers in the night, barely speaking. The tension was thick in the air, a heavy uncomfortable silence between them. Relief coursed through Jessi when Monday came and she woke to find herself alone in the house.

After a quick breakfast, a white paper lying on the table caught her attention. How did she miss it before? Picking it up, she recognized Michael's handwriting. *Jes, one of my clients was taken to the emergency room. I have an appointment with a new housekeeper at lunch. I'll be home around three.* It was just before eleven.

"Girls," she patted her stomach, "I guess we'll see about washing your clothes."

Upstairs Jessi found the nursery pretty much in the state as yesterday. The only difference was the bags were piled around the room. She grabbed one of the larger bags and sat on the rocker to remove the tags to wash them.

Rocking gently, she separated the clothes and once again tears threatened to fall. She couldn't help but wonder if things would have been different if Peg didn't file for divorce. Would the nursery be complete? Would she still have the unease in her stomach about giving up the twins? There was no way to tell, but she believed it would have been different and not as emotional. Michael's emotional upheaval only made things harder. Still, she couldn't separate herself, to deny him the help he needed. She just wasn't sure if her actions were for the sake of the girls, or because she still had unrealistic longings for Michael.

Jessi's cell phone rang. With an arm full of clothes she stood, and snatched it off the dresser and put it to her ear without checking the caller id. There were only two people who would call, James or Michael. "Hello?"

"Hey, Jes." Her brother's voice filled the line. Like Michael, James was a pediatrician. The only difference was James accepted a position in Denver after he graduated while Michael chose the quieter life in Clearwater.

"How's my big brother? It's an odd time for you to call."

"Can't I miss my sister?" he asked innocently.

She laughed. She and James were never the average siblings, they shared a close bond. "No. Not in the middle of the day when you're supposed to be working. What's up?"

"I hoped to catch you before you left for Clearwater. Maybe we could do lunch today?"

"I left Friday, but you'll join us before Christmas, right?" Since James was the only family she had left, part of the agreement was he'd join everyone in Clearwater for Christmas. She didn't want him to spend the holidays alone, and honestly she wanted his support through the holidays. Maybe even then she realized that she'd have some regret and wanted James there.

"Oh."

The tone of that one little word let her know it meant so much more. "What is it, James?"

"You know about Peg?" In the background papers shuffled, he had to be in his office, patients waiting on him.

"I found out when I arrived. How do you find out? You didn't know when I was home, did you?" Her anger flared to life. If James knew and didn't tell her she wasn't sure who'd she would be angrier with, Michael or him.

"Give me some credit, I'd have told you. No, I just learned this morning when I went into the coffee shop. She was there, with another man."

Another man? Did Michael know his ex-wife was seeing someone else already? "What did she say?" She made her way down the hallway to the laundry room.

"Hold on." He covered the phone with his hand and said something to someone Jessi assumed was his nurse. "Sorry, sis. Mother of a sick kid wanting to know if I can squeeze her in. Anyways, she explained they split. She took a job here at a law office, and she's engaged. What will you do?"

"Oh, James." She opened the lid of the washer, tossed the clothes inside, and vowed not to cry.

"I'll support you no matter what you want to do. If you want to fight him for custody we'll get the best lawyer I can find. I'll help you raise them." When she didn't say anything he added. "Tell me what you want to do. I know Clearwater is under another blizzard, do you want me to come get you?"

"Running away from this won't fix it. I made a commitment and I'll stick by it." Even to her own ears the sadness was thick in her voice.

"Jes, you know the kind of hours this job requires. Mine are long and I rarely have to do any hospital rounds. Whereas Michael he's the only pediatrician in Clearwater, the hospital relies on him every time there's a sick child. That makes for even longer hours. How will he care for twins by himself?"

"They're his children. I'm sure he'll get a nanny. I don't know, James, we haven't talked about it." She decided not to mention the fact the nursery wasn't even set up because her brother would use that as a sign that Michael wasn't ready for fatherhood.

"They're yours as well. More importantly I thought you never wanted to have children who were raised by a nanny and that's what these children will be if Michael does it alone."

Their own mother died when they were infants, leaving them to be raised by a nanny while their doctor father worked day in and day out until he died of a heart attack three years ago, at only forty-nine. It was one of the main reasons instead of following her father and brother into the medical practice Jessi chose teaching. Now that she taught college courses online she'd be there to raise her child and be a good wife when the time came.

"Michael is my best friend, but you're my sister and these are my nieces or nephews we're talking about. This needs to be about what is best for the children." His words brought little comfort. She made a decent living, but she could never provide some of the things Michael could for the girls.

"Nieces." She added the laundry soap and turned on the machine.

"You're having girls? I thought he didn't want to know." There was a hit of excitement in his voice.

"Peg didn't want to know, but Michael did, so we could do some additional shopping before the delivery." She tried to keep her own excitement out of her voice. She wanted girls, to dress them in all the cute little outfits.

"Jes, I have to go, but think about it and let me know what you decide. I don't want you to regret it later."

"I'll let you know. But you'll still join us for Christmas, right?"

Christmas was in less than two weeks and her delivery date was December thirty-first, so they had to work out something soon.

"I'll be there. If you need anything just call me. Think about what I said."

"I will and I'll see you soon. I love you, James. You're the best big brother a girl could ask for." He was amazing to her and now he was willing to stand by her if she chose to fight his best friend over the girls.

"Love you too, sis." He hung up, leaving her with even more to think about.

Life threw her one curve ball after another, but this one had to be out of the park. No matter what she chose, someone would get hurt. Hopefully whatever happened would work out in favor of the girls she brought into the world.

* * *

Michael strolled through the door at a little after three, with two large teddy bears in his arms. Eager to show her what he found for the girls, he shrugged out of his jacket and draped it over the rail. His gaze quickly searched the family room looking for Jessi before he headed upstairs. At the top of the stairs he heard the faint tumble of the dryer, but didn't see her anywhere. He peeked into guest room that had become hers. He still didn't find her.

"Jessi?" he called out on his way down the hall.

"In here."

He continued to the nursery. There she stood next to the cribs, installing a mobile above one of them. The room was completely different from when he left. The two cribs formed an L shape in the one corner. The pink and white rug defined the space. Each of the cribs were decorated with the pink bedding with white roses scattered over it. The mobiles above each of the cribs matched the bedding, with pink and white roses dangling from each. The changing table on the opposite wall and the dresser closer to the door left enough room for the second dresser that would be delivered soon. The rocker that had been in his family for generations sat cattycorner to the cribs.

He stepped into the room. "Wow! You shouldn't have done this."

"I didn't have anything else to do. All the clothes have been washed and are put away. You'll need to pick out an outfit for the girls when we bring them home and I'll add it to my hospital bag." She turned on the mobile, testing it.

"Whatever you think would be best is fine." He held up the bears. "Look what I found in the hospital gift shop. They're so cute, I couldn't not get them."

She smiled at him, shaking her head. "They're bigger than the girls will be."

"They'll grow into them." He stepped closer and placed a bear in each of the cribs. "I hired a housekeeper today. She'll start on Wednesday. I hope you don't mind dealing with things around here for another day."

"No, it's fine. I have a roast in the oven for dinner. I better check on it." She stepped past him before he had time to stop her.

"Can it wait for a few minutes?" He followed her down the steps.

"Sure, why?"

"I want to talk to you. Come sit." He led her to the sofa in the family room.

"Michael, I don't know what this is all about, but you're making me nervous." She eyed him with uncertainty.

He swallowed his nerves and wrapped his hand around hers. "I know the situation with the girls isn't what either of us planned, but we have to adjust to it for their sakes. For days I've wracked my brain to come up with the perfect solution to the mess I created—to find the best thing for the girls. *Our* girls deserve both of us in their life. I'm asking you to stay here, to help me raise them. What would be better than for the girls to have both of their parents in their lives? Will you stay and help me raise the girls?"

She sat there and stared at him. "What?" Her voice was whisper quiet as if she couldn't quite grasp his suggestion.

"I want you to stay here in Clearwater to help me raise the girls," he repeated.

"I heard you the first time." She shook her head, for a moment he wasn't sure if that was her answer or if she was still just trying to take it in. "Is this because you're concerned I'll fight you for them? Or because you know you can't do it on your own? Do you see me as a cheaper alternative to a nanny?" He voice rose and he could tell he made her angry.

"What the hell are you talking about? Who mentioned a nanny?"

She pulled her hand from his. "It's a logical jump."

"I'm not asking you to stay because I don't want to hire a damn nanny. I'm asking because I want you to. Our girls deserve to have their mother in their life."

"So I'm supposed to give up my life now, because you screwed up? What about my life in Denver? What about James, my friends…everything?" Each word dripped with anger.

"Your job is online, you can do it from anywhere and James will visit. What about the girls? I see how hard this is on you. Can you honestly just walk away from them?" He tried not to get angry. After all, she was just reacting to the sudden bomb he dropped on her. He should have eased into it, but he couldn't come up with an easier way to put it.

"Isn't that what you hired me for?" Anger was gone, replaced with a tear-cloaked voice.

"Things were different then, but I'd have never asked if I thought it would have affected you like this. I knew giving up the children wouldn't be easy but you'd have been in their life and they'd have a happy family. You have to know I never wanted to see you so upset." He leaned close to her, her hand in his. "Jes, years ago I fell in love with you and to see you now with the pregnancy glow around you all those feelings are back. We can give our girls the family they deserve."

She leaned back from him, just enough to allow look at him again. "What are you saying?"

In that moment he realized what he wanted. "Marry me. Let's have the family we started eight months ago."

Her eyes fluttered as if she was unable to focus seconds before she collapsed back against the couch.

"I propose and she passes out. What a mess this is turning out to be. Can I do nothing right?"

Chapter Five

Jessi's eyes fluttered open. Looking around the room, she tried to grasp what happened. Michael sat on the edge of the couch next to her, a cool rag pressed against her forehead. Last thing she remembered she was on the couch, then everything went black. "What happened?"

"You passed out." He took the rag away, and leaned back just slightly. "Are you okay now?"

"Passed out? That's never happened before. Should we call Doctor Bowmen?" Worries of danger to her daughters raced through her mind. She realized she thought of them as *her* daughters for the first time. Then everything rushed back. *He proposed.*

"You're fine, it was just the shock. I'm sorry, I didn't mean for this to happen." She tried to sit up, but he pressed a hand to her shoulder. "I want you to stay there for a few minutes to make sure the shock has worn off."

"I need a drink." He brushed away the hair that clung to her face, before a straw came into view.

"When I got the rag I grabbed a bottle of water. Thankfully the straw was on the counter from takeout from the hospital a few nights ago," he explained and bought it to her lips for her to take a drink.

Minutes passed as she ran through what he'd said, yet he the silence hang between them, as he sat beside her, her hand in his. "Michael, I don't know about marriage, but I'll stay. I'll help you raise the girls at least until we can figure out something else."

He leaned closer, his face hovered just above hers. "Thank you." He pressed his lips to hers, the warmth of his mouth made her forget her worries for a moment. He used his tongue to gently slide her lips apart then explored her mouth, the spice of cinnamon drew her in.

She returned his kisses, eager for more of his tongue, when he pulled back. "I promise this isn't a mistake. It might be unconventional and we might have been thrown together because of circumstances beyond our control but I think this was always had it was supposed to be and I'll prove it to you with time."

Reeling from his kiss, she watched him for a moment. "Why did you never make a move before?"

"James…he was always so protective of his little sister. Plus I was an intern. You deserved better than somebody under that kind of pressure—both physically and financially." He cupped his hand along her cheek. "I planned to ask you out once my internship was over but you did the semester abroad and when you returned James mentioned you had a serious boyfriend. Then Peg came along. I always wondered how different things would have been if I wouldn't have waited. Now we have the chance to explore it."

"I know it might sound stupid, since we will have children together in a matter of weeks but it needs to be slow."

"Anything you want, as long as you give us a chance. Not just for the sake of our girls but for us. We deserve it too." He ran his thumb along her chin. "I've always loved you and finally I'll have a chance to show you."

She wasn't sure what she was got herself into but he was right. She couldn't just walk away from this opportunity. This might be Fate's way of giving them both a chance to explore what could have started all those years ago, this time with twins in tow.

* * *

The following days passed in a blur, until Christmas only a week away. With Michael busy at the office and his hospital duties she was left to break in the new housekeeper, do the final preparations for the twins, as well as finals for the online class she taught. Jessi had planned everything in advance. After the holidays she would take a semester off giving her nearly eight months with the girls before she had to teach the fall semester.

Jessi sat behind the desk in Michael's study where she had she had set up temporary quarters until they had time to refurnish Peg's old office for her to use, when Cathy entered. "Ms. Macis, you have a phone call. A man name James."

Cathy was an older woman, a little plump around the middle and she had let her hair turn gray adding a nice silvery white to her dark brown hair. With time she'd have that beautiful white grey that so many older women wanted if they let their hair remain natural. "Thank you, Cathy. James is my brother. Please, always put through his calls." She tried to put down the ground rules now while Cathy was still new, later they'd be harder to instill. One she tried was for

Cathy to call her Jessi instead of Ms. Macis but that was the only thing the woman refused saying it was respectful to call her employers Mr. and Ms. and Jessi had no comeback to that.

"Yes, Ms. Macis." She left to get back to her duties and Jessi picked up the phone on Michael's desk.

"James, once again a phone call in the middle of the day. What's up?"

"Michael called." He stated it as if she should know why.

She leaned back in the warm leather chair, waiting for James to say why he called. "I don't follow."

"Jessi Ann, don't play with me. You're staying in Clearwater with him. Dammit, you go up there a little more than a week ago and he's proposed." James didn't seem angry, just disappointed she didn't tell him sooner.

"I didn't accept his proposal, yet." It seemed stupid to defend only that part of his statement but that's the part she got from it. She wasn't sure why she added the *yet*, had she decided that she might accept it? Thankfully James didn't call her on that.

"So, you are staying?"

"Yes. We both know he can't do it alone, and the girls deserve better than we did. A nanny can't replace a mother." She loved her brother, but she really didn't want to have to defend her actions—not to him, not to anyone.

"I just don't want to see you hurt. I wish I would have never mentioned he was looking for a surrogate."

"We both know Michael won't hurt me on purpose. This might be the best thing that's happened to us. Giving up the girls would have been harder than I realized. Now I don't have to." She ran her hand along her stomach, feeling feet kick beneath her hand. At least one of them, if not both, sure had a kick.

"It could make things harder later if you decide to fight him for custody. Maybe you should speak with a lawyer before you make any kind of commitment."

"No matter what happens between us, I won't take the girls from him. They deserve to have their father a part of their life. If things don't work out with Michael, I'll get my own place here in Clearwater and we'll raise the girls together, even if in different houses. We'll remain civil to each other for the sake of the children." She'd do whatever had to be done to give the girls two parents.

"Sister, you have high expectations. I just hope it works out for you." He was silent for a moment she thought they were disconnected. "Michael is a good man and you're an even better woman, so if any two people can make it work it's you too. I'll miss having you around here. It will seem odd not seeing you a few times a week for lunch, dinner or just coffee."

He had her there that was the one thing she'd missed. "Me too. When will you be here for Christmas?"

"I'm flying in Friday night. Michael is picking me up at the airport."

"Five days before Christmas." Shocked he was taking that much time off work, she leaned forward to look at the calendar. "That's nearly two weeks. I don't think you took more than a weekend off since you graduated medical school."

"I'm about to be an uncle. I want to be there to see my little nieces when they're born. Plus, if you're moving, the least I can do is spend Christmas and New Years with you. You'll be so busy with the twins, who knows when I'll get to see you." There was a touch of sadness in his voice. It wasn't just she was moving away, it was they were both losing their best friends due to the miles that separated them.

"We'll see each other regularly. I'll come down and you'll come up here. After all, the girls need their Uncle James in their lives just like two parents." With another few minutes of small talk—she asked him to pick up a few needed things from her apartment—they ended the call.

Jessi sat and made a list. She had to figure out what she'd do with her furniture. Was it worth bringing it here to put into storage? None of her furniture would fit into the elegance of the house, so it was either storage, or get rid of it. If she got rid of it and things didn't work out she'd have to start all over again. So many decisions to make.

* * *

Michael stepped into the house, not bothering to take off his coat. "Jes!" He hollered up the steps, hoping she wasn't resting.

Cathy stepped out of the kitchen, her apron bore splotches of flour. "Mr. Johnson, is everything all right?"

"Nothing could be better. I just wanted Jes here before I bring in the surprise from outside."

"She was working in your study. I'll get her for you." Cathy turned to go.

"No need. I'm here. What's all this fuss about?" Jessi came down the hallway toward them. Without another word, Cathy left them.

"I have a surprise." He stepped out the door and grabbed the Christmas tree he had leaned against the house only moments before. "I didn't see the point to put one up before you arrived, but I want to now. I thought we could decorate it together."

"Only if we have hot cocoa and listen to Christmas music."

"Deal." He lugged the tree into the family room. It was the first time he had a real Christmas tree since he was a child. It was also the first time he'd decorate a tree since he did it with James and Jessi when he was an intern. Peg never wanted a tree. She hated the mess they created... *How did I ever end up with such a woman? We were so different.* He pushed the thoughts away and focused on making this a Christmas both Jessi and he would remember always.

"I have decorations in the truck, as well as a tree stand." He leaned the tree against the wall before he turned to go back out into the cold. "Ask Cathy to make some cocoa. I'll get the Christmas music on when I get back."

Bag after bag he carried in before finally he turned the stereo on with the jazz instrumental Christmas CD she bought him on the last Christmas they spent together in Denver. With the tree in the stand they took a moment to drink their cocoa while she separated the decorations he purchased.

"When did you find the time to get all this?" She set another string of Christmas lights into the pile that was already larger then they'd need for the tree.

"Confession...I bribed my office assistant Melissa. I told her what I wanted color-wise and she did the rest, thankfully, because I would have never known what all to get. Who'd think a tree would need a skirt?" He held up a red velvet one with white snowflakes decorating it.

"Everyone knows that. You need to hide the hideous tree stand until the gifts are put there." She unfolded it and handed it to him. "Being as big as a whale, if I get down there I might never get back up, so it leaves you to put it around the base."

"You're beautiful." He kissed her cheek then did as she had asked.

"I love that you find me beautiful even when it looks as though I've swallowed a beach ball." She pressed her hands against the cushions of the couch for extra momentum to get up.

"You've always been beautiful to me, but now you have a glow around you like nothing I've ever seen. It makes your beauty radiate."

His words alone would sweep her off her feet if she let them. But knowing he meant them meant more to her than just the words. He'd told her years ago she was beautiful, but after that one kiss they'd shared he seemed to erect a wall that no matter how much she tried she couldn't scale. It was what prompted her to sign up for the semester abroad. Would things have been different if she hadn't? That she would never know.

Chapter Six

The snow was coming down heavily again and was forecasted to only get worse through the hours. Jessi's nerves were shot as she waited for Michael to get back from picking James up at the airport. In Denver she had to deal with snow, but not like this. This was more than just a snowstorm, it pounded the sleepy town with ice. The roads were a disaster.

"Ms. Macis, can I get you anything?" Cathy asked from the doorway.

"I'm fine, thank you, Cathy." She pulled back the curtains to look out upon the driveway again. Even though Michael had used the snow blower on the driveway before he left it was covered again. The snow was at least three inches thick already, with the possibility of four feet over the next few days.

"I know you're worried, but Mr. Johnson will be home soon. Maybe you should rest. I don't want you going into labor without him here. I don't think we could make those roads in either of our cars."

"I'm not due for over a week." With her hand rested on her stomach she turned to face Cathy.

"I've been around long enough to know that in multiple baby pregnancies the mother rarely make it to their delivery date." Cathy scooted one of the chairs closer to the window. "Humor me and sit."

Jessi nodded and obeyed. How could she argue when the woman was looking after her?

"I'm just in the kitchen. Holler if you need me." With that Cathy returned to her duties leaving Jessi alone with her worries.

Her cell phone vibrated on the coffee table, tearing her gaze from the window. "Please don't let that be bad news." She eased her hand toward it like it might bite.

"Hello." There was a hesitation to her voice as she tried to push the Pause button on her fears. She didn't remember to be this full of worry before the pregnancy, had this brought out her motherly instincts, forcing her to worry more about those she loved.

"It's me." Michael's voice came through the phone.

"Oh Michael, is everything okay?"

"We're fine, I didn't mean to worry you. We stopped to help a car that ran off the road just on the other side of town. I didn't realize how long it took us to get it out of the snowbank. I just wanted to let you know we'll be there soon." She heard the engine start up.

"I'm glad you're both okay. Drive carefully." She didn't care how long it took him to get home as long as he made it safely.

"Will do. I love you."

The first time he said it she wasn't sure how to respond but in that minute she knew she shared his feelings. "I love you too."

"I'll see you soon." By the tone of his voice she knew she caught him off guard. He hadn't expected her to return the sentiment.

* * *

Most of the evening Michael hung back giving Jessi time with her brother, biding his time until they were alone. When James finally retired for the night, Jessi snuggled up on the couch.

He rose from his chair, wanting to be closer to her. "May I join you?" She moved her legs to give him space to sit. "I was thinking the other side. I enjoyed when you snuggled against the chest last night. Scoot down and let me sit behind you." Last night they sat in the light of the tree talking of Christmases past.

"With the weight of me and my stomach against you I don't know how you could have been comfortable." She moved enough for him the room to squeeze in beside her to cuddle.

"You're light as a feather. Now come here."

After they were comfortable, his arm around her body, he finally brought up the earlier call. "Did you truly mean what you said before?"

"About my weight?" She leaned back enough from his chest to look up at him.

"No. That you love me." He felt as nervous as a schoolboy waiting for her answer.

"Yes. I think part of me always loved you, but you were always out of reach. Now well, we can finally have what we wanted." She yawned and he knew they should call it a night.

He ran his hand down the length of her arm with the knowledge that he had everything he wanted right there with her by his side.

"Come upstairs to my room. Sleep beside me so I can feel you next to me. Allow me to wake with you beside you to know none of this was a dream."

"Okay. I'll change and meet you in your room." She rose from the couch headed toward the steps.

"I'll be up after I check the house." Clearwater was a safe town, with very little crime, thanks to Sheriff Ryder, but growing up in Denver instilled habits of locked doors. He moseyed around the house checking the doors before making this way back to the living room to unplug the tree.

He took a final look at the tree before unplugged it. "If this Christmas goes well I'm going to have more than I ever knew I wanted." With only days left before Christmas he had a few final things he needed to finalize to tie everything up in one big Christmas bow.

Chapter Seven

Christmas morning Jessi woke in Michael's arms, his fingers gently gliding along her shoulder blade. "How long have you been awake?"

"Only a few minutes."

She twisted her head to look up at him. She wasn't sure what she would have said, but before she could he kissed her. The unsaid words died on her tongue. His kiss was full of heat and need. She opened her mouth, meeting his kisses with her own desire.

When the kiss ended she snuggled tight against his body. Wishing her large stomach wasn't in the way so she could lay the length of his toned body, feeling him pressed against every inch of her.

He stared at her so long she started to feel nervous and had to ask, "What?"

"You're beautiful." His face told her he wasn't lying, he honestly found her beautiful. Her cheeks heated with a blush she couldn't restrain.

He reached under the covers and pulled out a small ring box. "I asked you once before, but this time I want to do it right." He tried to slip out of bed, away from her.

"Yes."

"I haven't asked yet." He smiled at her a twinkle in his eyes.

A light laugh escaped her lips, taking a bit of her apprehension with it. "Stay here, ask me where you are."

"I wanted to get down on one knee, but if you insist." He opened the box, taking the beautiful diamond ring from its bed. "Jessi Ann Macis, years ago when I was just a measly medical intern I fell in love with you and over the years that love has only grown stronger. Will you do me the honor of being my wife? Marry me and make me the happiest man alive."

"Yes. I love you and it would be my pleasure to be Mrs. Johnson." He slid the engagement ring on onto her finger. "You have any connections that could see us married quickly? I'd love to do it before the girls are born, to give them a proper family right from the start."

"Tomorrow I'll see what I can do. Until then, we have a Christmas to get to and you have to break the news to James—preferably before we got to the Christmas party at the hospital."

"I'll deal with him." She got out of bed ready to get dressed and tell her brother. Hopefully he would be as happy for her as she was.

* * *

Later that afternoon, the gifts were opened, the news of their forthcoming marriage had been delivered to James, and now they gathered in the family room. Michael was content with Jessi's head resting against his chest, while James took the chair cattycorner to them, each relaxing before the night's excitement was upon them.

"James, I know you have a promising practice in the city but have you ever thought of settling for the slower life?" Michael took a drink of his coffee.

"Sure, from time to time. To get out of the city, away from it all. It sounds like Heaven but that means starting all over, and positions like yours don't come up often. Most small towns want family doctors not pediatricians."

"So if something came available, would you be interested?"

"Michael, what's this all about?" Jessi inquired before her brother could answer.

"Let him answer and I'll explain. I promise." He kissed the top of her forehead and looked back at James.

"Maybe if it was a good fit."

"I want to offer you a job. Now with twins due any day to have another doctor in the office to share the workload and hospital duties would be a blessing. It would give me more time to spend with Jes and the girls. It would also keep you close for Jes. You'll be able to play a bigger part in your nieces' lives." When James started to speak Michael added. "Just think about it, that's all I'm asking."

James laughed. It was deep and full of life. "I was going to say I'll take it. I'll need time to give notice in Denver, but it would be perfect." He rose from his seat and walked across the room to stand by the window. "The other night when we were on our way back from the airport and you stopped to pull that lady out of the snowbank. I realized this was the type of place I wanted to be. No one would have done that in Denver. More importantly, Jessi is here.

We've always been close and to think of her gone... Well, she's all the family I have left."

"Oh, James." She tried to rise, but didn't have the momentum to get up. "Damn stomach always in the way." Finally able to get up, she went and hugged him.

"Last night, I looked to see if there were any openings for a pediatrician in the area. I'd change my life, to stick close to you and be a part of my nieces' daily lives. I don't want to be the uncle they only see once or twice a year."

"I'm sorry. I never meant for this to change your life. I thought you loved your job," Jessi told him.

"None of this is your fault. I want you happy and Michael does that for you. He's a good man. I couldn't have picked a better one for you."

"Thank you. Jes is an amazing woman, I'll do my best to make sure she's always happy." Michael came up behind her, placing his arms around her until they slid overtop hers on her stomach, before steering the conversation back on track. "So when can you start?"

"If you're serious I'll call tomorrow and give my notice. My contract says I need to give thirty days, so I'll need a month to close things up back in Denver before I could start."

Michael nodded, excited about the possibility of working with his former medical school roommate and best friend. Back before they went their separate ways that had been an unstoppable team. His father always told him work to live not live to work and that was exactly what he what he wanted to do.

"You're really going to move here?" Jessi asked, her voice holding a touch of surprise.

"Why little sister, the way you ask that, someone might think you wouldn't want me intruding on your happiness," James teased.

"It's not that. I mean I'd love you close. I'm just surprised. You've worked so hard to establish your own clients and now you're willing to give it up?"

Michael spoke up. "Sometimes it's more about living your life, than working it away. James was a mess when you were studying abroad. If it weren't for medical school and the long hours, he wouldn't have known what to do with himself. Now he's back in almost the same position and he doesn't want to miles to separate you both."

"He's right," James agreed. "Thank you, Michael. I truly appreciate this opportunity."

"We'll finalize the paperwork and get you hospital privileges before you leave. In the meantime, we have a party to attend. You'll get to meet some of your future co-workers." He ran his hand on Jes's stomach. "You still up for the party? We don't have to stay long but I promised I'd stop in."

"Who doesn't love a good Christmas party? I'm fine, but are you sure the weather's okay?"

He kissed her neck. "It will be fine. The plows were busy getting the roads cleared this afternoon, and I doubt we'll be there long enough for this to do any real accumulation. We'll keep an eye on the weather. If it gets too bad we can leave. The hospital isn't that far."

"If you say so." She didn't seem convinced.

"For a woman who lived in Denver all her life you sure don't like to go out in the snow, do you?"

"It's not the going out in it. I'd gladly go win a snowball fight against both of you again. I just don't particularly like driving in it. I guess working from home all these years has spoiled me."

Michael and James laughed, until James finally gained enough control to speak. "Dear sister, next year I'll challenge you to a rematch for you cheated on that particular snowball fight you're remembering."

"I'll take you on now and still win." She tried to slip out of Michael's embrace as if to go to the door.

Michael pulled her back against his body. "Oh no you don't. You're pregnant and so not having a snowball fight this year."

"Party-pooper." She nestled her head against his shoulder.

He might be just that but he wouldn't let his fiancée run around in the snow with only a week before she was due. He hoped the girls would wait another few days to give them a chance to get married before they came into the world.

* * *

The hospital Christmas party flew by without a hitch. Jessi met Michael's co-workers and James mingled easily with his future co-workers. Everyone welcomed him on board with eager enthusiasm. Things were coming together for Jessi better and faster than she ever imaged. Taking a seat at one of the tables, she arched her back trying with all her might to take the strain away, but nothing seemed to work.

"Maybe a backrub would help?" Michael came up behind her, laying his hands on her shoulders, gently rubbed her shoulders before he worked down the back that wasn't pressed against the chair. "How is tomorrow evening for us to get married?"

She laid her hand on his. "Tomorrow? How did you manage that?"

"Father Donavan does rounds most night to see his parishioners and anyone else who might like a visit. I caught him as he was leaving. Does that work for you? I know you wanted to do it before the twins were born, and who knows when they might decide to make their arrival. Hopefully they'll hold off another day."

"Tomorrow's perfect. I'd marry you now if I could."

"Don't think I didn't think of that. But we can't get our marriage license until in the morning, and Father Donavan has other commitments, he's squeezing us in tomorrow as a favor."

She rose from the chair to stand before him, her hands in his. "Tomorrow will be soon enough. I can't wait to be your wife. I love you."

"I love you too." He wrapped his arms around her.

The girls kicked as if they could feel her excitement, and she wondered if the inside of her body was one large bruise from her active daughters.

"I'll love when they kick. It's almost as if they're telling me to get away from their mother," he teased, his hand glided along her stomach to feel their kicks.

"They're excited about their daddy." She placed her hand over his, and moved it to the other side to feel their other daughter, the one with a seriously powerful kick. "Our girls are excited we've worked things out." They weren't the only ones excited about the way things were turning out. In under two weeks she'd have the family of her dreams and she couldn't wait.

Chapter Eight

Epilogue: Two months later

Jessi grabbed the baby monitor and quietly eased her way out of the room, leaving Kari and Kami to sleep. She was exhausted, but today James was joining her and Michael for lunch. Not wanting to miss it, she'd forgo a nap with the girls.

Outside the door she found James at the stairs. "Tell me I'm not too late to see them."

"I just put them down, but you can look in on them if you're quiet." She eased the door open and let him step in.

"Can't I just hold one of my nieces?"

"No!" She nearly cried with the thought of one of them waking so soon. They were good babies but it seemed like when one woke the other did too. "You can see them later. Now let's go eat before they wake up again."

Downstairs, her husband, Michael had just stepped out of his study. "Tessa's daughter Rosalie is having allergies issues again and has been taken to the hospital. I need to go."

Jessi had come to think of Tessa as a close friend over the last few months. Learning different motherhood tricks from her had been a blessing. "Go. Let Tessa know if she needs anything to call me." She hoped her friend wasn't alone dealing with a sick child. Months ago she wouldn't have thought twice about someone dealing with it alone, but now a mother herself she realized the stress of seeing your child sick. She hoped Tessa's husband, Cameron, or Jordan and Chloe were with her.

"I can go," James offered.

"You can come with me. We might have to run some more tests. This sounds more like it could be a food allergies," Michael told James before he turned his attention back to her. "Jordan's with her, but I'll let her know of your offer. Are you sure you will be okay alone?"

"I'll be fine. Cathy's here if I need any help, you know how she loves those girls. Go take care of Rosie, she needs you now." She took a step towards him and wrapped her arms around his waist. "I love you."

"I love you too." He pressed his lips to hers.

After years of solitude, Jessi finally had the man she always loved and two beautiful girls to show for it. There was nothing better than that. Waiting proved she could have her very own happy every after.

Marissa Dobson

Born and raised in the Pittsburgh, Pennsylvania area, Marissa Dobson now resides about an hour from Washington, D.C. She's a lady who likes to keep busy, and is always busy doing something. With two different college degrees, she believes you're never done learning.

Being the first daughter to an avid reader, this gave her the advantage of learning to read at a young age. Since learning to read she has always had her nose in a book. It wasn't until she was a teenager that she started writing down the stories she came up with.

Marissa is blessed with a wonderful supportive husband, Thomas. He's her other half and allows her to stay home and pursue her writing. He puts up with all her quirks and listens to her brainstorm in the middle of the night.

Her writing buddies Max (a cocker spaniel) and Dawne (a beagle mix) are always around to listen to her bounce ideas off them. They might not be able to answer, but they are helpful in their own ways.

She love to hear from readers so send her an email at marissa@marissadobson.com or visit her online at http://www.marissadobson.com.

Other Books by Marissa Dobson

Tiger Time
The Tiger's Heart
Tigress for Two
Night with a Tiger
Storm Queen
Snowy Fate
Sarah's Fate
Mason's Fate
As Fate Would Have It
Learning to Live
Learning What Love Is
Her Cowboy's Heart
Half Moon Harbor Resort: Volume One
Passing On
Reaping Good Time
Restoring Love
Winterbloom
Unexpected Forever
Losing To Win
Christmas Countdown
The Surrogate
Clearwater Romance: Volume One
Secret Valentine

www.ingramcontent.com/pod-product-compliance
Lightning Source LLC
Chambersburg PA
CBHW021947170626
46808CB00001B/57